I'M
WITH THE
BANNED

I'M WITH THE BANNED

AUTHOR OF THE BESTSELLING **DEAD IS** SERIES

MARLENE PEREZ

Entangled Publishing, LLC
10940 S Parker Road
Suite 327
Parker, CO 80134
rights@entangledpublishing.com

Entangled Teen is an imprint of Entangled Publishing, LLC.

Visit our website at www.entangledpublishing.com.

Edited by Stacy Abrams and Liz Pelletier
Cover design by Covers By Juan
Cover images by
FlexDreams/shutterstock and
Arra Vais/GetttyImages
Interior design by Toni Kerr

ISBN 978-1-64937-009-9
Ebook ISBN 978-1-64937-010-5

Manufactured in the United States of America

First Edition October 2021

10 9 8 7 6 5 4 3 2 1

entangled teen
an imprint of Entangled Publishing LLC

"Listen to them, children of the night. What music they make!"

—*Bram Stoker's* Dracula

To my favorite twins. I hope you do the things you love, even if it's not hunting vampires.

At Entangled, we want our readers to be well-informed. If you would like to know if this book contains any elements that might be of concern for you, please check the back of the book for details.

Chapter One

This summer, I'd become the queen of the vampires. When I'd killed the king, I got the royal title—and yeah, he'd been exceptionally awful, even for an evil vampire—but now I had a crown I didn't want and a kingdom I didn't know how to rule.

But even teen vampire queens had to finish high school, so that's why I was striding down the halls of Golden West High.

It wasn't all bad news, though.

It was the first day of my senior year. My best friend, Skyler, was back home; Vaughn, the guy I'd crushed on forever, was now my boyfriend; and I was learning to manage my allergy to the sun.

Since I was a striga vie—a vampire-witch hybrid—I didn't turn to ash in the sun, like other vampires, but without my tonic, I did get violently ill, which was why I'd guzzled down a big glass of it right before school. The tonic, my granny's recipe, was what staved off the worst of my vampire vulnerabilities, but it only managed the symptoms.

I still needed a cure.

I was getting better at taming the monster inside me, at least in public, but my fangs would descend involuntarily when I got angry or upset.

I had high hopes that today would be fang free. I might even go as far as to say it was going to be a great day. I would see Vaughn, who was finally back from Texas.

I hummed as I waited for him at the lockers. We hadn't talked much while he was gone, but I knew he had been busy training. And a vampire queen constantly checking in on her boyfriend while he's off learning how to be a vampire hunter? That would be as clingy as Saran Wrap.

The warning bell rang, but Vaughn still didn't show up. My good mood deflated faster than a popped birthday balloon.

"What's wrong?" Skyler asked, slamming her locker door shut.

I didn't want to sound like I'd been just hanging around waiting for my boyfriend, even though I clearly had been.

"I miss sunshine and the water and spending the whole day at the beach," I said as we started walking to class. "We live in *California*. Beach time is practically the law."

"You miss Vaughn, huh?" my best friend asked.

"It feels like he's been gone forever," I said. No use trying to hide my worry now. "And it's not like him to skip the first day."

"He probably just overslept or something," she said.

"Maybe," I replied, but I wasn't convinced.

"You should take the opportunity to remind Vaughn what he missed," she replied. She wiggled her brows as we took our seats in the classroom.

"What's with the eyebrows?"

"Just remind him what he left behind when he went to Texas."

I flinched at the reminder that he had left me behind. I knew she wasn't trying to hurt me, but the comment stung.

"How exactly am I supposed to do that?" Again with the eyebrows. "Skyler," I chided. So much had happened between Vaughn and me. We'd spent the summer chasing a vampire rock band—and it wasn't to get their autographs—but somewhere during all the chaos, Vaughn and I had gone from friends to a couple.

Vaughn Sheridan was my boyfriend. The thought still brought a smile to my face.

"Senior year is looking up," I said.

Class started before Skyler could respond to me, but Ms. Ferrell's lecture on nineteenth-century poets was quickly interrupted when the classroom door opened. Principal Townsend stepped inside and cleared her throat.

"Sorry to disturb you, but we have two new students joining us today, Rose and Thorn…Assassin." She paused. "Unusual last name."

Someone in the back row choked on a laugh.

What the hell? Skyler mouthed to me.

My sentiments exactly. What were two vampire hunters doing at my high school?

Rose and Thorn were identical twins who, at first glance, looked nothing alike. Rose's hair was pink, and Thorn's was black. The blue highlights were new, though. Rose wore floral dresses and looked like woodland creatures would do her laundry, while Thorn preferred leggings and leather jackets and looked like she'd hunt and eat those woodland creatures for breakfast. Rose's weapon of choice was poison, and Thorn's was her pointy dagger.

I eyed her up and down as she strode across the room; I had no doubt the blade was concealed on her somewhere.

When Ms. Ferrell turned her back to us to write something on the board, Thorn glared at the guy at the desk in front of me until he got out of his seat, then took his place. He shot her a look that was part confused, part annoyed, before finding an empty desk in the back of the room.

"You are not enrolled here," I hissed at her.

"My queen, I hate to contradict you, but yes, we are," Rose whispered. She was sitting right behind me.

Queen. Whenever someone used that word to describe me, my body felt as though I'd guzzled about a thousand cups of coffee.

I wasn't 100 percent certain whether the sisters were my friend or foe. They'd been helpful this summer, but I could never be too sure where their loyalties were.

"Why are you here?" I asked.

"In English Literature?" Rose sounded confused.

"Why are you *at my school*?"

"We go where you go," Thorn said. "Until further notice."

"Why?"

"For your protection."

Great. So now I had two bodyguards I hadn't asked for.

I waited until Ms. Ferrell had turned her attention to the other side of the room before whispering, "You can't kill anybody. Not unless you absolutely have to."

Thorn frowned but nodded that she understood.

They didn't work for me. They worked for the Paranormal Activities Committee, aka PAC. The PAC ruled over the supernatural world, or what Granny and her coven called the hidden world. They had oversight in every supernatural realm, including mine.

Why had the twins been ordered to stick so closely to me? Did they know something I didn't? It wasn't a reassuring thought, since I knew their entire job was *exterminating vampires*.

"We're not only here to protect you," Thorn said. "We're also going to *train* you."

"For what?"

"Survival," she said.

I was embarrassed by the relief I felt, but if I was really in danger, whether it was because someone wanted to hurt me or because this was standard for any queen, I couldn't think of anyone better to help than the twins.

Ms. Ferrell ordered us to form into groups of four and work on a project about Bram Stoker's *Dracula*. Rose, Thorn, Skyler, and I went to a back corner of the room and pushed our desks together. With the class allowed to talk now, it would lessen the chance of being overheard. I had more questions.

"How was vampire hunting in Texas?" I asked in a low voice. They'd been there with Vaughn over the summer. Maybe they knew why he wasn't here today.

"Unexpected," Rose said.

"Unexpected how?" I asked. When a frown crossed her face, I sat up straighter.

"We had to leave a week early," Rose said. "I did not even get to have any barbecue while we were there."

"Why did you have to leave?"

"To report to PAC headquarters," she replied.

"Did Vaughn go with you?"

"No," Rose said. "Haven't you talked to him?"

I shook my head. "He isn't back yet."

"He did leave Texas when we did, though…" Thorn said. She and Rose exchanged a glance, which did absolutely nothing to calm me down.

Then Thorn clamped her lips shut and pretended to be fascinated by what Ms. Ferrell was writing on the blackboard. Unlike the twins, I needed to pass this class, so I actually paid attention to what the teacher was writing.

"Who can tell me who wrote this?" Ms. Ferrell asked.

I raised my hand. It was a quote from Bram Stoker's *Dracula*. Having a librarian for a grandmother came in handy.

Where was Vaughn? And where had he been while Rose and Thorn went to PAC headquarters? My stomach felt like it was full of shards of glass. I told myself I was overreacting, but I slid my phone out anyway. I kept one eye on Ms. Ferrell while I texted Vaughn. **Where are you?**

He didn't reply. I waited a few minutes…and still nothing.

When I realized Ms. Ferrell was looking my way, I pocketed my phone and pretended to be writing something down, but my mind raced. Why wasn't he answering my texts?

"Where did Vaughn go when you guys left?" Skyler asked.

Rose shrugged. "He said he was going to head home."

I frowned. What if something had happened to him?

Thorn gave me a long look. "Now that we're back, we'll begin your physical conditioning." She started going over a long and tiresome-sounding workout regimen.

I exchanged a look with my best friend. My idea of exercise was a long walk on the beach. Thorn's was an hour of burpees followed by a fifty-mile run.

Senior year was not looking so *up* anymore.

Skyler and I met for lunch, and since we were seniors, we could go off campus. In the parking lot, I held my parasol over my head to block the sun, feeling kind of foolish walking around with an open umbrella and no rain, but most people were eager to leave, so nobody seemed to be paying me any attention. Skyler drove, but she put the top up on her convertible once we were in her car.

"Thanks for this," I said, gesturing to the roof as I rolled my window down to get some fresh air. "And that reminds me, time for my tonic." I dug the Thermos out of my bag and took a sip before recapping it. The strong licorice taste still made me wince a little.

"We never decided where we're eating," Skyler said. "Anywhere but Chicken Clucks."

Skyler's dad owned the Chicken Clucks chain. She'd eaten enough there in her lifetime that I'm surprised she hadn't turned into an actual chicken.

"Understood," I said. "How about Janey's? They have a drive-thru." Janey's was a diner at the pier, but the building had been there so long that it had its own tiny parking lot and could offer quick to-go service.

When we pulled into the drive-thru, there was a bright orange muscle car in front of us with its music blaring. The passengers were dancing in their seats to what my granny called "old-school country."

"Is that Dolly Parton?" I asked.

The driver was wailing, "Jolene, Jolene, Jolene, Jolene," at the top of his lungs. More masculine voices joined in, harmonizing faultlessly.

"They don't sound too bad," Skyler said.

I sucked in a breath. "You don't think it's The Drainers, do you?" The vampire band had disappeared after I'd killed the lead singer's father, the vampire king, but I kept imagining I saw them everywhere. I don't know, something in my gut told me it wasn't over.

"It's not The Drainers." She sounded certain. "First of all, they're in tune. Then there's the more obvious issue."

I slapped a hand over my forehead. "Sunlight." The Drainers were *vampires*—of course sunlight was out for them. Also, unless someone was compelled, there was no way anyone would believe The Drainers sang that well.

"Connor used to sing that song to me," Skyler said. Her ex. She'd been mentioning him more often ever since she'd snapped out of the hold that Travis, The Drainers' lead singer, had on her.

I craned my neck to see who was in the other car, but it moved forward before I could get a good look.

Then the driver started honking the horn, followed by a deep voice shouting, "Skyler!" There was something familiar about the tone of his voice.

I raised my eyebrows. "Someone you know?"

She shrugged. "I have no idea." She put her head out

the window to see and then whipped it back seconds later.

"Who was it?" I asked.

"Nobody." Her lips were set in a straight line.

"Skyler, seriously," I said.

"It's Connor," she said. "I only caught a glimpse, but it was enough to know."

"Connor, really?" Her rat fink ex who'd abandoned her and broken her heart?

She nodded.

When it was our turn, Skyler rattled off our order like it was no big deal, but her voice shook when she said, "Thank you," and handed the cashier her card.

"It's already been taken care of," he said. "The car in front of you paid for your food."

"That asshole," Skyler whispered. "What should I do?"

"Eat your food," I advised. "Not like a Janey's deluxe is enough to make up for what he did."

Skyler waited until we were back in the school parking lot before taking a bite. "Okay, I'll admit it," she said. "Apology burgers *are* delicious."

I had to agree. Part of me wondered if my boyfriend was doing something he'd need apology burgers for, but I had to believe Vaughn was better than that.

Chapter Two

When the final bell rang, Rose and Thorn trailed Skyler and me from our lockers to the big double doors at the front entrance.

I'd dressed up this morning for the first day of school, but I was ready to change into my comfy clothes. Normally, I lived in band tees, faded jeans, and sunscreen. So. Much. Sunscreen. As a redhead, I'd learned my lesson during a seventh-grade beach trip, when I'd stayed in the sun too long and fried my skin. My classmates had called me Rock Lobster for six months. Christian even did the song's choreography from *Just Dance* every time he saw me.

And that was *before* I turned into a vamp hybrid.

Rose and Thorn stayed on our heels as we walked to Skyler's car.

There were a bunch of guys crowded around a souped-up orange Challenger. I was almost sure it was the same car that had been in front of us at lunch, the one that had ordered enough food for thirty and had been driven by

Connor Mahoney.

I caught the scent of Axe body spray and, underneath that, something like wet dog. Rose and Thorn stopped and sniffed the air, but before they said anything, the boys piled into the Challenger and took off.

"Thorn and I will see you tomorrow, Your Majesty," Rose said. "After your morning training, would you like a ride to school?" Everyone knew my old car, the Deathtrap, was unreliable, but lately it was in the shop more often than not. Like right now.

"I'll take her," Skyler said.

Rose gave me a tiny nod in acknowledgment, and then she and Thorn left.

My best friend and I had carpooled to school. She lived a few houses down from me, and Vaughn lived two streets over.

"Want to come over and raid Gertie's *going to Goodwill* bag?" Skyler asked.

"Who am I to turn down free clothes?" I replied. Gertie, Sky's stepmother, had a credit card with no limit and a serious shopping addiction, which was a bad combination. Well, bad for Gertie—not so bad for me. Since Gertie was a former Vegas showgirl with showgirl curves, her hand-me-downs didn't fit Skyler's slimmer build. I had what Granny Mariotti described as bounty. Or maybe she meant booty. Either way, I had it, so Gertie's clothes were a close-to-perfect fit on me.

When we got to Skyler's house, I plopped said booty on her king-size bed while she rummaged through a bag of discarded clothing.

"This would look great on you," Skyler said, throwing

me a jade-colored top. I held it against me and looked in the mirror. I had to admit, that shade of green did something wonderful for my eyes. I also snagged a pair of expensive, downy-soft jean shorts with the tag still on them.

"Why don't you let me cut your hair?" Sky asked. One side effect of being a striga vie I hadn't anticipated was accelerated hair growth. I usually kept my hair shoulder length, but I'd been to a stylist less than a month ago and it had already grown to my waist.

"Thanks, Skyler," I said, "that'd be awesome. Do you have everything you need?"

She whipped out a pair of shears. "Let's do this in the bathroom, where it'll be easier to clean up." Skyler had her own bathroom, which was nearly as big as my bedroom. "I forgot the stool," she said. "I'll be right back."

I looked in the mirror, opened my mouth, and examined my teeth. Did my incisors look more pointy today?

She came back carrying a stool and motioned for me to sit, then tied a big fluffy towel around my neck and started snipping. Pretty soon, there was a pile of red hair at our feet.

Then silence. She hated when I brought it up, but I had to. "Hey…how are *you* doing?"

"Not craving human blood, if that's what you're asking," she said. "Also not hooking up with vampire musicians."

"All good, then," I replied, but there was a look on her face I didn't like. "What?"

"You never talk about it," she said.

"It?" I repeated, but I knew what she meant.

"It happened to you, too," she said.

"I know," I replied. "I was there. I'm just not ready to talk about…what happened." My stomach churned when

I thought about it. Sometimes, it was hard not to wonder, *Why me?*

Travis had bitten Skyler multiple times this summer, but since she didn't ever become a Sundowner, which was what the vampires called the people near the final transformation, she and the other baby vamps had returned to being fully human. Because I was a witch, I hadn't fared so well. One bite from a reckless vampire and I became the creature I saw before me today.

Skyler wrapped an arm around me. "Okay." She paused and then added, "I know Connor's back, but I'm not ready to deal with him."

"Fuck Connor," I said, fury boiling out of me suddenly. If her ex hadn't bailed on her, she'd never have hooked up with Travis, the vampire asshole musician.

"Tansy," she said. "I just worry about him, you know."

"He doesn't seem to be worrying about you," I spit out.

She flinched. "That's not like Connor."

"Neither was dumping you without a word and taking off to another country for a year," I said.

"True," she agreed. "I honestly thought he…he loved me." Her ex's callousness toward Skyler had set off a chain reaction, one that had left me with fang marks on my neck and Sky enthralled to the vampire who'd bitten me.

"I know," I replied. "But sometimes, love isn't enough." I tried not to sound bitter, but I was woman enough to admit that I was.

Bitter was the new black.

Chapter Three

As much as I wanted to, I couldn't spend the entire night at Skyler's, so I headed home, where a pile of "ruler of the realm" paperwork waited.

Granny was in the living room, curled up in her favorite spot with a book and a cup of tea. "How was your first day of school?" she asked.

"The parasol helped," I said. "But get this—Rose and Thorn showed up."

"Hmm. Well, that's not necessarily a bad thing," Granny said. "I feel better they'll be there, just in case."

Just in case what? I vamp out in the middle of Calculus or something?

I grabbed my tote. I'd put everything vampire queen–related into my *I feel the need, the need to read* Teen Titan tote, and it was stuffed.

I plunked down the papers I needed to go over. Since I'd become queen of the California realm of vampires, Rose had been helping me, acting as an unofficial secretary, but the coffee table was covered in documents anyway. I stared, uncertain where to begin.

Granny peered over my shoulder. "You have that much homework already?"

"This is vampire queen paperwork," I told her. "Everything Jure owned now belongs to me. It's a lot."

The document I was staring at indicated I was the owner of the ranch where Jure Grando, who had been the previous ruler of my kingdom, had taken his victims. I wanted to burn the place to the ground.

"What are you going to do with it?" Granny asked.

"Have it disinfected and donated to a women's shelter," I said.

"Do you know how much that's worth?" she asked.

"I don't care," I said. I shuddered, the memories of that place creeping up on me. "I want to donate it to someplace it can do some good."

She nodded as I tried to clear my mind of the things I'd seen there.

"That reminds me," she said. "Something came for you today."

She went to the side table where we kept our bags and mail and the library books we wanted to return and held up a small package.

"Who's it from?" I wasn't expecting anything. The sender's name wasn't on the front, only a return address, which seemed familiar. I did a quick internet search. "It's from the ranch."

I wanted to drop the box, but instead, I studied it carefully before I opened it.

A black velvet pouch and a piece of paper roughly the

size of a business card were the only items in the box. *For the new queen* was written in ornate cursive.

"Thanks for the explanation," I grumbled. I picked up the pouch. Whatever was in it was heavy. I untied the strings, and because there was no way I was going to stick my hand into something that must have belonged to Jure Grando, I turned it over and dumped the contents onto the table.

A ruby the size of a golf ball tumbled out. The gem was dark red, the color of blood, and when I placed my hand on it, cold to the touch. Something about it was repellent to me. I wanted it out of my house, but I couldn't throw it away, not until I knew what it was and why it had been sent to me.

"Do you think it would look good added to your necklace?" Granny said.

I touched my necklace. Protective charms dangled from a long silver chain. Skyler had one that matched mine, and Granny added new charms to them often.

I couldn't add the ruby. The thought of the gem touching my skin made my stomach lurch.

"My neck couldn't take the strain," I joked. I hesitated, then admitted, "I actually don't want it anywhere near me. I don't like the way it feels."

"How does it feel?" Granny watched me closely.

I struggled to identify the source of the sickly, creeping dread emanating from the stone. "Evil."

She smiled like I'd done something that pleased her. "It's old, and it definitely has negative energy," she said.

Who would send me something so valuable and so dangerous?

"What are you going to do with it?" she asked.

I scooped it up and dropped it back into the pouch. "I can't get rid of it, at least until we know more about what it can do and why someone sent it to me. I don't want to keep it in my room, but I can't just leave it lying around, either."

She thought for a moment and then snapped her fingers. "I have just the thing. Be right back."

When she returned, she held a book out to me. "It's hollow," she said. "A gag gift from Evelyn. Open it."

I opened the pages. The hollowed-out middle contained a flask. I lifted it up to show it to Granny, and she laughed. "I'll be taking that."

I set the ruby into the hollow. "It fits." I slammed the book shut.

"Just stick it on one of the shelves in the library," Granny said. "That rock is probably worth more than this house."

"The library" was our grandiose name for the spare room. The walls were lined with overflowing bookshelves. The stacks would make the fake book harder for anyone to find.

After my task was complete, some of the sick feeling I'd gotten from the ruby dissipated, and I exhaled a ragged breath.

I returned to my paperwork. There were three months of bank statements, so I opened those next. They weren't in Jure's name, but in the name of the kingdom, which made it only slightly less hard to take. I didn't want the money, but maybe I could do some good with it.

Granny whistled when she saw the number on the bank statement. "That's a lot of zeros. What are you going to do with all that money?"

I hesitated about answering her. Things hadn't been

the same between us since I'd found out she'd lied to me about my dead mother, but Granny was the only family I had. I didn't count Vanessa, the woman who'd given birth to me and then abandoned me. The one Granny had told me was dead.

Technically, she hadn't been lying.

My mother was dead—or rather, undead, which I'd found out when I came face-to-face with her this summer.

"I'm not sure exactly," I finally said. "It doesn't feel right to keep the money."

"You are the queen," Granny said. "Everyone would understand."

"Jure Grando didn't come by any of it honestly. I want to give money to the people he abused, but I'm not sure how to decide who gets what."

"How about asking someone in the PAC for help?" she suggested.

"Possibly," I said. "I'll ask Rose and Thorn."

Maybe someone from the PAC could enlighten me, because I had questions. A lot of questions. Such as, why was Vanessa a full-on vampire while I was a striga vie? From what I'd heard when I eavesdropped on Granny and the Old Crones Book Club members, Granny had trained Vanessa in the art of witchcraft just as she'd trained me. My mother probably knew more spells than I did, plus she could kill someone with one bite.

I reviewed the list I'd been working on, which was short and sweet. Rose and Thorn had assured me that every vampire within my realm had received a copy.

I showed it to Granny to read. "Do you think this will be enough?"

Queen Tansy's first rule was NO KILLING, EXCEPT IN SELF-DEFENSE, which I'd written in big block letters with a Sharpie. I knew I'd killed vampires myself, but I wanted to be better than that, to be someone Granny would be proud of.

NO COMPULSION was the second thing on my list, and finally, DRINK ONLY WHEN INVITED. ETHICALLY SOURCED BLOOD A MUST. Donors must consent without compulsion.

In unfamiliar handwriting, it said, IF QUEEN TANSY CATCHES YOU BREAKING HER RULES, YOU WILL BE BANNED. Underneath that was, IF I CATCH YOU, YOU'LL WISH THE QUEEN HAD FOUND YOU FIRST. The addition was signed *Thorn Alicante, PAC.*

"Uneasy is the head that wears a crown," Granny quoted.

"You have a literary quote for everything," I said.

"It's the librarian in me." She shrugged. "And you can't go wrong with Shakespeare."

I chuckled and leaned against her. I didn't want to tell her that sometimes the responsibility made it hard for me to breathe.

Granny read silently, then said, "Your rules would make a good cross-stitch pattern."

I sighed. "I'm not sure how I'm going to enforce them."

She put a hand on my shoulder. "You'll figure it out."

I hoped so. Picking through the details of the enormous wealth that Jure had managed to accumulate, the "ill-gotten gains" as Evelyn called them, made me tired. But I still had so many questions, and it couldn't hurt to try out a few on Granny.

"Why weren't you turned into a striga vie when Vanessa bit you?" I asked.

She frowned. "We're not sure," she said. "But Evelyn has a theory."

"What kind of a theory?"

"That you became a striga vie because you are a virgin," she said. "Or at least you were when you were bitten." She winked at me.

My face felt hot. That was not what I'd been expecting her to say. "Why does Evelyn think…?"

"The research is solid," Granny assured me.

"The humiliation is solid, too," I replied.

"I wasn't going to mention it, but you asked."

I really wished I hadn't. "Now I know," I replied. I hoped we were done with this topic.

"It's just a theory," she added. "Besides, it's your body, your choice."

"Have there ever been any striga vies who were cured?" I asked. Granny and the Old Crones Book Club had been searching for a cure, but there weren't many study cases.

"You might have to kill your maker," she said.

"I'd have to kill Travis?" I asked. Despite having killed before, and despite knowing it had been in self-defense, I still couldn't sleep some nights. Sometimes, the urge to hunt down and kill the guy who'd ruined my life was overwhelming, but I just couldn't bring myself to do it—not in cold blood.

"If you want to be free, yes," Granny said.

"Why did this happen to me?"

She put her hand on my shoulder. "I don't know. Sometimes we don't know why something happens; we just have to accept that it did."

I sighed.

Granny put a hand on my forehead. "You look tired. I'm going to cook up a new batch of tonic."

"Sounds good," I murmured, already back to reviewing paperwork.

"I've been experimenting with the flavor," she added. "I think it's almost there."

"Flavor," I repeated. "That's one word for it." Granny's tonic, although lifesaving in the extreme, both for me and for any potential victims if I vamped out, tasted like licorice. It wasn't my favorite, but it could have been much worse. The first batch had tasted like nettles and soap.

She gave me a quick look. "Beggars can't be choosers."

"I know," I said. "I'm just frustrated." It was hard not knowing what would happen to me, to my body.

Money couldn't make up for what Travis and his father, Jure, had done to those girls, but it would help them get their lives back. I frowned. Maybe I could sell another property and use the money for scholarships or something?

"Anyway, it's just a theory," Granny said, "don't be embarrassed." She was obviously assuming I was hung up on the virginity thing. But I wasn't.

I went to bed still thinking about the strangest summer of my life. I'd almost died, but Vaughn had given me his blood to save me. I tried not to remember how much I'd liked my lips against his skin, his warmth filling my mouth. The more I thought about him, the more worried I got about where he was and what could have happened to him.

I wasn't going to be able to sleep, so I turned on the light and grabbed a novel from my nightstand. *A History of Vampyres*—a little light reading before bed. I was still searching for information about the hidden world, but this book wasn't much help. There were two mentions of vampire-witch hybrids, both citing obscure texts that I wasn't even sure Granny could get a hold of. My eyes grew heavy, and I yawned.

Then I heard a laugh. It was my mother's laugh, low and vicious.

My mouth was filling up with blood, coating my teeth. Hot and thick, I gulped it eagerly, but blood continued to flood my mouth until I was choking on it, drowning. In Vaughn's blood. He tried to push me away, but I clung to him, even as his heartbeat slowed and then stopped.

I sat up, my throat still working from the dream, breathing hard. I was covered in a cold, clammy sweat.

It was just a dream, but I couldn't shake the hunger it had awakened in me.

Chapter Four

By Saturday, there was still no word from Vaughn. I didn't count the two-word "*I'm okay*" text he sent in the middle of the night—when he knew I'd be asleep. I paced in my living room while Skyler studied me from the couch.

"Maybe we should go look for him?" I suggested.

"Where, exactly, should we look?" Skyler replied. "We've already gone by his house three times."

"Something's wrong," I insisted. "He hasn't been at work, either. His dad didn't seem worried when I asked, but Mr. Sheridan's been a little distracted lately."

"Maybe they're not getting along," she said. "Maybe he just needs time to decompress. If he were really in trouble, he wouldn't have sent you a text saying he was okay."

Part of me knew she was right, but the other part wanted to find my boyfriend and force him to tell me what was going on.

Granny came home, still dressed in her work clothes.

The library usually closed early on the weekend. "Long day?" I asked her.

"We had cake for Jennifer's birthday," she explained. "What are you two doing sitting around here on a Saturday night?"

"Nothing," I replied quickly.

But Skyler said, "Vaughn's ghosting Tansy and we don't know why."

"That doesn't sound like him," Granny said. She gave me a quick kiss on the top of my head. "Why don't you come out with the coven tonight?"

"I'm not really in the mood," I said.

"Tansy Morgan Mariotti, I did not raise you to sit around feeling sorry for yourself," she said. Granny rarely scolded me. Now I felt like I had to go just to prove I wasn't pathetic.

"You're right," I said. "Maybe a night out is what I need. Where are you going?"

"A cowboy bar," Granny said. "Yeehaw!"

"Can Rose and Thorn come, too?" I asked. "If they find out I went somewhere without my security detail, they'll take it out on me in my next workout. I might not survive it."

"Well, we wouldn't want that," Granny said with a laugh.

I sent the twins a text and got a thumbs-up emoji back from Thorn.

Then I put my red hair in a long braid—the haircut Skyler had given me was already growing out—and borrowed a cowboy hat from Granny, who just so happened to have a couple of extras for Skyler and me. At least we would blend in.

The twins and some of Granny's coven slash book club members showed up while Sky and I were getting ready.

Evelyn was wearing a purple maxi dress paired with bright teal boots. Edna was in skinny jeans, a T-shirt that said *Love is Love*, and a rainbow cowboy hat.

My grandmother was in jeans and a *Librarians are Magical* T-shirt, which wasn't that different from what she usually wore, but she had on a white cowboy hat and a belt with a buckle in the shape of an open book.

Granny and her friends rode with the twins in Edna's minivan, and I rode with Skyler. Before heading out, I secured my drumstick—the one I'd used to kill Fang, The Drainers' original drummer, when he'd attacked me—in my back pocket. My long top helped to conceal it. The drumstick was perfect for staking, and it fit there without being noticeable. Since the sun had already set, Skyler left the top down on her convertible.

The bar was in the canyon. We followed Edna's van through the winding roads. There were cow pastures, cattle and horse ranches just a few miles from the city, and even a winery up in the hills.

"We're here," Skyler said, pulling into a gravel parking lot full of pickup trucks, motorcycles, and cars with bumper stickers with sayings like *Buy at Feeders: Drain and Grain*.

"This doesn't look like a place the coven would hang out," I commented. "It has more of a vampy vibe than a witchy one."

A sign hanging on a wooden post read Ultima Parada. I'd taken four years of Spanish and still couldn't roll my Rs correctly, but I could translate that. *The Last Stop*.

We joined our group, who were waiting for us by the front door.

"There's a cover charge," the bouncer said. He wasn't

wearing his cowboy hat because he was using it to hold the money he was collecting.

"Why?" Skyler asked.

"Band comes on at nine," he said.

"What's the name of the band?" I asked.

"Thirsty Thieves," the guy said. "You in or out?"

I'd never heard of them. "In," I said and handed him some money.

They inspected our bags and tried to confiscate my tonic, but Granny wasn't having it. "That's my medication," she lied without batting an eye. "You wouldn't want me to have an episode, would you?"

The bouncer gave her a look but waved us through.

The interior was dim and smoky, even though technically it was against the rules to smoke inside. The crowd didn't look like the kind of people who cared about rules.

It smelled kind of yeasty, like beer and sweat had soaked into the walls. I took a step forward, and something both crunchy and sticky was under my heel. Along with spilled beer, there were peanut shells on the floor.

"Yummy," Granny said, looking around. "I like a man who knows how to wear a pair of Wranglers."

Most of the guys here seemed to be wearing high-end jeans, and I doubted most of them had ever been on a horse, except the ones on a merry-go-round.

"Is that a mechanical bull?" I asked. As we watched, the guy riding it got thrown off and landed on the mat, laughing. More than half the people in the bar wore cowboy hats, and the others mostly wore trucker hats.

It was larger than it looked from the outside. There was a jukebox in the corner and a beautiful antique bar that ran across the entire length of one wall.

We snagged a long table but had to hunt for more chairs.

"Thanks for dragging me out tonight," I told Granny. "A night of friends and live music is just what I needed."

"There are some hot guys here, too," Skyler said. She was sitting next to me and smiled at someone in the crowd. "Like that tall, dark stunner." Her smile faded. "Incoming," she added in a low voice.

I followed her gaze and was shocked to see Vaughn approaching. My heart immediately went into overdrive. His skin was golden brown from his month in the Texas sun, which made his gray eyes shine. His dark hair was longer than he normally wore it.

"What are you doing here?" I asked, then I noticed Connor walking next to him. He was taller and his hair was buzzed short, but it was him. And I wasn't the only one who noticed. Skyler was peeking at him, but I couldn't tell what she was thinking.

Connor Mahoney stood there, smiling at my best friend like he'd never broken her heart. "Hi, Sky," he said softly. His amber eyes glowed. "It's good to see you."

She said nothing and looked past him. Score one for Skyler.

Behind Connor were three other guys I didn't know, including the guy Skyler had been drooling over earlier.

"You've been blowing me off to hang out with Connor at a dive bar?" I crossed my arms and glared at my boyfriend. I trusted him, but I was starting to wonder if he trusted *me*.

There was a chorus of "ooohs" and "Vaughn's in trouble" from the guys. Vaughn ignored them. "I'm sorry," he said.

Some of my anger dissipated. There were dark

smudges under his gray eyes, and his hair was tousled like he'd been running his fingers through it. Vaughn didn't smile widely very often, but there was usually something sparking in his eyes. Tonight, even that spark was noticeably absent.

"Do you mind if we sit with you?" he asked hesitantly.

The rest of the group tried to pretend they weren't listening in. I was still a little mad at him, but I was also worried. Where had he been? At least he was here now and he could explain.

"I don't mind," I said, studying his face for clues. "As long as we talk later."

He nodded.

"Promise you'll tell me everything that's going on?"

"I promise."

"Good." I tilted my chin at the other boys. "Who're your friends?"

Connor made the introductions. "This is Lucas, Beckett, and Xavier," he said. They squeezed in at the table.

A low growl sounded, and I realized it came from Lucas, the blond. He was taller and even broader than Connor and the redhaired guy. His hair was short and spiked on top. It kind of made him look like an angry porcupine.

"I'm Beckett," the redhead said, waving at me. His long hair was the color of fire, and his blue eyes were full of mischief. "You're a hot ginger," he said to me. "Almost as hot as me."

I couldn't help but smile. "Yeah, almost."

"Beckett, quit flirting with my girlfriend," Vaughn said. "You should be calling her 'Your Majesty.'"

"Girlfriend?" Connor stared at Vaughn. "*Your Majesty?*

It seems like you left a few things out during our last chat."

"Yes and yes. Tansy's the queen of the California realm of vampires," Vaughn said evenly.

The news didn't faze the guys, except for Lucas, who seemed to have not just a chip on his shoulder, but the whole damn bag.

"You're dating a vamp?" Lucas wrinkled his nose. "I thought I smelled something bad."

"I'm not a vampire," I said. "I'm a striga vie. Jeesh, do I need to make a T-shirt?"

"Queen Tansy," Xavier said with a warm smile. "A pleasure to meet you." Xavier was a tall guy with dark brown skin, who looked a few years older than the rest of the pack.

I smiled back at him, stunned silent by the sheer beauty of his laughing brown eyes.

"Tansy's also my girlfriend's best friend," Connor said.

"Ex-girlfriend," Skyler clarified.

His eyes didn't leave hers. "My loss."

Skyler made a scoffing sound, then deliberately turned her back on him and addressed Xavier. "Why haven't I seen you around before now?"

"Xavier is in med school," Connor said proudly.

"I feel like all I do these days is study," Xavier said. "I'm glad I came tonight. I needed a little stress relief."

Skyler raised her hand. "I volunteer as tribute."

She was joking, but Connor frowned.

"What?" she challenged him. "I'm single."

"Are you?" he asked.

Their gazes met and held until she looked away.

A silver fox stopped in front of Granny and smiled at her.

"Very *Urban Cowboy*," Granny said, looking him up and down.

"What's an urban cowboy?" I asked.

Vaughn, with his love of Netflix, old movies, and trivia, beat her to an answer. "John Travolta in a cowboy hat."

My granny's admirer held out his hand. "Care to dance?"

"There's no music," Granny said, then shrugged playfully. "Not like that's ever stopped me before." Was she *flirting* with him?

As if on cue, the jukebox started playing an old country song. He grinned at her. "Now there is."

Granny took the silver fox's hand, and they hit the dance floor. Edna and Evelyn watched for a moment before hopping up to join them. I watched them intently, purposely avoiding Vaughn's looks. Until we had a chance to talk privately, I didn't know what to say to him.

After the song ended, Granny said something to her dance partner, and he laughed before he rejoined some older guys in the corner booth. Granny came back to our table, flushed and smiling.

"He's cute. Did you get his number?" Skyler asked.

Granny blushed, but she didn't deny it.

Evelyn and Edna went up to the bar and came back with a pitcher of beer and several glasses, which I knew weren't for me or my friends, but Beckett didn't get the memo.

He reached for one of the glasses, and Granny slapped his hand playfully. "Get your own," she said. "And make sure it's the kind you're old enough to drink."

I laughed, but I was conscious of Vaughn's gaze on me.

I had to keep ignoring him, though. It was either that or flash my fangs.

Xavier and Granny got into a deep discussion about holistic medicine. Beckett danced around the table, making the Old Crones Book Club laugh, and I sat next to my boyfriend, caught between anger and relief. What the hell was actually going on with him?

Chapter Five

Something was different about Vaughn and it wasn't just his physical appearance. Could a month apart turn him into someone I barely recognized?

"What brought you all to The Last Stop tonight?" I asked the group.

"That's none of your business," Lucas snapped.

"You don't get to decide that," I replied. Sensing the tension between us, everyone else stopped talking as Lucas and I stared at each other. He was the first one to look away.

Then Vaughn's stomach growled, releasing us from the edgy silence.

"Let's order some food," he said. The Last Stop had a pretty decent menu for a dive bar. A server came by, then went around the table, taking orders.

Vaughn ordered a burger and an appetizer combo plate. "Can you throw in a Flying Dutchman and a four-by-four to that?"

I gaped at him. He'd just ordered ten pounds of hamburger, and that didn't include the fries and cheese on the Flying Dutchman. "Are we feeding a pack of hungry wolves I don't know about?"

He winced but then smiled at me, his dimples flashing. "I'm a growing boy."

We ordered enough to feed fifty people, but Beckett seemed worried that there wouldn't be enough. "Maybe we should get one more order of sliders?" he suggested.

Connor nodded. "Two please. And a couple of those french dip sandwiches."

"For me, too," Beckett ordered.

Even though the bar was crowded, it didn't take long for our food to arrive.

The server put the appetizers in the middle and handed out plates. Vaughn made sure I had my favorites first and then proceeded to load up his plate. Until our little communication blip, I'd thought he was the perfect boyfriend. Now I knew he wasn't perfect, but I appreciated how he always looked out for me.

I checked out Vaughn when he wasn't looking. He wolfed down his food like he hadn't eaten in weeks. His shoulders were definitely broader, and his arms had new muscles.

"Have you been lifting weights or something?" I glanced over at Vaughn, meeting his eyes for the first time.

He took a big bite of his burger, and cheese oozed out the side.

"Maybe I'm going through a growth spurt," he said. "I have been powering down steak." He didn't meet my eyes when he talked, just kept his focus on his burger.

"That must explain it," I replied. But I wasn't sure that was it. Vaughn had never been much of a red-meat lover.

"Anyone heard of the band performing tonight?" Vaughn asked.

"The bouncer said they were called the Thirsty Thieves," I told him. I was excited to hear there'd be live music tonight. My experiences with The Drainers hadn't destroyed my love of music. We were at a country-and-western bar, so I assumed we were going to be listening to a country band or maybe bluegrass.

I studied the crowd, checking out the customers a bit closer. I started to get a bad feeling when I noticed that some of them wore matching WANNA BITE? belt buckles. Maybe it was a coincidence, but it sure seemed like advertising that you were a vampire groupie to me.

The band was late taking the stage, and the crowd started to get rowdy. Until finally, finally, they came on and started picking up their instruments. The lead singer's hair was black, and an oversize mustache took up most of his face. Something about the shadowy figures, their faces obscured by the wide rims of their cowboy hats, made my skin prickle and the hair on the back of my neck stand up.

I squinted at him. "That guy," I said. "For some reason, I want to punch him in the face."

Skyler and I stared at each other. "Travis," we said at the same time. His name sputtered out like a curse.

Travis Grando had traded his tight leather pants for faded blue jeans and had grown a mustache. I didn't even know that vampires could grow facial hair.

I sucked in a breath. "No frakin' way," I growled. "We

are not getting the band back together, and this is *not* a comeback tour."

"We won't let anything happen to you," Granny told me. I appreciated the sentiment, but she should be more worried about what could happen to *Travis*.

What were The Drainers doing here, masquerading as a country-and-western band?

Chapter Six

The spotlight finally went on, and the rest of the band was illuminated on the stage.

"We're the Thirsty Thieves," Travis said. A cowboy hat hid most of his face, but I knew that voice. There were loud whistles and cheers from the mostly male crowd.

Travis Grando, the lead singer of The Drainers, the vampire who'd made me a striga vie and who'd used my best friend as his personal chew toy this past summer, was onstage. Behind him were the rest of his merry band of assholes. They may have changed their name, their sound, and their look, but I knew they were still bloodsucking fiends who had no trouble abusing those around them.

My drumstick was in my hand before I'd thought about it.

Vaughn covered my hand with his. "Not now," he said. With a sigh, I nodded and slipped it into the back pocket of my jeans.

"Do you know who that is?" I hissed.

"Yes," he said. "But there are too many people around."

I couldn't kill Travis, no matter how much I wanted to, unless he broke the rules of my realm. Or in self-defense. Or if he challenged me.

Thorn started to get up, but I motioned her back. "Wait," I said. "I want to see what they're doing."

When the cheers died down, Travis started talking. I guessed he was warming up the crowd by telling a story, like some musicians liked to do.

I slung an arm around Skyler. "Does it bother you? Seeing Travis again?"

She hugged me briefly. "It's fine, Tansy. The music seems to be different at least."

"I wrote this song when I was hanging out at my dad's ranch," he said.

Skyler reached out her hand, and I took it. She squeezed it convulsively as Travis put on his good ol' vamp act for the crowd. I braced myself but didn't detect the haunting music that made promises of eternal love.

"What's wrong?" Connor asked.

"We're about to hear a vampire band," Granny said. "That's what's wrong."

"Maybe we should find some earplugs," Skyler suggested.

"We know what he's capable of now," I assured her. "We won't get sucked in."

"That's Travis Grando with a bad dye job and a mustache," I said. "And that's Armando with…omigod, muttonchops."

Skyler flinched. "I'm sorry, Sky," I said. "I didn't know they were going to be here."

Travis was still monologuing, but the other guys finally

got sick of it and started to play their instruments.

Armando caught me watching and gave me his player smile, but I wasn't sure he even recognized me from this summer. There'd been so many girls on tour. I bet it pained him to trade his sharp-dressed-man look for blue jeans and a Western shirt.

I spotted Ozzie, too, but there was a new drummer— because Vaughn had been their last drummer when we'd infiltrated the band to save Skyler. All of The Drainers, who were now apparently called Thirsty Thieves, were good-looking, but this drummer was a stunner.

Black leather gloves concealed his hands, but over his gloves, a heavy gold signet ring gleamed from his ring finger. I'd never seen a drummer wear gloves while performing.

I searched the audience, looking for the faces of the girls I'd met while on tour with The Drainers, and spotted Natasha at a table not far from ours. Her dark hair was longer than before, but she was the same old leader of the Bleeders. She was pretty, even though her bad attitude was written all over her face. She was with two guys, humans, who didn't look away from the stage once.

I went to do some snooping. There was an exit near the bathrooms, and I wanted to see where it led, but Natasha stepped in front of me.

"Hello, Tansy," she said.

I raised an eyebrow. "You can call me Queen Tansy," I said. During the summer, I thought I'd had a chance to convince Natasha the band members were up to no good, but here she was, still following them around, like the number-one fangirl she claimed to be.

She sneered at me. I was getting tired of bad attitudes

tonight. "It must be nice to have a blood donor on speed dial."

She was talking about Vaughn. "He's not a blood donor," I replied. "He's my boyfriend." It was useless to try to reason with her. I'd tried and failed before, so I wheeled around and went back to the table.

There was a brief pause between songs while the band drank what seemed like sports drinks, but I had my doubts. The next song was something I'd never heard before, moody and slow. Travis had unusual powers for a vampire, and one of them was the ability to compel through song. I listened but couldn't detect it.

"The drummer is a fraction of a second off-beat," Vaughn said.

"Who cares?" Skyler said. "Look at him."

I couldn't look away. His long raven hair flowed down his back, his powerful arms moving like pistons. His gloves went all the way to his forearms.

The lyrics to this song were mostly about a tear in his beer. Sad cowboy vampire was sad.

I relaxed just a little. Maybe Travis and the guys had reformed? The Thirsty Thieves didn't seem to have a bunch of female super-fans in white, but there *were* a lot of dudes in hats and blue jeans.

But then the song ended and the next one began. Travis sang an upbeat and peppy rhythm, but the lyrics were misogynistic and mean, the worst kind of bro-country music out there. There was something underneath the happy sound, something dark and sludgy. It was anger. So much anger.

The music was calling to the worst inside humans, but

I couldn't quite make out the message underneath, until I realized it wasn't meant for *me*. I watched the rapt faces of the men and boys. Their cheeks flushed, muscles flexed, hands clenched into fists. The compulsion coming from Travis was saturating every note, every breath they took.

"Boris is gonna hit you with a drum solo," Travis said into the mic. The drummer's name was Boris? I wondered where they'd found him.

When his drum solo ended, Boris took off his sweat-soaked tee and flung it at Natasha. Then he twirled his drumsticks and stared at me for a long moment before he sent a stick sailing right to me. Reflexively, I caught it. Vaughn scowled at the other man.

I tossed the drumstick to Natasha, who clutched both souvenirs to her chest.

"Why did they change their name?" Skyler asked. "What does it mean?"

"Nothing good," Vaughn muttered.

"Why are they back?" Skyler was full of questions tonight, but I didn't have any answers.

"Stupidity or overconfidence," I guessed.

"Are you going to kill him?" she asked.

"I might have to," I said. "You don't know what you're capable of until someone has their fangs at your throat."

Examining the crowd, I searched for signs of cloudy eyes, stunned adoration, or familiar faces, and found obvious signs that Travis was using his unique vampire ability to entice the listeners into thinking he was the next best thing to a Greek god.

He hadn't spotted me yet, but I knew the second he did. His hand holding the mic started to shake, and he stuttered out what seemed like the wrong lyric before he caught himself.

I glanced over at Skyler. Why had I brought her? I'd never dreamed that Travis would have the nerve to show his face anywhere near us again.

They announced the band would be taking a short break, and the guys passed us with their entourage. It was a familiar scene, but this time, they were surrounded by men.

The dudes were walking like ducklings in a row behind Travis, but when he stopped abruptly at our table, the rest of the group almost ran into him.

"Travis. So nice to see you." I gritted my teeth, trying to prevent my fangs from coming down, then gestured to the men following behind him. "I thought we talked about this."

"The fans are all willing," Travis said. "To be absolutely factual, I am assiduous in my inquiries."

Why was he talking like he'd been cuddling up to a dictionary?

He smirked at me. "You heard them. They were *asking* me to sing," he said. "That's permission in my book."

"That's just a loophole," I protested.

"Is it?" Travis asked. "I'm obeying your law to the letter. I don't think the PAC would look too kindly on a vampire queen who broke her own laws. You need proof. Good luck with that."

I gritted my teeth. He was right. I was a new leader, and he was the previous leader's son. I finally said, "I'll be watching you."

"You do that," he replied.

"I even got a nibble of one of those Real House-honeys of Orange County," Ozzie butted in.

"Tasted like too much Botox for me," Armando said.

"I dig it," Ozzie said. "Older women know how to suck."

I forced down a gag. "You better not be making any vampires," I said. "Especially not reality TV stars."

"Vamps need love, too," Travis protested. He gestured to his drummer. "Werewolves, too." Vaughn flinched, and I gave him a puzzled look. Was he surprised that werewolves existed?

"What's the new look and sound all about?" I asked.

"We wanted a change," Travis said, but he stared at a spot over my shoulder instead of looking me in the eye.

He was lying.

"I'm reformed," he said. "You can't kill me without provocation." Again with the big words.

"I know that, Travis," I said, my patience at an end. "I made the rule. I can't kill you unless you give me a good reason." I had to stick to the laws I'd already created or I'd be no better than Jure Grando.

The gold belt buckle he wore had to be ornamental, since there was no way he needed that belt to hold up his tight jeans. I didn't want to stare at his crotch region, but the belt buckle was enormous, and I could clearly read the words BITE ME.

"You mistake my intentions, Tansy," he said mockingly. Travis sounded like he'd swallowed SAT flash cards.

I raised an eyebrow. "That's *Your Majesty* to you." I wasn't really into the whole title thing—what you did was what really mattered. But Travis didn't need to know that.

He bowed, but it seemed sarcastic. "Your Majesty... the girl who killed my father," he said. There was a gleam of something dangerous in his eyes, but when I glared at him, he gave me a bland smile.

"Exactly. I'm your queen now," I said.

"Of course," he replied. He turned his attention to my best friend. "Skyler, you are looking as tasty as ever."

"Don't talk to her," I said. I didn't put any vampire compulsion into the words, but I wanted to.

"And Johnny Divine," Travis continued.

"My name's Vaughn," my boyfriend replied.

"You were my drummer," Travis said. "We had fun on the road, didn't we?"

Fun? That's not how I'd describe it.

"Can I stake him now?" I asked. I was joking, mostly, but then he had to open his mouth.

"No, you can't," Travis said. He smirked at me, like he knew something I didn't.

I couldn't kill him, but I didn't have to like it, either. "Been reading the vampire newsletter, have you?" I narrowed my eyes at him. "What are you up to?"

"Not a thing," he said. He gestured to the crowd. "Do you see any Bleeders?" Skyler winced at the term.

"That doesn't mean anything," I said.

"But they donate blood."

I snorted, and he added, "Voluntarily. No compulsion. All according to your rules."

I waved him away. "Get out of my sight. If you step even a single toenail out of line, there will be consequences."

We all watched him as he hopped back onto the stage in one fluid motion. I hadn't detected any enchantment in the music, but maybe they'd gotten sneakier about it. If the Thirsty Thieves were using their vampire powers to lure new victims, I'd find out.

And I'd make them pay.

"Can you believe it?" I asked.

"That Travis dared to show his face?" Skyler asked.

"That he used the word 'abide' correctly," I replied.

We all snickered, but then something occurred to me. Travis didn't use vocabulary words. It wasn't that he wasn't capable—he was crafty and charming, which meant he had brains. He just didn't like to use them. He couldn't be bothered to improve his vocabulary or anything else—if tonight's ensemble was anything to go by, certainly not his wardrobe.

"Travis has been talking to someone who uses their SAT flash cards," I said.

Vaughn nodded. "I thought so, too. I was stuck on a bus with him this summer, and his vocabulary is more of the bro variety."

Hmm. But what did it mean? I'd have to think on this more.

The night only got more confusing from there. After another set by the country band from hell, I needed additional refreshments. The thought occurred to me that I might need another weapon before the night was over, so I ordered a Diet Dr Pepper. Vaughn followed me.

"Did the band take off?" he asked, his mouth a straight line.

"Just on a break, I think."

"I hate that guy," he said. His hands clenched into fists.

"Vaughn, sit down," I said. "Please."

I raised my eyebrow beseechingly at Skyler to back me up, but to my surprise, it was Connor who came to my rescue.

"So, lovebirds, when did this happen?" Connor waved a hand between Vaughn and me.

"This summer," Vaughn said.

"You finally found your balls, then," Connor teased. "Asked her out properly. Told her how you feel."

Vaughn blushed as I gave him a surprised look. Connor had been gone for a year, yet even he knew that Vaughn had liked me before I did?

"How is it that you knew something I didn't?" I asked Connor.

"Vaughn tells me everything," he said.

"Not everything," Vaughn said. The husky note in his voice made me feel hot all over.

"What else did I miss this summer?" Connor asked casually.

Vaughn and I exchanged looks. There was no way our misadventures this summer were any of Connor's business, and it wasn't our story to tell anyway. It was Skyler's.

"Why did you come back?" I asked, avoiding his question.

"I missed my friends," he replied. "I missed Skyler." She flinched when he said her name. He seemed to be telling the truth about his feelings for Skyler, but Connor Mahoney was hiding something, and I was going to find out what it was.

Chapter Seven

I needed a break. When I noticed the deserted patio, I made an excuse and slipped out through the back.

The air was sharp and clear. There was a hint of pine in the air, probably from the tree farm a few miles away. The patio lights were off, but the full moon provided enough illumination.

I felt someone watching me. "Vaughn, I want to be alone for a few minutes."

"Not Vaughn," a voice said. I whirled around.

The Thirsty Thieves drummer was leaning against a wall. There was something reptilian about the way his tongue darted out to lick his thick lips.

"Want some company, darlin'?" the drummer asked in that same faux accent the whole band used since they morphed into the Thirsty Thieves.

"You don't know me well enough to call me anything, but *especially* not darlin'," I said.

Boris dropped the fake twang. "I don't mean any harm,"

he said. "Please excuse me, Miss Tansy Mariotti."

Why did his presence make my stomach clench anxiously? Because it answered the question about why he was here. He was here to see me.

"Shouldn't you get back onstage?" I knew he was a werewolf, but now that I was up close, there was something different about him. His eyes were flat, emotionless.

"Go out with me," Boris said. He caught my hand, his gloved fingers pressed hard against mine. Despite the warmth of his hand, I shivered, then jerked my hand away.

"I have a boyfriend," I said. Technically still true and he was headed our way. From the set of Vaughn's shoulders, he had seen Boris touching me and did not like it. I wasn't a fan, either. But I could take care of myself. I gestured to Vaughn to stand down. He knew I could handle myself, and I wasn't going to be intimidated by another wannabe musician like Boris.

"I don't care," he replied.

I stared at him, surprised and uneasy. "The answer is still no," I said. "Have a good night." I was not going to take crap from guys anymore, even hot ones.

"I can change your mind." His jaw jutted out.

"Others have tried," I said. "And failed."

"I don't fail." He didn't take his eyes from mine. Great, now he saw me as a challenge.

"You'll have to excuse me, then. I'd like a moment alone."

He looked like he was going to argue but finally went back into the bar.

Tonight was supposed to be a way to forget my problems, to relax and have some fun. But my problems had found me. It seemed like they always did.

Vaughn stepped out of the shadows. "Are you okay?"

I glared at him, crossing my arms. "Do you care?"

"Tansy," Vaughn said. "I missed you."

"You barely even texted me when you were gone," I said. "And then you just ghosted."

"I answered you," he protested, but his argument was weak, and he knew it.

"A two-word reply is not an answer," I said. I felt angry tears welling up, but I tried to blink them away.

"I'm sorry I didn't return your messages," he said.

"Did you even know I'd be here tonight?" I asked.

"No," he said.

We hadn't seen each other in over a month, and he'd been ducking my calls. I turned to leave before I said something I'd regret, but he put out an imploring hand. "Let's talk about this."

"Oh, *now* you want to talk," I said. "That's not how you treat a friend."

"Is that all we are now? Friends?" he replied, looking shocked.

This reunion was not going how I'd imagined it. I still wanted to kiss him, but I kind of wanted to smack him, too.

"I'll tell you everything," he said. I melted when he linked his hand in mine. "But first, can I kiss you?"

I nodded.

He cupped my face in his hands, his thumb brushing over the scar on my cheek, another permanent memento from Travis, before he leaned down to kiss me. His lips felt so good that I could barely stand it. I forgot I was mad at him, forgot that I deserved an explanation. He broke the kiss, but I leaned in for more, and he chuckled.

"You did miss me." He was smiling. I always felt like I had won a prize when Vaughn smiled at me, even back when we'd simply been friends. He hoarded smiles like librarians hoarded books.

But then I remembered I was fuming mad and said, "That makes one of us."

"You think I didn't miss you?" he asked.

"You barely responded to my texts," I said. "I thought you were going to break up with me."

He sucked in a breath. "I'm sorry. Something happened in Texas. I was just trying to figure out how to deal with it."

It wasn't like Vaughn to be dramatic, so I tensed, expecting him to tell me something heartbreaking. Dating while deadly was complicated enough, but when you were a vampire and your boyfriend had spent the summer learning how to be a vampire hunter, "complicated" was an understatement.

"You shut me out," I said. "You hurt me."

"I didn't mean to. You're the last person I'd ever want to hurt."

I leaned into Vaughn, and he rubbed my back comfortingly. He buried his face in my neck. "I missed you so much, I felt sick," he said. He planted tiny nibbling kisses along the curve of my neck. He reached the bite scar, his tongue flicked out, and he licked the slightly raised abrasion.

When our lips met, he showed me how much he had missed me. I ran my hand through his hair. The ends curled, which Vaughn normally ruthlessly controlled with regular haircuts, but he'd clearly been too busy for a visit to the barber when he was gone.

He seemed to realize how our bodies were pressed together and took a step back. Ouch. I had to admit that stung. "Tansy, I'm sorry. As much as I'm enjoying this, I need to talk to you."

We were both breathing heavily, and I wanted nothing more than to continue our reunion, but he was right. We needed to talk.

"Do you want to get out of here? It's a perfect night for a moonlit stroll."

"The moon?" Vaughn glanced up and swore.

"Why are you swearing at the moon?" I asked.

"It's full," he said meaningfully, but at first I didn't get what he was trying to say.

"And a full moon is bad because..." My brain was catching up.

He raised his eyebrows and gave me a meaningful look, but before he could either confirm or deny my suspicions, Vaughn doubled over.

"Find Connor," he said. "Now! Nobody...else." His jaw clenched with the effort to control the pain, and sweat beaded his forehead.

I didn't want to leave him, but I didn't have any other choice. He was shaking so badly I was worried he was having a seizure.

Vaughn's gray eyes had turned silver. There was something happening to his lush lips. His sharp jaw elongated.

I ran inside and grabbed Connor's arm. "Vaughn's hurt."

"Xavier," Connor said.

"Already on it," he replied.

I didn't wait to see if they followed me; I just ran back to Vaughn.

Before I could react, there was a wolf—a creature that used to be Vaughn—on the patio, and it had me by the throat. Our eyes met, his black and wild, no trace of my boyfriend. His hand that held me was covered in fur with long, jagged claws. He was standing on two legs, not four, but all traces of human were gone. He didn't even smell the same.

"Don't move, Tansy," Connor said.

"He won't hurt me," I said. His hand was wrapped loosely around my neck, not squeezing. Vaughn let out a feral growl.

"You don't know that," Connor said. Out of the corner of my eye, I saw that he was inching closer. The moon would be fully out soon.

"I do," I said. "Vaughn would never hurt me."

Carefully, I put my hand over Vaughn's. The hair on his hand felt coarse and wiry. For a moment, his grip tightened. It wasn't painful, but I kept my eyes on his, and gradually, his eyes returned to their normal gray. He didn't shift back completely, but he was returning to his human form, just with more hair and a lot more attitude.

"We need to get him to the hospital," I said.

Connor shook his head. "Xavier is on his way. He just went to get the first-aid kit."

"We need a real doctor," I said. "Not just a med student."

"We can't take him to a doctor," Connor said. "Pack law. And besides," he continued, "if you take him to a non-supe doctor, they might do more harm than good. He just needs to make it through the first shift."

"What are you talking about?" I asked.

"Keep up, Tansy," Connor said. "Vaughn was bitten by

a rogue werewolf."

"A werewolf bit Vaughn?" I asked. Cold dread settled in my stomach. "What does that mean?"

Connor kept his eyes focused on Vaughn. "In Texas. Vaughn didn't say anything to you?"

I shook my head. "He hasn't exactly been chatty." My eyes narrowed as I realized something. Connor seemed unusually calm about the whole thing. "Why are you so unfazed?"

"Xavier is pre-med," Connor said. "He'll take care of Vaughn."

"What's taking him so long?" I replied.

Long minutes later, Xavier jogged to the patio, clutching an oversize first-aid kit. Skyler followed on his heels.

"I thought I told you not to let anyone else know," Connor said.

"Like I could stop her," Xavier replied. He turned his attention to Vaughn.

"Lucas is blocking the door," Skyler said. "What's going on?"

"Vaughn is going through his first shift," Connor said. His tone was bleak, his eyes black with repressed emotion. "Some werewolves don't make it through."

"Connor," Skyler said. "He's one of your best friends. You can't let him die."

"He's not going to die," Connor said.

"And you know that for sure how?" I said, panic and disbelief seething behind my words.

"We'll take care of him," Connor argued.

"He didn't tell me," I said. "A rogue werewolf bit my boyfriend, and he didn't tell me. Why would I be angry?"

Connor looked away as Vaughn screamed and then went limp. "What's he doing to him?" I tried to keep my voice from trembling, but I could barely get out the words.

Vaughn started to pant, and then a low, feral growl came from his throat. There was the sound of crunching bones, flesh ripping and tearing.

"He's helping him," Connor assured me. "The flesh will re-form."

"Xavier is helping him shift," I said accusingly.

He studied my face. "Yes."

"How did this happen?"

"Vaughn made a mistake," Connor snapped. "Haven't you ever made a mistake?"

My anger faded. "You're right."

"A bite doesn't always turn someone," Connor explained. But it did this time because Vaughn started to howl, and when I looked over at him, his face was covered in fur.

"How do you know so much about werewolf shifts?" I asked him, but I was pretty sure I knew the answer anyway. There was a reason Vaughn had turned to Connor for help.

Connor ignored the question. "Skyler, you and Tansy need to stay out of the way." He kept his attention on Vaughn.

Panic sweat oozed from my body, and I felt my fangs descend.

"Jesus, get her out of here," Connor said. "I can't deal with her vamping out when my best friend is going through his first shift."

His words cut through my growing bloodlust, and I snapped back into my body. I'd been thinking about blood while my boyfriend lay in agony.

My fangs retracted, and I took some deep, slow breaths until I was calm again.

The calm didn't last. Vaughn let out a terrible howl, and then his whole body shuddered. He fought Xavier's hold.

"Connor, I need your help," Xavier said. "He's too strong. I can't hold him without shifting."

I was focused on Vaughn. He sounded like he was in pain. When I glanced at Connor, he was gone, and a werewolf stood before me. Connor's eyes peered out at me from the body of a creature of myth, a creature of the hidden world.

Just like my boyfriend.

Chapter Eight

Skyler wrapped a comforting arm around me as we watched Connor, his big frame shuddering with the effort of holding Vaughn down, restraining his best friend.

When the clouds obscuring the moon lifted, the moonlight shone upon the three werewolves, but the moon's rays didn't seem to affect Xavier. Only Vaughn and Connor had gone full wolf, and it seemed that Connor's transformation was voluntary, Vaughn's less so.

Xavier pulled out a needle from the first-aid kit.

"What's that?" I asked.

"Tranc," he said succinctly, before he injected it into Vaughn's arm. He went limp, his body still.

"Is he breathing?" I asked. My palms were sweating. My heart was beating so fast I thought I was going to faint. "It doesn't look like he's breathing."

Vaughn's entire body convulsed, but when I tried to go to him, Connor stopped me. "Give Xavier a minute."

Xavier picked up Vaughn and laid him gently on one

of the patio tables. "He's coming out of it," he murmured. "Skyler, can you bring me a pitcher of water? But don't let anyone follow you."

She squeezed my hand briefly before darting back into the main part of the bar.

With a groan, Connor shifted back into human form, and I quickly averted my eyes as he bent to pick up his discarded clothing.

Skyler came back with the water and handed it to Xavier. He poured a glass and drank it while we stared at him.

"What? I was thirsty," Xavier said. His quip lessened the tension in my spine. I didn't think he'd be joking if Vaughn was in trouble.

Vaughn roused slowly and sat up.

"Careful," Connor said.

Vaughn groaned and put his hand to his head. "What happened?"

"First shift's a bitch," Connor said.

"Do you think they'll fight now?" Skyler asked.

My eyebrows knit together. "What do you mean?" My brain was still processing the fact that Connor Mahoney was a werewolf and I hadn't had a clue.

"You know, two werewolves in a brutal battle to decide who will be alpha," she replied.

Connor smirked. "That's not the way it works," he said. "No fights to the death." He didn't say it, but I knew he was thinking it. Not like vampires.

"So how do werewolves decide who is boss?" I asked.

"We arm wrestle for it," he said, deadpan.

"So you've never had to kill anyone?" I asked.

"I didn't say that," he replied. "Vaughn will be okay. He has to learn to control the wolf inside him."

"What happens if Vaughn can't control his wolf?"

"Then we'll help him," Connor replied.

"We're a team," Xavier added. "There's no fighting for dominance."

"Then how do you choose your leader?" I asked.

Xavier's dimples made an appearance when he was amused. "We vote on it, like normal people."

"Good thing, because I don't think Vaughn's in any shape to challenge anybody right now," I said. He groaned as his bones seemed to settle back into his human form. I wasn't sure he even realized we were there with him.

"His clothes are trashed," I said.

"I have some sweats that should fit him in the gym bag in my car," Connor said. "Tansy, would you mind getting them?" He tossed me the keys.

"I'll go with you," Skyler said.

"It's okay," I said. "While I get the clothes, could you go check in with the Old Crones? Tell them that we're hanging with Vaughn and Connor for the rest of the night or something." It wasn't a lie, but I also wasn't ready to face Granny right now. She'd take one look at me and see the freak-out written all over my face.

I spotted an exit that I thought would lead to the parking lot. From there, I followed the sidewalk, which led to a dark corner. Connor's orange Challenger was easy to spot, but I had to pass by what looked like a tiny outside break area next to the Dumpsters. There were a couple of chairs, and the ground was littered with cigarette butts. The streetlight had either burned out or had been busted out.

I found Connor's gym bag and grabbed it. No way was I touching anything in there, even if it was just a pair of clean sweats. The shoes he wore to the gym were probably in there, too.

When I got back to the patio, I was relieved to see Vaughn was more alert and was now sitting at the table instead of laying on top of it.

I handed the gym bag to Connor, and he rummaged through it before pulling out some clothes and handed them to Vaughn.

I started to turn my back, but Vaughn reached for my hand. "It's not anything you haven't seen before," he reminded me in a low voice.

My face felt hot, but I stayed next to him, just in case he lost consciousness or something. Connor must have had the same idea, because he stayed at Vaughn's other side.

Vaughn dropped my hand so he could remove his torn clothing. He shrugged on a new shirt and pants and put the torn items on the chair.

"I'll put these in the trash," I said. Then I quirked an eyebrow at Vaughn. "Unless you'd rather save them?"

He grinned at me. "I don't think I need them for a memory book or anything." His smile faded. The reality of what had happened was probably hitting him.

Nobody said anything, and I realized Connor and Xavier were waiting for me to leave. They obviously wanted to speak to Vaughn alone.

I exhaled loudly. At least now I knew why Vaughn had been acting so weird. I caught the scent of fresh blood and froze.

I scanned the area, looking for the source. My fangs

extended, my heart sped up, and my stomach growled. So gross.

I followed the metallic scent. In the shadows of an old oak at the edge of the property, I saw someone bent over a prone figure. The smell of blood was stronger here.

I dropped the gym bag. "Hey, what are you doing? Let go of them."

I flicked on the flashlight on my phone and aimed it at them, then wished I hadn't. Travis Jure, alleged reformed vampire, was standing over a bloody werewolf. And I was pretty sure that whoever it was, they were dead.

I screamed.

Chapter Nine

Unfortunately, it wasn't like I'd never seen a dead body before, but this was a particularly gruesome sight. The woman had been killed mid-shift. Her hands were curled into claws, and her jaw was elongated, teeth bared, but her face was still human. There was a gaping hole in her chest where her heart should be.

I finally regained control and clamped my mouth shut, but my scream had drawn attention. Luckily, it was just Skyler along with Connor and his pack, including Vaughn. He moved quickly over to me. He looked much better than he had ten minutes ago. Less hairy, too.

Vaughn pressed my face into his chest, but I couldn't block out what I'd seen. Travis Jure standing over a dead werewolf whose fur was soaked with blood.

Mixed in with the smell of blood was a heavy, floral scent. It was probably the victim's perfume, but something about the smell made me shiver with dread. It wasn't perfume, I realized. It was magic. Bad magic.

Just when I thought my life couldn't get any more f-ed up, Travis seemed determined to ruin it. Only Travis would kill a werewolf in front of Connor's entire pack. Vaughn had barely regained control, and I was worried Travis was going to set him off again.

But when I looked up at Vaughn, his eyes were fixed on me. "You okay?"

"I didn't do anything," Travis stubbornly insisted.

"Travis, you're covered in blood, and you were standing over a dead werewolf," I said. "Your alibi is weak." I tried to infuse my voice with every bit of power I had as I said, "Tell me the truth." It was either that or let the werewolves rip him apart.

"Her blood smelled delicious," he said. "I wanted it. So I took some."

"Was she alive?" I asked.

"This is a waste of time," Lucas snapped.

"Shut up, Lucas," Vaughn said.

Out of the corner of my eye, I watched Vaughn. His big body strained with the effort of not ripping Travis apart, and I was grateful he was letting me handle it. His eyes went silver, though, and I realized I didn't have much time left.

Travis made a move and tried to pin Xavier against the trunk of a tree. I snapped my fingers at the vampire.

"Come here," I said.

"Make me," Travis snarled.

I extended my index finger and beckoned him. I summoned every bit of my power to command and said, "Come here." I tried not to use my vampire powers too often, because it was a slippery slope. When I used my witchy powers, I tapped into something that was part of nature, alive, fresh, and green. But when I used my vampire ability, it felt icky, artificial, and dark, like I was channeling the worst part of myself. The part that craved power.

His forehead crinkled in confusion when his feet obeyed my command and brought him in front of me.

"Travis, was she alive when you drank her blood?"

"No, she was dead," he said.

Vaughn sucked in a breath, and Connor growled, low and threatening. The hair on the back of my neck stood up. One wrong move and he would tear Travis limb from limb.

The moon had decided it was time to shine, and I could tell the moonlight was making the werewolves more edgy than they already were, which was a hair's breadth away from snapping Travis like a twig.

"Do you know anything about any other murders?" Connor asked. "There's been a werewolf murder on the first night of the full moon every month for the last three months."

The vampire pressed his lips together and shook his head.

"Do you, Travis?" I echoed, then again, "Tell me the truth." I pushed up against his vampire will. "Now."

"I've heard rumors," he finally said. "Nothing concrete."

"What kind of rumors?"

"That it was another werewolf," Travis spit out.

I felt the hot fury coming off Connor in waves. "He's lying," he said.

For a long, tense minute, he and the vampire locked eyes. Skyler put a hand on Connor's arm, and his body relaxed minutely before she managed to lead him away.

"Travis, go home," I ordered. I realized I might need to get ahold of him again and added, "Where are you staying?"

He jerked his head, and I noticed a familiar tour bus parked near the front of The Last Stop. It hadn't been there when we'd arrived.

"Don't leave town," I said. "As your queen, I command you."

"I can't leave," Travis said. "We have a bunch of gigs here. Our country-and-western band is really taking off."

"Just make sure *you* don't," I replied. "Now, you may go."

And just like that, Travis went back inside the bar.

I turned to Connor. "I don't think he did it."

"Because he's not a killer?" he asked sarcastically.

"No, he's a killer," I replied. "But I believe him."

"You believe him?" Vaughn asked. His brows furrowed. "After everything?"

"Why would you protect someone who tried to kill you?" Skyler asked.

"Because I'm the queen of the vampires," I said. "And like it or not, Travis is one of my subjects. I have to treat him fairly."

"You're sure he didn't do it?" Connor asked. "Someone's life may depend on it." I wasn't sure if he was talking about mine or someone else's.

"As sure as I can be," I said.

I still couldn't look at the body on the ground. I wanted to ask what we should do about her, but Connor took out his phone and dialed a number. "We have another one," he told whoever was on the phone, then gave them our location and hung up. "Vaughn, take Tansy and Skyler back inside," he said.

Vaughn took me gently by the arm. "C'mon, Tansy," he said. "You've had a shock."

"We can't just leave her there," I protested.

"Our pack will take care of her," Connor said. "And we will find whoever did this to her."

"We already know who did it," Lucas snarled. "And he has fangs and a cowboy hat."

He was wrong, but Lucas had made up his mind, so arguing with him wouldn't do any good. Instead, I let Vaughn lead me inside.

Granny and the OCBC were still on the dance floor, but Rose and Thorn were at our table, trying to talk with Beckett over the music. It felt like we'd been gone for hours, but it had been less than thirty minutes.

Vaughn pulled out a chair for me and then eased into the spot next to me. He looked pale and his mouth was in a tight line, but he was keeping his human form.

The Thirsty Thieves were back onstage, and the country-and-western version of a mosh pit had formed in the front. As Travis's voice got louder, guys started slamming their bodies against each other, and then the inevitable fight broke out.

A bouncer, the same one who'd been at the door earlier, broke up the fight and made the group go back to their tables.

"We'll leave as soon as Connor gives us the all-clear," I said. I touched his hand with just the tips of my fingers. "I wish you would have told me," I said in a low voice.

"I was hoping it wasn't true," he admitted. "That it'd all just go away. But it didn't."

Finally, the night started to wind down. The band left

the stage, and a few minutes later, Granny returned with her silver fox still trailing behind her. "That was fun," she said. "Let's settle up the tab and get out of here."

Her dance partner, whose name I still didn't know, said, "Your tab's already been taken care of."

Granny went pink. "You didn't have to do that."

"My pleasure," he said. "I hope you had a lovely evening. I know I did."

I wanted to talk more with Vaughn, but Connor came back to the table. "Ready to go?" he asked Vaughn.

Vaughn met my eyes. "I'm spending the night at Connor's place," he said. "With the rest of the p—the guys." His arm went around me, and he gave me a brief hug. "I'll call you tomorrow."

"Famous last words," Skyler muttered.

Vaughn glanced at her. "I'm going to call Tansy tomorrow," he said. "And then she can tell you all about how I groveled."

"You plan on groveling?" I asked.

"Yes," he said firmly.

"Good." We smiled at each other before he leaned in and kissed me, just a peck. "Drive home safe."

"Why don't we walk you to your car?" Connor suggested, which I assumed meant the coast was clear.

We left as a group, and I noticed that Beckett, Lucas, and Xavier scanned the parking lot as we walked. Vaughn grabbed my hand and held it tightly.

After Connor's pack, which now included my boyfriend, escorted us to Skyler's car, they walked the rest of our group to Edna's minivan. I watched them as Skyler pulled out. They didn't get into the Challenger until we'd left.

I sat back in the seat and exhaled long and loud. "What a night," I said. "Can you believe The Drainers are back?"

"It's pretty ballsy of them," Skyler said, "even with the new look and sound. Did they think we wouldn't be able to recognize them?"

"Who knows how Travis's mind works?" I had no doubt that Travis was the driving force behind the Thirsty Thieves. "When his father was king, Travis got away with murder. But that's not going to happen during my reign."

"Why didn't you just stake him?" Skyler asked. "Problem solved."

"Have you ever killed anyone?" I asked. Fury made my voice shake.

"No," she admitted.

"It's not so easy," I said. "It stays with you, even when it's self-defense, even when you know they deserved it. I don't want to become the kind of ruler who can kill without thinking twice."

"Like Jure," she said. She was quiet a long time. "I'm sorry. I shouldn't have suggested that you just kill someone. Even Travis."

"We need to solve this," I said. If I didn't find out who was behind the murders, I'd have a vampire-werewolf war on my hands.

Chapter Ten

Sunday morning, I stumbled into the kitchen, still yawning, in search of my tonic. Instead, I found Edna, Evelyn, and Granny with plates of cake and cups of tea.

"Did your reunion with Vaughn go well?" Evelyn asked.

"Of course it did." Edna nudged her. "Don't you remember when we were seventeen?"

I gaped at them, floundering for an answer. I couldn't reveal Vaughn's secret without his permission. Finally, I settled for, "I was surprised to see him."

Granny held up a plate with a piece of cake on it. "Want a slice?" she offered. "It's lemon and lavender pound cake."

"Isn't it a little early for dessert?" I asked. I rummaged in the fridge until I found my Thermos. I opened the lid and sniffed it.

"This is our afternoon snack, Tansy," Evelyn said.

I frowned. I'd had a late night, but it was getting harder for me to wake up before noon even on the best of days. I had to set three alarms to make it to school on time.

"No, thanks," I said. "I'm not hungry." I gulped down the nasty beverage that kept me semi-human.

"I got you something." Granny dug into her book bag and then handed me a new charm. It was a tiny silver moon.

"It's so cute," I said. "What's this one do?"

"That one is special," Granny said grimly. "Something tells me you might need this. It's protection against certain creatures of the hidden world. Wear it next to your cornetto."

"Thanks, Granny," I said. I kissed her cheek. "I need to take a shower." I still smelled like sweat and fear from the night before.

"We've got to go," Evelyn said. "Edna wants to paint the bedroom, so we're off to look at color samples."

"Rose should be here any minute," Granny said.

"Rose is coming over?" I asked. "By herself?"

Granny nodded. "I told her she could use a corner of the backyard to plant an herb garden."

"What kind of herbs?" I asked. Rose's specialty was poison, so I was curious what kind of plants would end up in my backyard.

After I got out of the shower and changed into my favorite Saturday outfit, a worn tee and shorts, I wandered into the backyard. I stayed under the pergola and watched Granny and Rose bond over gardening.

Rose was on her hands and knees, digging in the dirt, while Granny handed her the seedlings. They were both wearing gardening gloves and hats.

"What kind of herbs do you plant in the fall?" I asked curiously.

"Peppermint, rosemary, thyme," Rose replied. "And a few others."

"What kind of others?"

Before Rose could answer, Granny held up a plant and cooed in delight. "This is a rare one, and it's so pretty," she said. "What's it used for?"

Rose glanced up. "I believe that an extract from that plant's blooms will render someone unable to move or speak within seconds."

"Oh, that kind of others." The deadly kind. Rose was so sweet that I sometimes forgot that poison was her choice of weapon.

Granny handed it to her quickly. Granny used plants to heal, and Rose used them to kill, but that didn't seem to bother either of them.

Granny glanced over and saw me. "Why don't we take a short break? There's something I want to show Tansy."

Witchcraft was about learning the secrets of the universe, the things only the hidden world could reveal to those in the craft. So whenever Granny wanted to show me something, I listened.

She handed me a small golden cylinder. "You can hang it on your necklace," she said. "But open it."

Inside was a piece of chalk, except instead of the typical white, this had a muddy color to it.

My brow furrowed. Why was Granny giving me chalk?

"It's mixed with Mariotti native soil," Granny said. "I'm going to teach you something new. We've been neglecting your education."

While Vaughn had been learning to hunt vampires, I'd been in California, learning to be queen. I was looking forward to learning a new witchy skill, which I hoped would be something slightly more useful than the ability to cast a spell to find a parking spot.

Rose brushed off her hands and came over to observe.

I picked up a piece of chalk and waited for further instructions.

"Draw a flower," Granny said.

"What kind?" I asked.

"Whatever you want," she replied.

I found some blank sheets of paper and then sat at the kitchen counter and sketched a daisy, which was the simplest flower I could think of. When I finished, I looked at Granny. "Now what?"

"Now you use your powers," she said. "Tell it to bloom. Magic has its own language. You need to find yours. Try it in Italian."

At my blank look, she prompted me, "Fiorine."

I wasn't fluent in Italian, but I copied her accent the best that I could. "Fiorine."

Nothing happened. "Bloom, dammit!"

The dull chalk began to glow, to change color, from muddy-white to pale yellow to brilliant lemon, the stems bright emerald. I blinked, and then the two-dimensional drawing was a living plant reaching toward the sky.

Apparently, my magic involved the use of sentence enhancers, as my granny called swear words. Words to be used sparingly, if at all.

Rose let out a gasp. "I've never seen that before."

I stared at the flower. Swear words and a bad Italian accent were the key to success, at least in my case.

"Very good," Granny said. She held out her hand, and I put the chalk in it. She put the chalk back in the box and gave it to me. "It's yours."

I glanced back at the flower, but it was already withering. "Was that supposed to happen?"

"Things die, Tansy," Granny replied.

"What kind of magic is that?" I asked. "And how am I supposed to use it?"

She studied my face for a long moment. "My grandmother used her chalk in emergencies, but once it's gone, it's gone."

"What would happen if I drew a dragon?" I asked.

"I believe a dragon would appear," she said. "But you don't have that much chalk."

"That's all it would take?"

"There's always a cost to magic," Granny reminded me. "You can also use your chalk for protection."

"Does my mother have one of these?" I asked, holding up the box.

"Your mother is beyond this kind of magic," she replied.

"Because she's evil?" I asked.

"Because she's drained a human of blood, felt their heart stop, and reveled in it. She can't come back from that."

"But I've been thinking about something. What if Jure was her maker? Now that he's dead, wouldn't she become human again?"

"Possibly," Granny Mariotti said and shifted uncomfortably. "It's not like vampires share information with witches."

My grandmother didn't like talking about my mother, so I changed the subject. "Rose, did I tell you someone sent me a ruby the other day?"

I didn't think it was a big deal to tell her, since she and Thorn were helping me get the realm in order.

I glanced over at Rose, who was staring at me. She

looked like she was going to be sick.

"Are you okay, Rose?" I asked.

"Just a little too much sun," she said.

"Sit in the shade and have something cold to drink," I said, but she shook her head.

"I have to go." She rushed out, abandoning the plants in their trays.

I gave Granny a perplexed look. "Was it something I said?"

"That *was* odd," Granny replied.

I stared after Rose for a minute. Neither twin was great at talking about emotions, so I decided to let it go for now and returned to grilling my granny.

"Did your friend from Italy ever find that book you were looking for? The one that mentioned a cure?" There hadn't been many striga vies in history, mostly because vampires were smart enough not to bite witches.

"It was a dead end," she said, but she avoided my eyes, which meant she'd probably discovered bad news instead of the solution I'd been hoping for.

Where did that leave me? I was part vampire, part witch, all alone with no one to talk to.

I would find the information. I had to, before I turned into a monster myself.

Chapter Eleven

Tuesday, Mr. Robinson announced there would be a huge Chem test at the end of the week, so that night Vaughn, Skyler, and I were studying in my living room. Granny brought out snacks and then sat in her favorite chair to read a biography of a dead president.

Vaughn chugged a big glass of water before I'd had more than a few sips of mine. Then he started on the mini meatballs, which were little balls of deliciousness.

When I looked up, the food was gone. Granny stared at Vaughn for a minute. "Still hungry?"

He nodded. "I didn't have much lunch."

I raised my eyebrow at Skyler. Vaughn had eaten an entire meat lover's pizza at lunch. The pack's grocery bill must be unreal.

Vaughn caught us staring and blushed. "If that's okay," he said. "Why don't I order something for delivery instead?" he asked, clearly embarrassed.

"We have plenty," Granny assured him. "You know I

love to cook."

Granny bustled off to the kitchen and then returned with a heaping plate of food for my boyfriend.

"There's something different about you," she said.

My head snapped up. We hadn't told Granny or anyone about what had happened at The Last Stop. Part of it was because I didn't want her to worry, and part of it was because Vaughn becoming a werewolf wasn't my secret to tell.

Vaughn took a gulp of his smoothie. "Like what?"

"Like your appetite," she said.

He laughed, but it sounded forced. "Growth spurt, I'm sure."

"Didn't they feed you enough when you were in Texas?" Granny asked. It was a casual question, but Vaughn's whole body went tense.

Whenever someone mentioned the vampire hunting portion of the summer, Vaughn's expression went blank. The last time I'd seen him trying to hide that much pain and fear was when someone mentioned his mom.

Granny went to her bedroom to read, and I decided it was time to ask my boyfriend a few questions.

"Are you ready to talk yet?" I asked Vaughn. "Because I am."

Skyler scooped up her backpack and stood. "That's my cue to make a quick exit. Night!" She left like she was being chased by bears. Or werewolves.

After she was gone, there was a long silence, then Vaughn started talking, stumbling over his words in his haste to get them out. "It happened the first time I was on patrol alone," he said. "I-I knew. Knew it was a werewolf.

Knew that the legends were true."

"But you didn't tell anyone? Not Rose or Thorn? Or anyone from the PAC?"

He shook his head. "I didn't trust anyone." I winced. Including me. I tried to cover it, but he noticed. "Tansy, I trust *you*, I do. I was just freaking out."

"Where'd you go when you left Texas?" I asked. "The twins said you didn't go with them to PAC headquarters."

"To talk to Connor."

"Why Connor?" *Why Connor and not me?* That's what I really wanted to ask but didn't.

"When he came back to the States, he told me the truth about why he'd left, so I already knew he was a werewolf when I left to train."

"When was he bitten?" I asked then added, "Or is that impolite to ask?"

"He was born a werewolf, not made."

"Connor has been a werewolf for as long as we've known him?" I asked.

"Yes. You can be bitten and turn, or you can be born a werewolf. Like the Mariotti witches are born witches."

"And then what?"

"I holed up at Connor's, feeling sorry for myself," he said. "The guys in the pack taught me how to control the shift, so that when my first shift happened, I'd know what to do."

"It looked painful," I said.

"It was." He hesitated, then asked, "Does it matter to you?"

"Does what matter to me?" I'd lost track of the conversation.

"That I'm a werewolf."

"Why would that matter?" I asked. "Does it matter to you that I'm a striga vie?"

Instead of answering me, he put his hands on my hips and drew me close. "Not. One. Bit," he said, accentuating each word with a brief kiss.

I wound my arms around his neck and tangled my fingers into his hair, massaging his scalp.

"That feels good," he said in a low voice, his lips a breath away from mine. I leaned in and pressed my lips to his. Vaughn was a great kisser, and he spent some time reminding me just how good.

After Vaughn and I said good night at his car, which involved a good ten minutes of him leaning me up against his Camry and kissing me senseless, I went back inside. I threw myself on the couch and fiddled with my phone for a few minutes. I put the name of the dive bar from the other night into the search engine, but there wasn't a lot of information. It had been open since late spring. It had previously been a family-owned restaurant called Ultima Parida, but it had closed suddenly and then reopened as The Last Stop. I googled the previous owners and found a small article about their sudden departure. In its previous life, The Last Stop had been a Mexican restaurant owned by a husband-and-wife team. I couldn't find much information about who the new owners were or what had happened to the old ones.

The online police blotter showed there'd been a few

fights at night when the restaurant started serving more alcohol than food. It wasn't technically a dive bar, but it was definitely a close relative.

It seemed like there had to be more to the story. What was I missing? I wasn't Nancy Drew, but the next full moon was only a few weeks away, so I was about to go all girl detective.

Granny was hosting the Old Crones Book Club, but it hadn't started yet, because they were waiting for Mrs. Nelson, who was habitually late. Not just for book club, but for her life. Granny must have invited Rose and Thorn, because they were lounging on the chaise as they flipped through the book club's latest read.

"I'm glad the full moon is over," Edna said.

"Strange things occur during a full moon," Granny said. "It's not just when werewolves come out."

I stared into space. I had approximately four weeks to figure out who was killing werewolves in my realm and why. It didn't seem to be nearly enough time. I glanced up and noticed she was staring at me. "What?"

"Just making conversation," she said mildly, but I was pretty sure Granny suspected something.

"Speaking of werewolves," I said casually. "Did you hear anything about a werewolf getting murdered?" I wasn't revealing Vaughn's secret by that question, and I was smart enough to know I'd need all the information I could get. The OCBC had a wealth of knowledge among them, and I needed to tap into it if I had any hope of figuring this out.

Before she could answer, a loud, mournful howl echoed throughout the hills to the east.

"That doesn't sound like coyotes," I said.

"It's not," Thorn said. "Don't you know the sound of a wolf's howl?"

I shook my head. I didn't, but I had a feeling I was going to get used to the sound.

"Vampires and wolves are natural-born enemies," Thorn replied.

I glared at her, then pointed at my chest. "Again. Not a vampire."

A second howl and then a third. More voices joined the others. The sound continued for several minutes until all but one dropped away.

"If they aren't coyotes, what are they?" I asked. "There aren't any wolves running around the suburbs of Southern California."

"Not wolves, either," Granny replied.

"Are you trying to tell me that my neighbor is a werewolf?" I shouldn't be surprised, but something about the news made me jittery. I tapped my foot while I waited for her answer.

Another howl rang out, and the sound sent a shiver up my spine. The low, mournful sound was full of sadness, but mixed with it was a clear feeling of rage.

"How many werewolves live in Southern California?" I asked. "And who's in charge of them?"

"They're part of the PAC, too," Granny said. "At least that's my understanding from Rose. But I don't know who the head of the local werewolf pack is."

My life was just getting back to the new version of normal. Sure, I couldn't stay at the beach all day, but I could still go to school, eat garlic, and hang out with my friends. Nobody knew why the rules didn't apply to striga vies, but I was grateful I didn't have all the vampire weaknesses. At least as long as I refrained from drinking someone dry. And now I had to deal with werewolves?

"I'll ask Rose and Thorn for more details," I said, but I wondered what else the twins had told my grandmother that I didn't know about. It wasn't like I hadn't figured out that there were other paranormal creatures. The existence of the Paranormal Activities Committee assured me that there were more than vampires lurking.

I grabbed every book Granny owned regarding werewolves and settled in to learn more about their history.

We spent the rest of the night in near silence, reading and listening to the werewolves mourn their dead.

Chapter Twelve

It was Friday night, and Granny was out dancing with Edna and Evelyn and some of the other Old Crones Book Club members. For all I knew, she was meeting her silver fox from The Last Stop. He'd been texting her, and although Granny was trying to play it cool, her smile got wider every time she heard from him.

Skyler, Vaughn, and I were having a movie night, like we used to before Vaughn and I had started dating.

Vaughn came out of the kitchen, carrying bowls of popcorn. He handed one to Skyler and then took a pack of M&Ms out of his pocket.

Skyler's face lit up. "Popcorn and M&Ms are my favorite," she said.

He smiled at her. "I know."

He sat next to me, and I snuggled into him to better appreciate his familiar scent, which was sunshine and sand and a little bit of sweat. My nose twitched when I detected something new. He smelled a little wild. It wasn't unpleasant, just unfamiliar.

We bickered over what movie to watch like we always did but finally settled in to watch a Marvel superhero movie.

"You haven't told us much about Texas," I commented.

"You haven't told me what you and Skyler did while I was gone," he countered.

"I'm just going to say it," Skyler interjected.

"What?" We both turned to look at her.

"It's kind of weird that my two best friends are a vampire and a werewolf," she said, giggling.

"Don't forget about your ex-boyfriend," I said. "Who seems to want to take the ex out of the equation."

"We're not talking about Connor." She sniffed. "Vaughn asked what we did while he was gone. I started a new business," Skyler said. "Selling Bloodsicles to vamps."

"Bloodsicles?" Vaughn quirked his eyebrow.

"Bloody frozen treats," Skyler said brightly. "Tansy loves them."

Vaughn frowned. "Is it safe?"

"They're made with blood from animals," I said, trying not to feel defensive.

"I meant safe for you and Skyler to be dealing with vampires at all," he said.

"They're my subjects, Vaughn," I said. "I have to deal with them." I crossed my arms over my chest. It wasn't like I wanted to take care of a bunch of blood-sucking fiends.

I still needed to figure out what to do about Travis and the other Drainers, the werewolves, and the potential feud. And find a werewolf killer. The one thing I was pretty sure of was that the killer was some sort of supernatural creature. It would take an inhuman amount of strength to rip someone's heart from their body.

Skyler got up. "I think I'll grab more soda," she said. She went into the kitchen and stood in front of the closed refrigerator for a long time.

I shifted in my seat. "Maybe we should just watch the movie before it gets too late."

"Is it safe to come back yet?" Skyler yelled from the other room.

None of us wanted to talk about the bad parts of the summer, so I faked a cheery tone. "C'mon, let's just watch before Vaughn has to go."

He groaned. "I hate Saturday morning shifts," he said. "It's like Dad can't stand to see me sleep in." Vaughn's dad owned the catering company where we both worked.

I gave him a sheepish smile. "I did the schedule this week." I had to because Vaughn's dad had been too distracted. He had some new girlfriend who had him all dreamy-eyed and dazed.

I glanced over at my boyfriend. I knew the feeling.

"We have another hour," I said. "We'll watch the end of the movie, and then we can walk Skyler home."

"Deal," he said. It looked like he wanted to say something, but instead, he picked up the remote and hit rewind. "I missed a bit of it."

We watched the rest of the movie in silence, partly because Vaughn couldn't talk while he was busy powering down an entire bowl of popcorn.

There was a knock at the door. *Weird*. It was after midnight.

"I'll get it," Vaughn said.

"It's okay," I said. "My leg's going numb. I need to

move." I carefully slid out of Vaughn's arms, then grabbed my drumstick from my bag and slid it into the waistband of my yoga pants before going to find out who was pounding on my door late at night.

Standing on my front porch was a young stranger. I took a closer look and caught a familiar scent.

No, not just a stranger. A vampire.

"I seek amnesty, my queen," he announced. He clearly didn't have the nerve to say it aloud, but from the way he eyeballed my outfit, I could tell I wasn't his idea of a vampire queen.

I had on a pair of yoga pants—but in my defense, they made my ass look amazing—and a tee Granny had brought back from a library conference that read, "*Check out my big books.*"

Judging by the way he was staring at them, I thought it was the pink hedgehog slippers on my feet that really threw him. "You *are* Tansy Mariotti? The vampire queen of California?"

"Yep," I said.

He took a step closer to the front porch light, which gave me a clearer view of him. He was young when he'd been turned and still resembled someone on the brink of puberty. He was trembling, and blood soaked his T-shirt and jeans.

"What did you do?" I asked. I didn't invite him in.

"Your Majesty?"

"What. Did. You. DO?"

He looked blank. "Does it matter?"

It seemed inconceivable to him that I'd actually care if he'd killed someone.

"Yes, actually, it does," I said, crossing my arms, but then I sighed. I was the queen; it was my job to show mercy. "You can come in," I said, holding the door open. "But no biting." I used my vampire ability to make the last part an order, one I knew he'd have to obey.

I led my visitor into the family room.

"Who was it?" Vaughn asked. "Did your grandmother forget her key or something?"

"Not my grandmother." I gestured to the vampire. "One of my subjects. He says he needs help."

"Is that blood on your jeans?" Skyler asked the guy. It was. The sweet, thick smell was making my head spin, but there was something unusual about it. It smelled earthier than other blood, but wilder, too.

"It's werewolf blood," I said before he could answer, "isn't it?"

He nodded, looking at his shoes. This young vampire seemed more scared than evil.

"Tell me what happened…" I paused and cocked my head in inquiry, since I didn't know his name.

"My name is Jared," he said. "I was at The Last Stop. They have live music on the weekends, and I was having a drink with some friends."

I narrowed my eyes. "What kind of drink?"

Someone pounded at the door, and his eyes widened. "Don't let them in," he begged. He was one of my subjects, but vampires weren't exactly trustworthy.

"I have to see who it is." I went to the door, irritated that my friends hang was turning into major drama.

The last person I expected, or wanted to see, was on my doorstep—Connor.

"What do you want?" I held the door open, but only a crack. I glanced back, hoping that Skyler had stayed put and wasn't going to have her night ruined by the sight of her ex-boyfriend.

"Tansy, where's the sucker?" Connor asked.

Skyler's laugh carried to us, and something like pain passed across his face. "Is Skyler in there?" Connor craned his neck to see inside the house.

I didn't have the energy to get into it with Connor, at least not tonight. Instead, I slammed the door in his face.

"Who was at the door?" Skyler asked.

I opened my mouth when the knocking started again. "Don't answer!" I finally said.

"Why not?" Skyler's brows knitted together.

"It's Connor," I admitted. The knocking continued, but I ignored it.

She started to smile but then went pale as it hit her, the reminder of all that had happened between them. Her eyes narrowed. "What does he want?"

The sound went from polite knocking to insistent pounding.

"I'll go," Vaughn said.

I watched Jared the vampire while Vaughn went to get rid of Connor. "Start talking. Quickly," I said.

"She was already unconscious when I found her," he said. "I just took a little drink. I didn't know she was a werewolf or I would never have…" His voice trailed off when my nostrils starting quivering. I had to clench my jaw to stop my fangs from coming down.

"You bit an unconscious werewolf. Tell me, Jared," I said, low and deadly. "Did you get a copy of my new laws?"

He gulped. "I did."

I held up a hand. "Please stop talking." He did, and I took a deep breath as I tried to figure out what he'd gotten us into. One of my subjects had bitten a werewolf. And now Connor was at my door, looking for "a sucker."

I wasn't thrilled with his terminology, but I knew one thing: this vampire had admitted to my face he'd broken vampire law and brought an angry werewolf to my door. The only thing in my favor was that it wasn't a full moon and the girl was alive. Or at least that was Jared's story.

"Jared, do you know the consequences for drinking without consent?"

"Banishment?" He said it like a question.

"Who is your ruler, Jared?" I asked.

He started to sob. "Please, Queen Tansy. I was so hungry."

"You are banished from this realm," I said. "Eighty-sixed. Kicked out of my realm and never allowed back. If you ever return, the penalty is death."

"But the werewolves will try to kill me if you don't help me," he said. His voice shook, and despite myself, I felt a twinge of sympathy.

"You drank from an unconscious werewolf," I said. "You're lucky I don't give you straight to them."

Instead of relief, I was surprised to see anger cross his face. "Why are you siding with those walking Furbies?"

"I'm not siding with anyone yet," I replied. "I'm trying to find out what really happened." A series of low growls came from outside.

"Don't move," I told him. "I'll take care of the werewolves."

Connor's voice rose. "We want the vamp, Vaughn."

I stomped to the front door. "The answer's no." Then I realized Skyler's ex hadn't come alone. Lucas and Beckett stood by Connor's car.

Skyler had absolutely perfect timing as she walked up to stand shoulder-to-shoulder with me.

The guys ignored us as they continued to argue. Connor said something to Vaughn to low for us to hear, but I caught Vaughn's reply.

"Tansy asked me not to tell you anything about Skyler," Vaughn said.

"What does Skyler have to do with Tansy being the vampire queen?" Connor's voice deepened.

"Go away, Connor," Skyler said.

"I didn't know you would be here tonight," he replied.

"Or you wouldn't have dropped by?" she challenged, but there was a trace of disappointment in her voice.

"He's not dropping by for old time's sake," I said. "He wants to kill one of my subjects. But I won't let him."

"He attacked one of my pack," Connor said.

"Tansy's subject," Vaughn replied. "Tansy's decision."

"Rose and Thorn will escort him from the realm. He's been banned." It seemed like a perfect job for the two vampire hunters.

"That's it?" Connor asked.

"It's not a full moon," I pointed out. "The girl is alive, yes?"

He nodded.

"He broke my law, and he will be dealt with," I said firmly.

Connor sighed and then gave a jerk of his head in agreement.

"Would it be possible to talk to her?" I asked him.

"You want to me to let a vampire queen talk to someone who was attacked by a vampire? No way."

"You don't know for sure that it was a vampire," I said. "Maybe I can find out something that will lead us to the real culprit."

He studied my face, and I had to force myself not to squirm.

"Okay," he said. "Give her a couple of days to heal. And I have to be there the whole time."

"Fine," I said.

"I do want to talk to you, Sky," he said.

"You have a strange way of showing it," she snapped.

"I don't think that's a good idea," I said.

"Tansy, I got this," she said. She stepped outside onto the front porch. "What do you want, Connor?"

"Just to talk," he said. "I can be reasonable."

If so, Connor had changed while he was away. When he was dating Skyler, he'd been stubborn, used to getting his own way.

Skyler cleared her throat. "What did you want to talk to me about, Connor? We're in the middle of a movie."

"Just the three of you?" Skyler's ex looked around suspiciously.

"Who were you expecting?" I asked, glaring at him.

Connor ignored me and stared at Skyler. "No date?"

She flinched, and for a second, I wanted to punch him, but his muscles would probably only hurt my hand.

"Connor, it's time for you to leave," I said firmly.

I really wanted to punch him again when he said, "I'll go, but be prepared for the consequences."

"Is that a threat?"

Vaughn grabbed my hand. "Tansy, let it go for now."

I nodded.

Connor hesitated, staring at Skyler intently, but she shook her head. "Go home, Connor."

He finally left, but Skyler stood on the front porch, watching him go.

I didn't want to leave her out there, but I needed to check on the vampire anyway. I went back into the living room and froze.

Jared was gone.

Chapter Thirteen

Saturday morning, Connor texted me and told me I could talk to the girl who'd been attacked. He sent me an address and told me he'd meet me there in twenty. I barely had time to brush my teeth and grab my parasol and drumstick before I had to leave.

We met at a coffee shop with the short and sweet name Beans. I was still in my faded T-shirt, pajama bottoms, and mismatched flipflops, with my hair piled in a bun on the top of my head, which wasn't exactly a regal image.

Connor sat at a table in the back with a gorgeous Latinx woman who looked like she was college-aged or maybe a little older.

I slid into a seat next to Connor. They'd been in a tense conversation when I approached, but they stopped talking when I arrived.

I held out a hand. "Hi, I'm Tansy."

She stared at me. "She's the queen of the vampires?"

I smiled at her. "Not what you were expecting, huh?"

"How is it that you can walk in the sun?" she asked, then realized she hadn't told me her name. "I'm Amy."

"Is it okay if I ask you a few questions?"

Connor stood and then asked both of us if we wanted anything to drink before wandering over to order. I noticed he kept a close eye on us, though.

"I'm not sure I can help you," she said. "I don't remember much about the attack."

"Do you remember going to The Last Stop?" I asked.

"Sure," she said. "This guy was supposed to be there, but he never showed."

"Cute guy?"

"Really cute," she confirmed. "Anyway, I decided screw him, you know."

I nodded.

"My friends and I were dancing, but I was getting hot and sweaty, so I stepped outside to cool down. That's all I remember."

"Nothing else?"

She hesitated. "I did smell something odd," she said.

"Odd how?"

"It was this really sweet floral scent," she said. "Like a perfume my grandma would wear, but more intense."

Connor returned with our drinks, but I made the excuse that I needed to get home before the sun got any higher in the sky.

"If you think of anything else, Amy, here's my number," I said.

A heavy scent would hide that distinct vampire smell, but there'd been a strange magical scent at the murder scene. Jared may have interrupted the killer. Or it was possible he *was* the killer.

I spent the rest of the day looking up spells that involved scent but reached a dead-end. It was time to get ready, anyway. It was date night with Vaughn. I appreciated that he was trying to get us back to normal, or whatever the closest thing looked like for two supernatural beings who were supposed to be enemies.

Except that Vaughn was late. I used the time to reexamine my outfit. I'd dressed up my favorite jeans with a green camisole top and dangly earrings. My charm necklace went with everything, and I rarely took it off, so my look was complete. By the time I reapplied my lip gloss, he still hadn't shown.

I peeked out the window and scanned the street. No sign of his car, but something else caught my attention. I sensed there was a vampire out there, watching me. Waiting.

"Granny Mariotti," I hollered. "I smell vampire."

I didn't wait for her but snatched up my drumstick and rushed outside. I scanned the street, trying to spot anything out of place, but it was empty except for our neighbor, who was giving me a weird look as she watered her lawn.

The feeling was gone.

I went back into the house. "False alarm, I guess," I said. "I need to stock up on Diet Dr Pepper." It didn't always kill them, but soda would slow a vampire down. That was something that wasn't in any of the paranormal books, probably because Dr Pepper hadn't existed in Bram Stoker's day.

I didn't want my vampire subjects to get comfortable enough to just drop by any time, and now that I thought of it, how had Jared found out where I lived? I made a note to ask Thorn about added security and maybe using some of the kingdom's money to set up an office for me, somewhere away from my home. I didn't want a hungry vampire, or anyone else, wandering into my house and freaking out my grandmother.

"What's got you so on edge, Tansy?" Granny asked.

"Just jumpy, I guess," I said. "I feel like someone's watching me, but whenever I look up, no one's there."

"I'll add some protective spells at the end of the street," Granny replied.

"Can't hurt," I agreed.

I was slipping my shoes on when I heard Vaughn at the door, his knock distinctive.

"I like that boy," Granny Mariotti said. "He has enough manners to come to the door."

"I like him, too," I said. "But he is late."

I opened the door. "He likes you, too," Vaughn said, "and sorry I'm late." How had he heard us? "Windows are open," he said to my unspoken question.

He wore a navy button-down shirt with the sleeves rolled up and a pair of jeans. He'd made an effort with his outfit, which made me glad I'd done the same.

"You weren't supposed to hear that," I said.

"But I'm glad I did," he replied. I hadn't meant to confess my feelings for him in front of Granny.

I took a closer look at him and knew something was wrong. His lips were upturned, but his gray eyes were stormy. I raised an eyebrow, and Vaughn shook his head. *Later*, he mouthed.

"We should get going," I said. The sooner the better.

Granny Mariotti smiled at us both and then gave me

a little shove. "Have fun."

Vaughn was quiet in the car, one of his hands rapping nervously on the steering wheel. "So there's been a change of plans. Our date night is now a group thing. At The Last Stop."

He didn't seem happy about it, but still, I snapped, "Why?"

"I'm sorry," he said. "I wanted to take you on a real date. Spend time together, just the two of us."

"It's okay." I put my hand on his knee. "We can do a little snooping while we have some fun."

"Connor said they'd meet us there."

I tried to think of something to talk about so Vaughn would quit white-knuckling the steering wheel. The canyon road was a twisty two-lane highway favored by motor- and bicyclists, so I couldn't tell if Vaughn's tight grip was because of the road or because he was nervous about something else.

When we arrived, a line had formed at the door, with a few girls wearing white hats and cowboy boots paired with short skirts and skimpy tops and a lot of guys with big shiny belt buckles and bigger attitudes.

A small sign announced that the Thirsty Thieves were tonight's band. We paid the cover charge, and the guy at the door stamped our hands with the eighteen-and-under stamp. Like I wanted to drink around Travis and his band.

Once inside, it was standing room only. We found Skyler and Connor over by the bar. He had one arm draped over her protectively, shielding her from the crowd. They seemed more at ease with each other. Skyler had a tentative smile, and Connor's shoulders were relaxed.

"Where are the guys?" Vaughn asked him.

"On their way," Connor replied.

"We need to pool resources," I said. "Share information."

An older couple and their kids got up from a table, and Skyler managed to grab their seats before anyone else spotted them. The table was tucked into a corner near the hall that led to the bathroom and what I assumed were offices.

It was quieter back here. As soon as we sat, I said, "Connor, tell us everything you know about the werewolf murders."

"Why should I?"

Vaughn sighed. "Quit jerking her around and tell us."

"I'm going to figure out who the killer is and stop them," I replied. "With or without your help."

He paused, then swallowed hard and said, "We think it might be a witch."

"*Which* witch?" I glared at him.

"Not your granny. Did you know that in ancient times, witches used to hunt werewolves?"

I shook my head. "No. Why?"

"Nobody knows," he said. "The kind of witches who practiced the dark arts aren't around to ask anymore."

"Do you have any evidence that it was a witch?" I asked. "Or any evidence at all?"

"No," he said. "The killer hasn't left many clues."

"I'll start researching werewolf-witch history," I promised. "Maybe I can find something in one of Granny's books."

The guys went to the bar to order drinks and some food. The place was packed.

The jukebox was playing, mostly country songs I

was unfamiliar with, although I was able to identify a Johnny Cash tune.

I noticed a girl dancing near the jukebox. She wore a short white skirt, a Western shirt decorated with red snaps, and red cowboy boots and hat. The hat hid her face and hair, but I felt like I knew her. She looked up. Natasha again.

Skyler and I didn't talk much while we waited for the guys to get back with our drinks. I studied the crowd, wondering if the murderer was here tonight. I was going to find out who had been murdering werewolves, even if it turned out to be one of my own subjects. If the killer followed the pattern, there would be another murder attempt during the next full moon. The knowledge set my nerve endings jangling.

A guy hovered by our table. "Would you like to dance?"

"No thanks," I told him. He was cute, but not my type because a) he wasn't Vaughn and b) he was too old for me—by about twenty years.

He glared at me before stomping off. Why was I worrying about hurting his feelings? I had the right to say no without an explanation and without feeling unsafe. Still, I wished Vaughn would come back.

Twice, someone asked me if we were using the other chairs, but I managed to shoo them off.

Finally, Vaughn and Connor returned. Beckett and Lucas followed them.

"Where's Xavier?" I asked.

"Studying as usual," Lucas said. "Medical school is no joke, even for a genius."

Vaughn raised his eyebrow. "Do I have competition?"

"Of course not," I said. "You're the only wolf for me."

They set down our drinks and plates of appetizers. Werewolves and their appetites.

"Sorry it took so long," Vaughn said. "The servers are in the weeds tonight."

Beckett got a little too enthusiastic and started singing. It was another Dolly Parton song. "Islands in the stream," he crooned, using big hand gestures. He knocked over someone's beer.

"Hey, that was my beer." The speaker was a big guy with a red *Bite Back* tee and a glare.

"Are you saying you want to fight?" Beckett beamed at the angry man.

"Beckett, that's not what he said," I protested. Beckett turned a dazzling smile in my direction.

"That's what I heard." He looked like a kid on Christmas Eve, only Santa was a guy in a trucker hat with a short fuse. "You said you wanted to fight, right?"

The stranger's brows drew together, and he hesitated, like he was puzzling something out. "Yup."

"Fight!" Beckett replied before he threw himself at the guy.

"He's going to get hurt," I said.

"Werewolves heal fast," Connor said.

The bigger man grabbed Beckett by his long red hair and used it to slam his face into the bar.

When blood spurted from Beckett's nose, the bartender's fangs flashed. This cowboy bar was full of vampires, and I'd have to stake someone if they tried to drink from Vaughn's friend. The sound of breaking glass mingled with the snarls and thuds.

"I'm going to tear out your heart, puppy," the vampire

who'd started it all said to Beckett.

"Stop!" I screamed. Everyone else froze, but the vampire moved closer. I grabbed his hand as it drew back. "I am your queen, and I command you to stop or suffer the consequences."

It looked like we were in a weird wrestling match as he tried to bend back my arm.

His smirk faded when I flashed my fangs at him and said, "You don't want to do that."

"I don't?" He didn't sound certain, so I twisted his wrist.

"I am your queen," I repeated. "And when I tell you to do something, you will do it."

After a long moment, he nodded. "Yes, my queen."

The band finally showed up and were mobbed by their fans. After about ten minutes, Travis went by us with a gorgeous older man with curly blond hair, probably headed for somewhere more private. The Thirsty Thieves must not have known I was here. Or they didn't care.

They were probably headed for a tiny room with a couple of saggy sofas, stocked with goodies. Now that Travis was cut off from his father's money, I wondered briefly how the band was living. I'd left them their tour bus, but not much else.

One by one, the guys in the band left with their chosen donor. Except for Boris, since he was a werewolf and wouldn't need a blood donation.

Boris went past us. I thought he was probably on his way to the bathroom, but he didn't come back. What was he up to?

There was a roar of applause when the band took the stage. The sound of loud, angry country music filled the air. A faint hint of vampire compulsion was threaded through the lyrics. The song was loud and the lyrics were vaguely insulting to women. All about girls, dark roads, and moonshine. Not my favorite combination.

Vaughn wasn't paying attention to the stage. He stared down at his phone, frowning. "We need to go," he said. "Dad had an emergency at the office."

"Everything okay?" Skyler asked.

"The whole commercial kitchen flooded," he said. "Dad needs my help."

"I'm great with a mop," I said.

"It's okay," Vaughn assured me. "He already called the plumber. I'll take you home and then head over there."

"The guys and I will go with you to help," Connor said. "Skyler, I'll walk you to your car." So they hadn't driven together. Interesting.

Skyler's chin went up. "I'm staying here."

He opened his mouth to protest, I'm sure, but I said, "Why don't you guys go on ahead and I'll ride home with Skyler?"

"It's okay," Skyler said to Vaughn. "I'll fend off the guys and make sure your girlfriend doesn't get hit on too much."

"Like that's gonna happen," I scoffed, but Vaughn didn't look convinced.

I gave him a soft kiss on the lips. "I'm perfectly capable of standing up for myself."

"I know," he said. "I just worry." He tugged me closer and gave me a deep kiss. Vaughn had reason to worry. I'd almost died this summer, and he'd given me his blood to save me.

Neither guy looked like they were thrilled with the

idea, so I added, "Striga vie, remember? And I brought my drumstick along, just in case."

Connor and Vaughn stood to leave. Connor looked like he was going to try to kiss Skyler goodbye but settled for a touch to her shoulder. He whispered something that made her cheeks turn pink.

Vaughn bent down to kiss me again. "This is not how I wanted the night to end," he said against my lips. "I'll call you later."

After he left, the band played a few more country songs that had similar lyrics. When they paused, the crowd started making requests.

"Play 'Feeder'!" someone shouted.

"No, I wanna hear 'Breeder'!" another voice shouted. We stayed at the back of the crowd, where I hoped the band wouldn't spot us, and I watched them closely.

Travis opened his mouth and started to sing the lyrics about a bro-dude with a cowboy hat and a bad attitude that had raised my hackles before. I could detect the compulsion. When he'd been the lead singer of The Drainers, the melodies had been sad, haunting, but beautiful. This compulsion was all rage and testosterone. I noticed a few glassy-eyed stares from the guys in the audience.

Red-faced and sweating, the men crowded around the stage, and I fought the urge to snarl at them. They started to push each other, and as the song got louder and louder, bodies slammed against one another. By the time the song was halfway through, beer bottles were being thrown as well as fists.

A guy in a Stetson bumped into Skyler, and my fist went out before I could stop it, but I managed to force myself to relax and unclench my fingers.

I grabbed Skyler by the arm, and we made our way out of the rage pit. Our table at the back was still empty, so we sat there to catch our breath.

Someone had been teaching Travis to control his vampire talent, but who?

A broken beer bottle missed his head by a few inches, and the song abruptly cut off. The band exited the stage and didn't return. I wasn't sure if it was because he knew I wanted to talk to him or because the jagged beer bottle made him skittish. A few inches lower and Travis would have gone poof.

Skyler and I stared at each other.

"That was weird, right?" We discussed theories about why Travis was back but couldn't decide if it was ego or revenge that motivated his reappearance into our lives.

"Don't worry," I assured my best friend. "I won't let anything happen to you."

"Right back at you," she said. It was late when we made it out of the club. Most of the crowd had dispersed, and I was tired.

Travis was using his abilities to drum up anger in the crowd, but what was his motive?

"I wish I knew how to prove he was compelling through song again," I said. "Right now, it's his word against mine."

"Maybe one of his victims will talk," she said. She hesitated and then finished, "It's aimed at enraging the audience. He's still compelling them."

"I think so, too," I said. "I didn't catch it at first because it's so different from how he sang this summer."

We walked silently the rest of the way to her car, but

I stayed alert. It was scary sometimes to be a girl walking after dark on a deserted street. Even though I had powers, magic couldn't protect me from everything. Skyler seemed equally tense, scanning the shadows every few seconds.

I smelled vampire even before I heard their footsteps. Vampires, at least the ones I'd met so far, had a distinct smell of decay they couldn't conceal. It was like rotting apples mixed with milk that had turned chunky. Two of them, male, both wearing cologne, either to disguise the stench or because nobody had ever taught them that less was more.

Skyler and I were almost to our car when they approached us from behind. I whirled, drumstick concealed in my long sleeves, to find two good ol' boy vampires leering at us. They had blood-red trucker hats with the words I SUCK AND BITE on them.

So did their attitudes about women, which dripped with skeevy. Or maybe that was just the profuse amounts of sweat coming from their pores.

Their button-down western-style shirts were tucked into jeans that looked like they belonged in a museum.

"Hello, sweet thing," the taller guy said to me. What made guys act like that? Like they owned a girl, body and soul, even when they didn't even know her name?

"Does that ever work?" I replied.

"What do we have here?" Tall Guy said. "Something sassy."

"Looks like dinner to me," the other one said. They were both big guys with a resemblance that suggested they were brothers or maybe cousins.

The younger-looking vampire had the sleeves of his shirt rolled up, revealing a snake tattoo on his forearm. There was something repulsive about it.

He saw me staring at it and grinned. "You know what this means?" he asked, stroking the tattoo with a gesture that felt obscene.

"That you have no taste?"

The other vampire lunged for me, but I was expecting it. "Get back," I ordered. "Or you'll regret it."

His eyes narrowed. "Who died and made you boss, missy?"

I flashed my fangs at him. "Jure Grando."

"You're not the queen," he scoffed. "You look like you belong in the back of your boyfriend's Chevy."

Skyler and I exchanged a glance. "How do you expect these assholes to know you're the queen?" she asked.

She had a point. I gripped my drumstick. I'd hate to have to make my point with my trusty weapon, but I wasn't sure I had a choice. They didn't seem interested in letting us go.

"Do you know who we are?" The male vampires seemed offended that we weren't aware of their identities.

"Do you know who *I* am?" I replied. I flashed my fangs at them, but they weren't impressed.

"I don't see any mark on you," Shorter Vamp said.

"Mark?" I asked.

"Your mark," he said impatiently. "Where's your mark?"

"I don't have one," I replied.

"You're a vampire," he said. "Who do you belong to? Your den? Your house?"

"I belong to myself," I said.

"Who do *you* belong to?" Skyler asked.

To my surprise, he answered her. "Den of Snakes. California branch." That explained his tattoo.

"I would have guessed pig pen," I said. "From the way you smell. But looks like I'm your queen. So back off."

"You gonna let her talk to you like that, Jeff?" Shorter Vamp said. "Are you a leader or a bleeder?"

"Shut up, Lennie." Jeff made a grab for Skyler. He held her by the waist, but she stomped on his foot. It didn't work. Those cowboy boots were tough. He probably didn't even feel it.

"Let us go," I said. "And nobody has to get hurt."

"We're not worried," Jeff said. He grabbed Skyler by the hair and bent her neck back, his fangs gleaming.

I twirled my drumstick once and then threw it at the closest target, the shorter vamp, Lennie, who wasn't holding Skyler. "Fly true," I said. I didn't want to kill him, and I'd been aiming for his shoulder. But he moved at the last second and the drumstick went through skin and bone to his heart. At this rate, I wasn't going to have any subjects left. I didn't like killing, even though vampires were technically already dead. My hands were shaking, and the smell of decay made me want to throw up.

"You're going to regret that," Jeff said. He shoved Skyler, and she almost fell but managed to scramble to me. I leaned over and helped her up, then grabbed my drumstick from the puddle of goo that used to be Lennie.

"Jeff, do you know who I am?" I asked again.

Instead of answering, he lunged, but I'd been expecting it. I twisted away and then my drumstick was at his throat.

"I'm the Vampire Queen of California," I said.

And he must have believed me this time because that's when he ran.

Chapter Fourteen

The next weekend, Thorn knocked on my door bright and early. Early enough that the sun wasn't even up yet. Neither was I, but that didn't stop Thorn.

I staggered to the living room. I'd stayed up late, looking through reference books to see if I could find anything that mentioned witches hunting werewolves, but nothing came up.

Granny's books did yield a mention of the Blood of Life Ruby, but it was just about how it had gone missing when the owner died. Nothing about what it could do or why someone would want it, besides the obvious monetary value, of course. The description matched the ruby in my possession, but it still didn't explain the weird energy I got from it or even why it was called the Blood of Life.

"Why are you here?"

"Training," she said.

"But it's the long weekend," I wailed, only halfway kidding. Labor Day weekend should mean barbecues and the beach, not bruises. "I want to sleep in."

"Train now. Sleep later," she said. She crossed her arms over her chest. "You need to get into shape. Unless you want to be a lazy ruler."

Ouch. Thorn had no problem with honesty. Brutal, unnecessary honesty. "All right, what are we doing today?" I replied.

"Running." Thorn started to weave her long black hair into a braid, and I noticed there was a hint of another color showing at the roots. I knew that the twins both dyed their hair, since Rose's hair was a candy-color pink not found in nature and Thorn's was midnight black.

"What's your real hair color?" I asked curiously.

Her eyes flashed, and she bit her lip. For a second, I thought Thorn looked guilty, but that couldn't be right. Her expression cleared, and she met my eyes. "My hair isn't nearly as pretty as yours."

I touched a strand. "Thank you."

"Now, quit trying to change the subject. It's time to run."

I groaned. "I would never have agreed if I'd known what you had planned."

"Put on a sports bra and some self-respect and let's go," she snapped. I felt like I should have saluted her or something.

Instead, I did what she ordered, grumbling the whole time.

She was waiting for me outside, with two water bottles in hand. The sun wasn't even up, and there was a heavy fog coming in from the ocean.

"You need to learn to run," she said.

"I know how to run," I said. "I just don't want to."

It was starting to make sense why Thorn was here before the sun was even thinking of coming up. We had time for some exercise, which was sure to be long, painful, and grueling, before my unnatural allergy to the sun's rays made it hard for me to be outside.

"You got lucky when you killed Jure Grando," she said. "There are stronger, more vicious vampires still out there. If you come up against them, you will lose."

"Your faith in me is heart-warming."

She grunted. "You're…not the worst vampire queen I've ever met."

She waited impatiently as I stretched.

"Where's Rose?" I asked.

"Still sleeping," Thorn replied.

Which is what I should be doing.

Thorn and I had never spent much time alone together. I tried to make conversation. "It must be nice having a sister," I said.

She widened her eyes and then laughed. "At least I wasn't alone."

"Do you get along with your parents?"

A strange expression crossed her face. "It's just my father. My sister is his favorite."

Her lip quivered. I'd never seen Thorn look so vulnerable.

She cleared her throat. "What about you? Did you want siblings?"

"I did," I admitted.

"You can have mine," she said. She bent down to stretch out her calves, and I couldn't see her face, but it didn't sound like she was joking.

"I thought you and Rose got along well," I said.

Thorn twisted up to look at me. "We do. But my sister is everything my father values. She's beautiful, quiet, obedient. I'm not."

I frowned at her. "You're both beautiful." I didn't want to point out the obvious, but they were identical twins, even though they had completely different style and hair color.

"It's time to train," Thorn said abruptly. Clearly, our moment of bonding was over.

"Why are we doing this anyway?" I asked. "It's not like I can outrun a vampire."

"There are other things to worry about besides vampires," Thorn said.

I stopped moving. "Like what?"

"Werewolves, banshees, Medusas, Narcisi, and stupid people," she said. "Just to name a few. All of whom can run faster than you can. Your granny can run faster."

I wasn't going to argue with her. Granny Mariotti was in shape, not just for someone her age, but for anybody. She and the other Old Crones took yoga, spin, and kickboxing classes at the senior center. And she'd survived a vampire attack this summer. I rubbed my cheek. I'd survived, too, but not without a few scars.

"We'll walk to your friend's house," Thorn said. "She can come with us."

I thought about trying to get Skyler out of it, but my best friend might have to fight, too. Training would be good for the both of us, and if not, at least misery loved company and all that.

I sent Skyler a text, and then we headed to her house. The marine layer was thick, and I could barely see two feet in front of me. Or maybe that was because my eyes weren't all the way open yet.

I was surprised when Skyler bounded out of her house as soon as we got there.

I raised an eyebrow. "You're up awfully early."

"My stepmother was throwing up this morning," Skyler said. "It woke me."

"Is she okay?" I asked.

"She said it was too many margaritas," Skyler said, then paused. "But I haven't seen her drink in months."

"What else could it be?" I asked.

"Maybe she's pregnant," Thorn said. "Dad told us my stepmother barfed…" Her voice trailed off, and she frowned.

"Eww, gross," Skyler said. "My dad's old." She wrinkled her nose at the thought. "But Gertie isn't."

"Wouldn't it be nice to have a little brother or sister?" I asked. Then I realized what Thorn had revealed. "Thorn, you have a half sibling?"

She gave a curt nod and then shifted on her feet. "Why are we still talking about this? Let's go before the sun comes out," Thorn said.

I complained the entire time about how out of shape I was, but I had to admit it did feel good to be outside.

Skyler was full of pep when we started, but after a while, she and I lagged.

"She just keeps running," Sky marveled at Thorn between gulps of breath. "She's not even sweating."

"What did I do to deserve this?" I panted.

Thorn whipped her head around. "You are the queen now, and you have to be ready to take on those who would harm you and the ones you love."

Okay, then.

Since it was (barely) morning, there weren't very many cars on the street, but Thorn veered off and headed for the bike trail. The trees shut out most of the light. When I stumbled, Thorn made an exasperated sound.

"You don't have vampire vision," she said. She sounded disappointed.

"That's because I'm not a full vampire," I said. "Just some weird hybrid. And Skyler is fully human."

Because that's the way my life went. Sky had spent the whole summer acting as a vampire musician's personal blood bank, and *I* was the one who went vamp. And when the vampire thing combined with the witch thing, I became a vampire-witch, and I had no idea how to balance the two sides. The sight of blood used to make me woozy, but now it just made me hungry.

"Quit feeling sorry for yourself," Thorn said. "Lots of people have it worse than you."

I stopped running. "Who? Who has it worse than me? I can't even go to the beach during the day."

Skyler murmured something consoling, but I was sick of acting like everything was just peachy.

Before Thorn could answer, a sound I'd never heard before, a low growl that made the hair on the back of my neck stand up, came from somewhere behind me.

"What was that?" I asked.

"Probably a coyote," Skyler said.

The sound came again. "It doesn't sound like a coyote."

Thorn stopped running. "Quickly now," she said. "Skyler, you take the lead. My queen, I will follow you."

"What is it?" Skyler asked.

Thorn didn't answer her. "If you plan to eat breakfast, my queen, we must end our training for the day." Now her breath came in short gasps, like she was finally winded.

Or she was scared.

We left the trail and ended the run where we'd started, at my house. I was doubled over and wheezing, but Skyler was barely breathing hard. Thorn looked shaken, either by the animal we'd heard or by my lack of athletic prowess.

"Let's go to Janey's Diner," Skyler suggested. We both studied the sky as if it would give us the answer. "It's still early," she added. "We could get those breakfast burritos you like."

I made a face. "It's supposed to be sunny today. I don't want to chance it."

"It's foggy right now," she said. She looked so hopeful that I couldn't bear to say no. "They'll be open. Bring a hat."

I was sweaty but didn't want to take the time to shower, so I wiped off the sweat and sprayed on a little perfume before I grabbed my hat.

Thorn drove, and Skyler took shotgun so she could give directions to our favorite Saturday morning hangout, although we'd never gone quite this early. Thorn's car was a nondescript sedan, spotless, but there was something rattling around in the trunk. I hoped it was just her spare dagger.

Thorn ignored the sound as she pulled into the parking lot. Her eyes swept the area, searching for any potential threats.

All I spotted was the diner's mustard-yellow building. Even from the outside, I could smell butter and maple syrup. My stomach growled.

The diner was almost empty, except for a couple of

older men who were drinking coffee and reading the paper. Later, it would be packed with people, but not even the early birds had rolled out of bed yet, which was the one plus of Thorn making me train at a time when I'd normally still be burrowed under the blankets.

Janey's seventies decor needed an update, but the beige walls, the orange upholstered booths, and Janey's collection of vintage neon signs were comforting in their familiarity. People came for the food, not the atmosphere.

The only server was Dave, the owner's grumpy college-aged son, who looked like he hadn't bothered going to sleep the night before.

He was stocking the pie display on the counter, holding three pies along one arm while he opened the case with the other. The middle pie, which looked like blackberry, teetered, and then plopped on the floor. He swore and then noticed us watching him.

"Sit anywhere," he said, then disappeared through a door leading to the back, probably to get a mop to clean up his mess.

"I'm going to the bathroom," Skyler said. "I sweated off all my makeup. If Dave comes back, order me an orange juice."

The two guys at the counter left as we headed toward a booth. Then the bell above the door jangled, and on reflex, I looked over…and a monster walked in.

The thing was nearly seven feet tall, with black fur, enormous teeth, and a flat, catlike snout. But it was bigger than any cat I'd ever seen. Something had bitten off a good chunk of its left ear.

"Do. Not. Move," Thorn said, but I'd already started for the door.

Someone tackled me and threw me over the counter and onto the floor. A hand sealed tight over my mouth before I could scream.

I almost bit it off at the wrist before I realized it was Thorn. Her eerie lavender-blue eyes were full of something I'd never seen there before—fear. Thorn was afraid, which sent a shiver of dread down my spine.

"Hellcat," she mouthed. "It was tracking us on our run."

I had so many questions, like what the ever-loving frack was a hellcat, but I knew it wasn't the time.

When I nodded, she took her hand away and drew her blade.

I wasn't sure which smelled worse, vampires or hellcat, but this hellcat carried a distinct smell of brimstone and burned marshmallow.

"Don't hurt it," I said. She gave me a disbelieving look.

"It's starving," she said. "It'll rip us to shreds."

"Okay, *try* not to hurt it," I said.

"I may not have a choice," she said. Thorn handed me a fork.

"What do you want me to do with this?" I asked. "Have a snack?"

"A fork is a perfectly adequate weapon," she replied. Her voice was shaking.

I took the weapon slash eating utensil. "I won't let it hurt you."

Then it found us. The hellcat lunged at me, snarling and snapping, and Thorn smacked it hard on the muzzle. The hellcat swung its enormous bushy tail and sent her sailing.

"I thought cats liked witches," I said.

The cat knocked me over, its paws the size of my head.

It kept one paw on my chest as it held me down, saliva dripping along its snout into my face. I held up my fork, but weakly, because the animal weighed a lot and was pressing down on my chest, making it hard to breathe.

I tried to tell myself I was a badass striga vie and either the witch side or the vampire side could kick this kitty's ass. But when its sharp teeth narrowly missed piercing my skin, I just tried not to pee myself.

There wasn't much time before Skyler was going to return. What would Granny do? I dropped the fork, put one hand to my charm necklace, and tried to think of a spell, any spell, that would help.

I rolled away, but the cat followed. We'd landed near the exploded blackberry pie. I didn't want to hurt the big cat, so I needed a plan. Why did they hunt?

Hunger. I whispered a quick amplification spell and then added, "You know what might taste good? Pie. Would you like a slice?"

There was a huge chunk of it still in the plate. Time to play *Hungry Hungry Hellcats*. I scooped it up and threw it into the animal's maw.

It gave out what I thought passed for a happy purr and then licked the rest of the pie from the floor.

While the hellcat was occupied, I reached a hand up, opened the case, and fumbled around until my fingers touched a pie plate. I knocked it to the ground, and the animal lapped up the blackberry pie before trotting away.

I finally let out the breath I'd been holding.

Thorn and I stayed where we were. "See? Everyone likes pie," I told her.

I totally deserved the dirty look she gave me.

Chapter Fifteen

After the hellcat left, I was still prone, breathing hard, while Thorn lay next to me. I wasn't sure who was shaking more, Thorn or me.

I glanced at Thorn. "You all right?"

"Fine, Your Majesty," she replied.

"Have you fought a hellcat before?" I asked. Her face paled, and I hurried to add, "You don't have to answer that if you don't want to."

"No," she said. "It's okay. I met a pride of hellcats when I was much younger."

"What happened?"

She lifted the hem of her shirt up until her stomach was revealed. "This."

It was a mass of scars. I winced at the thought of how much pain she'd experienced.

"That looks like it hurt," I said.

"They tried to tear out my stomach," she said.

"Why would they attack humans?" I asked.

"I displeased the PAC leader, Mason Alicante," she said. "He sent them after me."

I turned over the information in my mind. "This Mason guy can control animals?" I asked.

"He's an animal telepath. He can talk to them."

"Like Doctor Doolittle?"

She shook her head slowly and emphatically. "No."

I flinched. "So, you think the head of the PAC sent Blackberry after me?"

"Blackberry?" Thorn asked.

"The hellcat liked blackberry pie, hence its name," I said.

"It could be someone else," Thorn said, but she didn't sound convinced.

Skyler came back from the bathroom. "Why are you still on the floor?" she asked. "It's probably filthy."

Thorn had been shaking, and it had seemed more important to help her, but Skyler was right. The floor was nasty.

"No reason," I said before I jumped to my feet.

Thorn stayed where she was. "Is it gone?"

I held out a hand. "It's gone. But how did it even get in here?" I asked.

"Doors aren't obstacles for hellcats," Thorn replied. "They can materialize right through them."

"What does keep them out?" I asked.

"Wards sometimes work. Salt mostly. When a hellcat comes for you, there's not much you can do," she said, then added dryly, "except, apparently, feed it."

Dave emerged from the back and stared at the mess. "I don't even want to know," he said. "But you're going to help me clean this up."

A trash can, a mop, and several scrubbings later, it was like it had never even happened. Then I used some of Jure's dirty money to pay for the pies the big cat had eaten.

Thorn still looked shaken, so I led her to a booth.

Now that the place was clean and Dave hadn't had to lift a finger to make it that way, he was appeased enough to bring us menus and some water.

I ordered hot tea with honey for Thorn and me, and Skyler ordered orange juice.

"What happened to you guys?" Sky said. "I was only gone a few minutes."

I told her about the hellcat, while Thorn stayed silent, staring into space.

When Dave came back with our drinks, Thorn was still in some kind of a trance. I ordered her a pile of pancakes with fresh fruit and whipped cream—the sugar would help with the adrenaline crash—and Skyler and I decided we'd have the same. I was shaky, too, and I didn't think my favorite breakfast burrito would cut it.

"Is she okay?" Skyler asked me.

I gave Thorn a sidelong glance, but she didn't seem to notice. "Do you want me to call Rose?"

"I'm fine," Thorn replied. "Stop trying to baby me."

Her surliness had returned, which seemed to be a good sign. It was better than the blank stare.

I shrugged. "The hellcat freaked you out." It'd freaked me out, too.

"What is that exactly?" Skyler asked.

"Like a Siberian tiger on steroids," I said. "A creature from the hidden world."

"Those beasts have one job," Thorn said tonelessly.

"What's that?" I asked.

"To kill," she replied. "The question is, who wants you dead badly enough to send a hellcat after you?"

I could think of a few people, including my own mother. "The list is long and getting longer," I replied. I tried to shake off the way my entire body was still trembling. "Enough about me. Let's talk about you for a change."

"Connor called the other day," Skyler said, way too casually.

"He did?"

"I'm not a hundred percent sure why," she said.

I opened my mouth to reply, but then Dave came back with my pancakes. I picked up a fork and shoved a huge bite in my mouth.

As we ate, I kicked myself for not warning her about Connor earlier, and finally I couldn't take it anymore.

"Skyler, do you think that's a good idea?" She was going to go nuclear. My voice squeaked, so I cleared my throat.

"What are you talking about?" she replied, but her usual smile was gone.

"Do you think it's a good idea to start talking to your ex again?"

She squinted, like she was either trying not to swear or not to cry. "He apologized. He asked me to forgive him, says he wants another chance. Would *you* give him one?"

"I don't know," I said. "I still want to give him a junk-punch so hard they'll feel it back in Ireland…or wherever he ran off to."

Her face went red, then pale. "It's not like your boy-friend handled it much better."

"Vaughn did handle it better," I said. "At least he didn't

move to Ireland and break my heart."

"Okay, fine," she replied. "But Connor says he wants a second chance. And part of me thinks I should give it to him." The sadness on her face made me want to find Connor and suggest that he take the first available plane back to Europe. But Connor had already proven that he only did what he wanted, with no regard to anyone else's feelings.

She clutched her phone. "Gotta go," she said. "I promised Gertie I'd go with her to the doctor."

I searched my mind for anything to keep her there a little while longer. I didn't want her to leave while she was still so upset.

"How's the 'cooking for vampires' plan going?" I asked.

"The what?" Her face went blank, then she snapped her fingers. "I'm still searching for a commercial kitchen. I could ask my dad, but he'd want to know about my customer base."

Since her customers would be anyone with fangs, I saw her point. I was still in awe that Skyler was willing to interact with vampires, after all she'd been through, but she'd always had an entrepreneurial spirit, which she'd gotten from her dad.

"You know," I continued, ignoring the face she was making, "I really like the Bloodsicles." She'd laced them with animal blood and thought it would be a good way to provide a service to vampires and earn a little extra money. She'd even worked up a logo with an image of a fanged mouth licking one of her frozen treats.

She smiled. "I thought maybe I could put them in the vampire newsletter."

"Maybe we can use some of the kingdom's money for a business training program, get you some help in expanding your venture," I said. "Not all of the Bleeders had somewhere to go after the band broke up. They could help you with production."

"Yeah, good idea," Skyler said. She seemed to have lost her sudden desire to leave, because she went back to talking about *my* problem. "Do you think the crones know anything about hellcats?"

I nodded, but my mouth was too full of food to speak.

"You have to tell your grandmother what happened here today," Thorn said. "Or I will."

Dave came by with our check. "Was that a jaguar?" he asked.

"You saw it?" I asked.

"Yeah, it just trotted off," he said. "There was someone with it. Maybe a trainer? Are they shooting a movie around here? That would be cool."

We exchanged looks. "What did the person look like?"

He threw up his hands. "I don't know. They had a hoodie on."

"Did you notice how tall they were? Anything about their face?"

"No," he said. "They looked like a normal person, you know. Someone you'd pass on the street without looking twice."

After Dave left, I asked Thorn, "Exactly how many people have access to a hellcat?"

• • •

When we got back to my house, Thorn said she had to call in the attack to the PAC and took off.

"I've got to go, too," Skyler said. "Gertie's waiting on me."

We said goodbye, and then I went inside to find out what my grandmother knew about hellcats.

I summarized the attack at the diner for her. Granny took the news fairly well.

"The important thing is that you managed to escape," she said. She hesitated and then asked, "Are you sure it wasn't a werewolf? No, it couldn't be. They can walk upright."

"It was a feline, not a canine. I saw its face up close," I said. "I think the PAC sent it."

"Let's not jump to any hasty conclusions," Granny said.

"Who else could it be?" I replied. "Thorn even said that when she pissed off the PAC, they sent hellcats after her."

"You are the ruler of a large kingdom now," she pointed out. "And vampires covet three things: money, power, and blood."

"You never really think about vampires saving for retirement, do you?" I asked.

Granny chuckled. "But why would they need a hellcat to do their dirty work?" she asked. "Vampires just kill people and take their stuff." She glanced at my face and added quickly, "Not all vampires, of course."

"You may be right," I said.

Who would send a hellcat after me? And more importantly...why?

Chapter Sixteen

The next day, Vaughn was leaning up against my locker, which meant he'd wanted to see me first thing in the morning. I liked seeing him there, until the thought occurred to me that it could mean he had bad news.

"Hi, Vaughn." I smiled at him, but he didn't return it.

"I need to talk to you," he said. "In private." He took my hand and was already steering me toward the supply closet when I noticed Ashley, Vaughn's ex-girlfriend, giving me the glare of death.

"First bell already rang," she said.

"Thanks for the heads-up," I replied. I was pretty sure she was more upset about Vaughn and me breaking a rule than she was that I was dating her ex.

I really wanted to flash my fangs at her, but Granny and I had agreed that knowledge that vampires existed would be shared on a need-to-know basis. And Ashley didn't need to know.

Instead, I gave her my best *I hope you swallow a stake*

smile, grabbed Vaughn's hand, and pulled him into the closet. It was tiny and smelled like bleach, but then Vaughn pulled me close, and I breathed him in.

He smelled like sunshine, salt, and freshly washed guy. "Did you go surfing before school?"

"Not surfing. Paddle-boarding," he said. "I missed our beach when I was in Texas."

"Don't they have beaches in Texas?" I asked. I missed spending the day at the beach with him, too.

"There wasn't any time," he said. "But you know what I missed more than the beach?" He stepped closer. "I missed you. We haven't spent much quality time together."

"I don't mind hearing that," I said. I liked where this was going. My boyfriend was looking hot in jeans and a gray tee with the words *I LIKE A GIRL WHO READS* across it.

"Did Granny give you this?" I used the question as an excuse to reach out and touch the letters on his chest.

He laughed. "Who else?"

His eyes were on my lips. "Maybe I should just show you how much I like a girl who reads."

"You should. You really should," I replied.

He didn't kiss me right away. Instead, he brushed a stray lock of hair back from my face. "You are so gorgeous," he murmured. "I don't think I tell you that enough."

"You've kind of had a lot on your plate lately," I said. I kissed the spot just below his Adam's apple, and a shudder went through him.

He pulled me closer, until our bodies were close enough that I could put my head on his chest.

"You know it doesn't make a difference to me, right?" I asked.

"That I turn hairy and howl when the moon is full?" he replied. "I know." He tilted my chin up until our eyes met. "Just like nothing could change the way I feel about you."

I nodded because my throat was suddenly too tight to speak.

But I didn't think Vaughn had pulled me in here to make out in the supply closet.

I cleared my throat. "What did you want to talk to me about?"

"I forget," he said. He nuzzled my neck, and I nearly forgot my own name.

"We have approximately five minutes before your ex either tattles to a teacher or starts spreading the rumor we're hooking up in here," I warned.

He looked like he wanted to argue but then said, "I talked to Dad about his new girlfriend."

"What did he say?"

"He wants me to meet her," he replied. Vaughn and his mom had been really close, so it must be hard for him to think of someone taking her place.

He buried his face in my neck. "I need some of that quality time we talked about. Let me hold you."

I stroked his hair gently while the embrace went on.

"He says they're serious," Vaughn finally said.

"How did they even meet?"

Vaughn choked out a laugh. "They met at a country-western bar."

"Like The Last Stop?" Vaughn's dad had always leaned more toward oldies rock and smooth jazz.

"Yeah." He snickered. "He says they have matching cowboy hats."

"What else did he tell you about her?" I asked.

"Not much," he said. "Just that she's great, and he thinks they're in love."

"So why are you worried?" I asked. "She sounds harmless."

"I've just never seen him so…into anyone besides my mom," Vaughn said. His mom had died when we were in fifth grade. I could understand why Vaughn would feel resentful about a new woman in his dad's life.

"Come over tonight," I said. He gave me a devilish smile that showed his dimples. "Not for that." Then I smiled and added, "Okay, maybe a little for that."

His dimples deepened as he leaned and nuzzled my neck. We were definitely going to be late for class. Someone yanked open the door. A tall, thin, frowning woman with glasses and a glare—the school principal. "Ms. Mariotti, Mr. Sheridan, my office. Now."

It didn't take a witch to know that Vaughn and I *would* be spending some quality time together. In detention.

Chapter Seventeen

The dismissal bell rang, but I wasn't quite ready to face my punishment yet, so I made a quick stop in the bathroom with Skyler.

"I need a haircut again," I told her as we both checked our images in the mirror. I pulled my hair up into a loose bun and then checked my fingernails. They were already getting too long.

"I can cut it again," Skyler said. "I like doing it."

"I love it when you help me with my hair and makeup," I said.

"That's what friends are for," she replied.

My classes were over for the day, but I had to hang around. Detention was not optional. As Sky and I walked down the hall, signs for the Homecoming dance were everywhere. I stared at one of the posters. This year's theme was I DON'T WANT THIS NIGHT TO END. Would Vaughn ask me to go?

I took a closer look at it. "Is that a cow?"

"The best artist in school is Christian G., and he got suspended, and the rest of the art crowd is preparing for a gallery show or something," Skyler said. "We had to make do."

"What did he get suspended for?" My mouth gaped open. Christian G. did the artwork for every dance, football game, and bake sale we had. More importantly, he was the most chill guy I knew. I'd never seen him angry.

"He was fighting with Lazlo," Skyler told me. "Christian called Esme a name."

Esme was Lazlo's girlfriend. "Christian actually insulted someone?"

She nodded. "And it was bad enough that Kellie wouldn't tell me what it was he said."

"That doesn't sound like him," I commented.

"Maybe you can ask him about it," Skyler said. "Since you'll both be in detention today."

"They didn't expel them for fighting?"

"No one saw any actual physical blows," she said. "Just a lot of yelling. So they both lucked out and got detention. Speaking of which, I can't believe *you* have detention today, you little rulebreaker, you."

I made a face. "Ashley saw Vaughn and me go into the supply closet and tattled."

"Figures," she said. "Remember in elementary when she told the teacher you were reading during class?"

"I forgot about that," I said. "I was worried that it was more personal."

"You mean because Vaughn's her ex?" Skyler shook her head. "I heard she has a new guy." She was in Associated Student Body with Ashley, so they served on a lot of committees together.

"Anyone we know?" I asked.

"She's dating Aiden Matsuda," Skyler replied. He was the ASB President and loved rules as much as Ashley.

"They're perfect together," I said.

Skyler rolled her eyes. "Perfectly perfect. How're things with you and Vaughn?"

"Vaughn is a tasty snack," I said, then started to backtrack. "I mean that in a he's so gorgeous I want to eat him way. Not, you know, in an actually eat him way."

Skyler giggled. "I knew what you meant," she said. "I'm really happy for you two."

"Me too," I replied. I leaned in and looked at a bump on my chin. Was I getting a pimple? Could vampires break out?

Skyler dug into her bag for some makeup and pulled out a tube of lip gloss. "Do you like this shade?"

"Cute," I replied. "Is it new?"

After she finished putting on lip gloss, she replied, "Gertie and I went shopping yesterday. She bought it for me." Sky frowned and then continued, "I'm starting to like her."

"Oh no," I said. "Poor Gertie."

Skyler and I had a running joke that her dad got twitchy about the same time that Sky started getting used to the new stepmother. Almost as soon as Skyler got attached, that stepmother was out the door and Mr. A was inviting another one in.

"Maybe it'll be different this time," Skyler said, but she didn't sound convinced.

"She is gorgeous," I said. "And nice." But that hadn't

mattered before, either.

"Dad's been 'working late' again," she said, using air quotes.

"Already?" I made a face.

"I don't know what else to think," she said. "But I really like her."

I wanted to call Mr. A up and tell him his revolving door of wives hurt Skyler, but instead, I gave her a side hug. "Sorry, Sky."

She shrugged. "Enough about me. When are you going to ask Vaughn?" Skyler pointed to another of the Homecoming dance signs we'd passed.

My shoulders tensed, and I shook my head. "You and I are going together, remember?"

"That's right," she said. "We planned it ages ago. But that was before you and Vaughn became 'you and Vaughn.'"

I didn't want Skyler to feel weird now that Vaughn and I were a couple. "That doesn't change anything. The three of us can go together." I smiled in relief, but it wasn't like Skyler to give up so easily. The smile she gave me back didn't ease my concern.

"Unless I find someone to ask to the dance," she said, a little too casually.

"Like who? Connor?" I wrinkled my nose.

"Things are kind of weird with us right now." She hesitated, then said, "He keeps asking me to let him explain."

I threw my lipstick in my purse so hard it ricocheted back out and fell to the floor. It was my favorite, but I called it a loss and tossed it in the trash. "What did you say?"

"I told him I'd think about it," she replied. "Maybe we

can all go together. A group of friends hanging out."

"You mean Vaughn and me, you and Connor?" I asked. "Don't you think he needs to explain himself before you go on a date with him?"

"Not a date," she said. "A group activity. Besides, you know his whole pack will go wherever he goes."

I checked the hall to make sure we were alone. We were. "What aren't you telling me?"

"Connor and his pack—well, everyone except Xavier, who's some kind of genius and is already in medical school at twenty—are enrolling here."

"At Golden West High?" I stared at her. "Where did they go before?"

"Virtual learning," she replied. "Since Connor took off, anyway. But now they're all coming here."

"Does Vaughn know?" I asked.

She nodded. At first I was hurt, but then I realized he'd been distracted by the situation with his dad or he would have probably told me already.

"I know Vaughn has a lot going on right now," she said.

That was an understatement. Connor and Vaughn had been best friends before Connor had taken off without a word to anybody.

"You and Vaughn were friends first," she finally said. "And you love each other. Just talk to him."

I sighed. "You're right," I said. I gave her a hug, which she wiggled out of. "I'm going to tell him everything I've been stressing out about."

"I wish Connor would have talked to me," she said. "Instead, he just dumped me and then ghosted. It hurt."

"I know." I hugged her again. "He's an asshole and

didn't deserve you anyway."

"Maybe," she said, but she didn't sound convinced. "Or maybe I was wrong about him."

"You think Connor was *right* to ditch you like that?"

"No," she said. "But it's more complicated than that. He was hurting. Sometimes, you do messed up stuff when you're in pain."

I knew she wasn't just talking about Connor. She blamed herself for what happened to me this summer, but it wasn't her fault. It was Travis's. "You're right," I said.

"And I'm right that Vaughn's going to ask you to Homecoming." She gestured to the poster.

"He hasn't yet," I replied.

"Then ask him yourself," she said, then gave me an assessing look. "Unless you're chicken."

"I'm not chicken," I said. "Little Miss Chicken Clucks."

Skyler had won a beauty pageant contest when she was ten that had been sponsored by her father's fast-food company, and occasionally, I liked to remind her of her tiara and feathered sash.

"He does like to dance," I said. "But there's a lot going on with this dad right now," I added. I checked the time on my phone and made a face. "Sorry, I have to get to detention. I don't want to get a detention for being late to detention."

"I'll walk with you," she said.

When we got to Mr. Robinson's classroom, he wasn't there, but Vaughn was waiting in the hall.

"We still have a few minutes," he said. "What's new, Skyler?"

"Not much since the whole Janey's thing," she replied.

"What Janey's thing?" he asked.

"Didn't you tell Vaughn about the giant cat who tried to eat you?" she asked.

"What?" Vaughn growled. Telling Granny about the hellcat attack wasn't as stressful as telling my boyfriend. He was not nearly as sanguine as Granny when Skyler spilled the tea.

I dug into my backpack for a snack and took a big gulp of my tonic to give me a few seconds to think about what I was going to say. I hadn't meant to keep it from him, but my class load was no joke. I'd been busy writing papers and studying. I'd also been training with the twins and trying to be a good ruler, which meant listening to vampires' complaints, which usually consisted of whining about my new rules. I'd had to settle an ownership dispute about an abandoned building in L.A., which was settled quickly when both vampires revealed they'd previously used it as a human hunting ground.

"It slipped my mind," I said. "I've had a lot going on."

"You forgot to mention that you were attacked." Vaughn's face was red, and he glared at me like I'd broken his favorite guitar.

"It wasn't that big of a deal," I said. "It liked pie."

"You were attacked by a demonic feline and fed it banana cream pie," he said.

"Blackberry," Skyler said.

Vaughn gave her a confused look.

"It was blackberry pie, not banana cream," she explained.

"It was both," I said. "That hellcat could eat a lot."

"Blackberry or banana is not the issue," Vaughn snarled. "The issue is that you were attacked."

"I'm okay," I said. "Skyler was in the bathroom and missed the whole thing, but Thorn was with me." I wrapped my arms around him and hugged him. He nuzzled my neck and took a deep breath, then nodded.

Skyler was grinning at us. "You two are the cutest."

"I've never heard of a hellcat before," Vaughn said. "What did it look like?"

"Bigger than a tiger, black fur, fiery eyes. Bad attitude."

He paused, thinking. "Who do you think sent it?"

"There are a few possibilities," I said. "Including Connor."

"It wasn't Connor," Vaughn said. "Or anyone else in the pack."

"You seem certain," Skyler said.

"I am," he said. "You don't really think he could do that, do you?"

I shrugged. "I'm not sure I know him at all anymore," I said. "He kept secrets from us." He wasn't the only one.

Mr. Robinson walked up to us and pointed at Skyler. "You, out. No socializing here." Then he gestured for me and Vaughn to get inside the classroom.

"Have fun in detention, you two," Skyler sang out before walking down the hallway to the outside doors and freedom.

Mr. Robinson was the teacher in charge of detention, and since he taught Chem, his classroom always smelled like singed hair and Bunsen burners.

Lazlo was at a table in the front while Christian was in the opposite corner in the back. Rose and Thorn were sitting in the middle.

"What are you two doing here?" I asked the twins.

"The same thing as you," Rose said.

"Names?" Mr. Robison asked dryly.

We gave him our names, and he frowned at Rose and Thorn. "You're not on my list," he said.

"We wanted to experience detention," Thorn argued.

Mr. Robison looked at them like they'd each grown an extra head. "You need to leave. Now."

They slowly filed out, and then Mr. Robison opened a drawer in his desk. "Phones in here until this is over."

One by one, we dropped our cells into the drawer. When Mr. Robison was looking down, counting the phones, Christian gave Lazlo a hard shove as they passed each other before they retreated to their corners.

I took a seat near Christian. Something about him was different. Vaughn sat next to me.

It was hard to remember at this moment, but Vaughn and I'd gotten off lightly with only one day of detention. Everyone liked Vaughn, even our grumpy, hard-ass principal.

Mr. Robison took out a crossword puzzle.

After a few minutes, Mr. Robison stood, crossword puzzle still in hand. "I'll be back. No talking."

We listened to the sound of his feet receding.

"He won't be back for at least ten minutes," Vaughn said.

"Vending machines?" I asked.

"Bathroom break," Christian said.

"For ten minutes? Ew." I made a face. I had so much to do and was stuck here. I couldn't even do homework.

"Your ex sucks," I said to Vaughn. We wouldn't be in here if Ashley hadn't snitched.

"That's chicks for you," Christian said. "More trouble

than they're worth."

"Chicks." I raised an eyebrow. "What year is it again?"

Christian smirked at me. "If you're not a breeder or a feeder, you should keep your mouth shut."

I sucked in a breath. WTF?

"Don't talk to her like that," Vaughn snarled.

"Don't talk to *anyone* like that," I said.

Christian tilted his neck when he shrugged, and that's when I noticed the bite mark above his collarbone. The blood froze in my veins.

"Where did you get that?" I asked.

"It's not your business," he replied. "You're a nosy bitch."

"It's with a w, not with a b," I told him. I'd never heard Christian call anyone a name before.

He muttered something foul under his breath.

"What's wrong with you?" I asked. "And where did you get that bite?"

"Stay out of it," he said.

I couldn't. Not if a vampire was compelling him. I took a closer look at him and realized the graphic of his shirt were two interlocking Ts.

"Are you a Thirsty Thieves fan?" I asked. "If you are—"

I broke off when I saw Mr. Robison standing in the doorway, glaring at us. That was not ten minutes.

Obviously, Christian doesn't know I'm queen of the vampires. But he does know a vampire. I'd stake my life on it.

Mr. Robison was known for leaving to raid the teacher's lounge for goodies about halfway through detention, so I waited until his stomach gurgled. Ten seconds later, he left with another short command: "No talking while I'm gone."

The door slammed closed, and Vaughn got up and sat

on my desk. He smelled delicious, like sunshine and ocean breezes.

I was still a little hurt that he'd gone through something life-changing and hadn't told me about it. I hated the doubts running through my brain.

"Want to do something this weekend?" he asked. He threaded his fingers through mine.

"Like a date?"

"Why do you sound so surprised?" he asked.

"I wasn't sure you wanted to," I said stiffly.

"You weren't sure I wanted to go on a date with you?"

Uh-oh. I'd hurt him. "I didn't mean it like that."

"I don't know how many ways I can say this. You're it for me. You're my one and only, and I hope I'm yours."

"You're it for me, too," I said, my voice husky. Christian made a scoffing noise, but I ignored him.

I had to kiss Vaughn after that, so I pressed my lips to his but made it quick because it wouldn't take Mr. Robison long for snacks.

Some of my anxiety eased. It was a good reminder; Vaughn kept his promises. What was the matter with me?

"Tansy…would you go to the dance with me?" The slight tremor in his voice told me he was nervous.

I beamed at him. "I'd love to." I was smiling so wide that my cheeks hurt. I squeezed his hand. "We could use a little fun." Then I realized something, and my smile faded. "Wait. We can't go," I whispered.

"Why not?" Vaughn whispered back.

"Full moon."

"I'm not going to let that stop me," he said. "Besides, Connor is asking Skyler, so I'll have backup if I need it."

We heard footsteps in the hallway, and Vaughn scrambled back to his seat.

By the time Mr. Robison dismissed us at five, it seemed like we'd been trapped there for a week.

We collected our phones, grabbed our backpacks, and bolted.

"Want a ride home?" Vaughn asked.

"If you don't mind," I said. "The Deathtrap was being stubborn, so I caught a ride with Skyler this morning."

We were almost to his car when Rose and Thorn appeared and fell into step behind us.

"Is it my imagination or have they been hovering lately?" I asked Vaughn.

"We can hear you," Thorn said.

I turned to face them. "That means you're too close," I said. "Back off."

They exchanged a glance and, without a word, bowed in unison before they walked to their car and got in, Thorn behind the wheel.

That car followed us all the way home. They'd done what I told them, and I hadn't even used my power of compulsion. It was a relief to know that, sometimes, people would listen to me without it.

"What was it like training with them?" I asked. We'd been dealing with a lot since he got back, and we'd never talked about his actual PAC experience.

"The twins?"

I nodded. "I can't help feeling there's something they're not telling me."

"Like what?"

I shrugged. "I don't know. It's just a feeling, but

whenever I ask questions about the Paranormal Activities Committee, they get weird."

"I don't blame them," he said. "I didn't learn much about the PAC when I was in Texas, but they do not play around."

"What do you mean?"

"We were following this group of vampires who were raising hell all over the place," he said. "The order was to take out the leader."

Interesting. "Go on."

"Thorn and I were ahead of Rose, closing in on the head vamp, when Rose was surrounded by six or seven vampires. We ran back to help her and fought our way out. We had to kill those vampires to save her, but the leader got away."

"The important thing was that you saved Rose," I said.

"Exactly," he replied. "But when we got back to the house where we were staying, Thorn reported in. When she told the head of the PAC, this asshole named Mason Alicante, that we'd lost the leader, he told her that she should have left her sister and completed the mission."

"You're kidding?" I asked.

"That's the kind of people you're dealing with," he said. "You're right to be suspicious of the twins. Thorn would do anything for her sister, but…"

"But what?"

He gave me a long, hard look, then said, "If the PAC leader ordered her to take you out, I'm not sure what she'd do."

Chapter Eighteen

Monday morning brought a new challenge when I saw Lucas and Beckett walking the halls of my school.

Beckett waved wildly at me while Lucas settled for a smirk. Beckett bounded over to me, his limitless energy not stifled one bit from being in a strange place. At least someone in the pack was happy to see me.

They were part of Connor's pack. Where he went, they followed.

Werewolves were loyal, I'd give them that.

The bell rang. I was relieved when they turned and walked in the opposite direction of my class. At least I didn't have to deal with Lucas first thing in the morning.

Several heads turned as they went, Beckett flashing his dazzling smile that seemed to stun several of my classmates. I hurried to class.

After class, the twins walked with me. I wasn't looking where I was going and bumped into someone.

"Sorry," I said and looked up. It was Christian.

His eyes were red-rimmed, and he was shaking.

"Are you okay?"

"Mind your own business, feeder," he answered with a glare and then marched off without a word.

"What's his problem?" Thorn asked.

"I'll go talk to him," I said.

I wasn't sure he'd listen to me, but I tried anyway, wondering if I could help. "Christian, wait up."

He ignored me and bolted away. I stared after him. I couldn't force him to talk to me, though.

The rest of the morning included a pop quiz and an assignment that I'd managed to forget at home.

At lunch, I was feeling frazzled, sitting alone in the cafeteria. Skyler was at a doctor's appointment with Gertie. The "food poisoning" was almost certainly a little brother or little sister for Skyler.

"Meditation can help with that," Connor told me. I'd been lost in thought and hadn't heard him approach. He took a seat next to me.

"To help with Vaughn's bad moods?" I asked.

Amusement crossed Connor's face. "I meant yours."

I punched him lightly on the shoulder. He rubbed it. "Meditation for sure."

I stuck out my tongue.

"I'm glad to be back," Connor said.

"If you ever hurt my best friend again, you won't be."

"I won't," he said. He hesitated. "At least, I will do my best."

"Do better than that," I replied. He nodded, and then I added, "I'm glad you're back, too."

We ate in silence for a few minutes, but then I asked,

keeping my voice low so we wouldn't be overheard. "What if the murderer is human?"

"Unlikely that a human could overpower a werewolf," he pointed out.

"Have there been any murders in any other part of the country?"

"Just here," Connor replied.

"And why do you think that is?"

"My uncle thinks it's because the paranormal leaders in Southern California are..." he hesitated. "Inexperienced."

I winced. "The inexperienced leaders being you and me?"

"Yep." He took a huge bite of his sandwich.

"What do you think?" I asked.

"I think it's personal."

I paused, my drink halfway to my mouth. *Personal? Does he mean him or me?*

"How's it going with Skyler?"

"She's changed," he admitted glumly. "She doesn't trust me."

"Do you blame her?"

He shook his head and returned his attention to his meal. I got the impression there was still something else he wanted to tell me.

"Spit it out, Connor," I said.

"Have you found any useful clues?" he asked in a low voice.

"Not yet." I studied his face. "Travis said he didn't kill her."

"And you believe a sucker?" he asked. "Vampires lie all the time. Especially that one."

I glared at him. I couldn't believe it, but I was defending *Travis*. "Don't call him that."

"Vampires and werewolves are enemies," he said. He crossed his arms, and the muscles in his arms tensed.

"Are *we* enemies?" I asked.

"Not yet," he replied. There was a warning in his voice.

I clenched my jaw and willed my fangs not to appear. I managed to control my inclination to respond to his unspoken challenge.

Vaughn, Beckett, and Lucas slid into the seats next to us, their trays piled high.

"We still on for yoga tomorrow?" Beckett asked Vaughn.

"Yoga?" I asked. Beckett was constantly in motion. I had a hard time picturing him staying still long enough to hold a yoga pose.

"It helps with the grr," he said.

I quirked an eyebrow at him.

"It helps us control the wolf," he said. "Meditation, too."

"You can control when you go full werewolf?" I asked.

He nodded. "Most werewolves can, after they learn coping tools." He hesitated like he was getting ready to tell me a secret—and maybe he was. "It's hardest to control during a full moon."

Then the bell rang, and Connor stood. "You should find the murderer, Tansy," he said. "Because you won't like what happens if we find them first."

No pressure or anything.

I hurried to my next class and was halfway through Calc before I realized that I'd forgotten to drink my tonic at lunch. My interaction with Vaughn's pack had been mostly positive, but there had been a hint of menace in

Connor's last statement that worried me, so much so that I'd forgotten my lifesaving tonic. And it wasn't just my life that it could be saving.

I raised my hand for a bathroom pass and managed to grab my backpack without the teacher stopping me, then rushed to the bathroom to gulp it down. I put reminders on my phone before I went back to class.

When school finally ended, I waited for Vaughn in the gym, since he was supposed to be giving me a ride home after his workout. I caught a couple of stares, probably because I was wearing a wide-brimmed hat and sunglasses indoors. Rose and Thorn kept me company while I sat there. The weight room was just off the gym, and through the open doorway, I saw Lucas, Connor, and Beckett lifting weights with Vaughn.

My attention was focused on my boyfriend. His shirt was off, and I watched a drop of sweat as it slowly descended from his neck to his glistening chest. I had to look away and fan myself. "It's hot in here, isn't it?"

"Something's hot, all right," Thorn said. "Hot and bothered." She snickered as she gestured toward her sister.

Rose was checking out Lucas. She couldn't stop staring. She bit her lip when Lucas caught her and gave her a head-to-toe examination before returning his attention to his friends.

"You and Lucas, huh?" I asked her. "He's got that hot werewolf bod going for him, but he's kind of an asshole."

"No, what?" Rose said. She was blushing, and I decided not to tease her.

"Vaughn's running late again," I said. I wasn't sure why I was dumping my problems all over them, but I was.

"Would you like us to take you home?" Rose offered. "It's no problem." Suddenly, she seemed eager to leave.

"He'll be out any minute," I said with more confidence than I actually felt. Vaughn had always been someone I could count on, no matter what.

I fished out my phone to see if he'd sent me a text. He hadn't.

"Why don't we get some of the vamp stuff out of the way while we wait?" I suggested. Rose had been acting as an assistant and had been helping me with Jure's ill-gotten wealth. Thorn had no interest in anything money or organization, but she was ready and willing whenever there was a fight.

Thorn picked up an abandoned basketball and started dribbling it. They were so different.

"Do people ever have a hard time telling you apart?" I asked them.

Thorn smirked at me. "Only at first. She's the suck-up and I'm the smart-ass."

I glanced at Rose, wondering if she ever got tired of Thorn poking at her. "I'm not a suck-up," she finally said quietly.

"You certainly jump when Dad snaps his fingers," Thorn replied.

"Unlike you, I choose my battles," Rose said.

"Priss," Thorn hissed.

"Psycho," Rose replied. I guess she did get sick of her sister sometimes.

As fascinating as this display was, I needed to change the subject before they came to blows.

"What happens if a vampire doesn't obey my laws?"

"You kill them," Thorn said.

"I can't do that," I replied.

"You can do anything you want," she said. "It's good to be queen."

I frowned. It was most decidedly not good to be queen right now, not when I had to figure out who was tearing out the hearts of werewolves.

"What do most vampire rulers do?" I asked.

"It isn't a long process," Rose said. "If they do something you find abhorrent, you tell them to leave your realm and never return, upon pain of death."

"Most rulers don't even bother banning someone," Thorn said. "If they get pissed off, they just kill them right off. Or shove them into the sun."

"And the PAC doesn't stop that sort of behavior?" I asked.

"Not usually," Thorn said, and suddenly she couldn't look me in the eye.

"What?" I asked. "What aren't you telling me?"

"The PAC," she said. "They can't figure you out."

"Why is that?"

"You don't want the money, you don't want the power," she said. "It's hard for them to understand."

"You mean it's hard for them to understand why I'm not an abusive asshole like the last one?"

"Exactly."

"Why do you work for them?" I asked.

"It's not exactly voluntary," she hedged.

Okay... "What are they holding over you?" I asked.

"There are..." Rose hesitated. "Repercussions if we refuse to do as they ask."

I hated the idea that either of them would be asked to do something against their will. "You know I'll help you any way I can," I said.

Her frown smoothed out. "I know."

"You guys don't have to hang out," I said. "Vaughn should be done soon."

Thorn studied me for a second. "I'll be at your house tonight at seven to train."

"For what?"

"Just in case," she said. Her ominous tone wasn't my imagination.

"Just in case what?" I asked, but I'd caught sight of my boyfriend hurrying toward us. Obviously, they'd seen him, too, because they were already striding off.

"Sorry I'm late," Vaughn said.

I tried to think of the best way to approach his unusual unreliability as Vaughn and I walked to his car.

"What's wrong?" Vaughn asked. He opened the passenger door for me, and I slid in.

"Nothing," I said, but I knew it wasn't true. My completely reliable boyfriend was acting pretty unreliable.

He gave me a searching look before he changed the subject.

"Want to study for the Bio test?" Vaughn asked. "We can hang out at your house if you want."

My grades had been tanking. I wasn't the kind of student who could read the material once and ace the test. It took hours of studying my butt off for a B.

"I can study for a few hours," I said. I'd completely forgotten about the test. "But Thorn is coming over later."

He lifted an inquiring brow. "What for?" He pulled out

of the nearly deserted school parking lot.

"Training," I said grimly.

"I thought you were already a badass," he said.

"Apparently, Thorn disagrees," I said.

"Any sign of the demonic feline lately?" he asked.

I sighed. "I can take care of myself. Stop worrying." Vaughn had gotten a little more protective lately. I liked that he was concerned, but I didn't want him to freak out, either. He was still learning how to handle the whole werewolf thing.

"Someone sent a hellcat after you," he said.

"To scare me," I said.

"Or worse," he said. This summer, Vaughn had given me his blood to help me heal. He could have been the one to die. My stomach churned at the thought of losing him, and I resolved to be more understanding. I'd give him time to work through whatever was bothering him.

Once we were in my room, I dug through my backpack and realized I hadn't brought my textbook home. "What is wrong with me?"

"Don't worry—I made flash cards." He handed me a stack, and I started going through them.

"You are a lifesaver," I said. "There's no way I would have passed without you."

"There's a lot going on right now," he said.

Something in his voice made me look up and study him instead. I didn't want to tell him that I wasn't sure the academic effort was even worth it. Could I go to college? I'd have to live at home and take night classes, which wasn't the worst thing in the world, but I'd been looking forward to the whole college experience. I couldn't imagine explaining my sun allergies to my new roomie or why I needed to drink my tonic or I'd probably want to bite her.

By the time Thorn arrived, I was fairly confident I would at least pass my bio test.

I gave Vaughn a quick kiss. "Thanks for being my study buddy," I said.

"I'll see you tomorrow. Go kick some ass," he said.

"More like I'm going to get my ass kicked," I admitted. I had a feeling Thorn wasn't about to go easy on me.

"Where do you want to do this?" I asked her.

"Outside," she said.

I thought she would teach me some fancy fighting technique, like maybe sword-fighting or Krav Maga, but instead, she sucker-punched me as I followed her into the backyard.

While I was still doubled over and sucking wind, she tried to hit me again, but I blocked her. It didn't deter her for long. She rained blow after blow down on me. I dodged most of them but took a few hard hits.

"What's wrong with you?" I huffed out.

"What's wrong with *you*?" she countered. "Do you think you can keep your crown with those weak-ass moves?"

"Where did you learn to trash talk?" I asked. "From a kindergartner?"

"From your best friend," she replied. "The one you were too weak to protect." Ouch, she was going for it. She knew my friends were my weak spot.

"You want me to kick your ass? Fine, I can make that happen." Seeing red, I struck wildly, but Thorn danced just out of reach.

"You're not only weak, you're slow," she crowed.

"If I'm so weak and slow, then how did I manage to get the best of Jure Grando?" I panted.

"Luck," she said. "And perhaps a tiny bit of skill."

I brightened. That was a compliment coming from her. "Thanks."

"A tiny bit," she repeated. "But you are undisciplined. You use your heart, not your head. Vampires will try to kill you to take your throne. Is that what you want?" She tripped me, and I went down hard.

Oof!

I just laid there, facedown in the grass.

"Get up," she commanded. I stayed still, but out of the corner of my eye, I saw her move closer. "My queen?" she asked. "Are you okay?"

Just a little bit closer. She bent down to check my pulse. I grabbed her by the hand and threw her to the ground, then jumped on top of her. "Who's weak now?"

She smelled like prey. My fangs descended, and I was a breath away from taking a bite when Granny shouted, "Wash up, girls. It's time for dinner."

Dang, I'd almost bitten my bodyguard. I jumped up and moved away from her slowly, my hands clenched into fists as I fought for control.

"Very good!" Thorn said.

"Please go inside, Thorn."

"Your Majesty?"

"Now," I said. My voice was gravelly. I didn't want to give an order, tried to make sure I wasn't compelling her, but I wasn't sure I could manage right now. I needed her to leave or I was going to lose control and drink her blood until it was all gone. Until she was gone. I'd be stuck as a vampire forever.

She didn't say another word, just went through the slider into the house. I stared after her.

I turned on the garden hose and splashed cold water on my face until my fangs retracted and I didn't feel like killing something was the best idea ever.

Thorn and I had started to become friends. Had I ruined it by almost going full vamp on her?

When I finally regained control, I went back inside. Thorn was at a barstool, snacking on a dinner roll while she scrolled through something on her phone. She didn't look up when I entered the kitchen.

I cleared my throat, but she still didn't look at me. I'd really screwed up.

"I'm sorry, Thorn," I said. I'd nearly tried to eat her. The least I could do was apologize.

"No apology necessary, Queen Tansy," she said stiffly.

"I'd really like it if you dropped the queen bit," I said. "Please."

Thorn was tough, but nobody liked it when someone tried to kill them. I knew I was forgiven, though, when she finally looked at me. "I'll try to remember. You are getting better at fighting," she added.

I smiled at the compliment.

"You couldn't get much worse," she added, and my smile disappeared.

Chapter Nineteen

Granny Mariotti was in the kitchen, standing in front of an enormous copper pot. "What's wrong?" she asked.

"Everything's fine, Granny," I replied. Everything was not fine. I'd been seconds away from losing control, but at least Thorn seemed to have forgiven me. "Something smells good," I said. I picked up a big spoon, but she smacked my hand.

"It's not ready yet."

"But I'm starving," I said.

She took out a smaller pot and used a ladle to portion some into it, then took out a glass container and poured it into the pot before stirring it all together. "This one's yours," she said.

I couldn't identify the smell, but something in the beef stew was making me ravenous. I took a small bite, and my tastebuds did a little happy dance. "What did you put in this?" I asked. "It's delicious."

"I've been experimenting with herbs that are supposed to help with cravings," Granny said. "Xavier suggested a few things."

"It's working," I said. "All I'm craving is more of this stew."

I fidgeted a bit, then sat down at the kitchen counter.

"What's new with you?" Granny asked.

"Vaughn asked me to Homecoming," I said. "We're doubling with Skyler and Connor." Connor had managed to convince Skyler to go with him, but just as friends.

Granny beamed at me. "You'll need a new dress."

"I'll just borrow something of Skyler's," I said. I knew we didn't have the budget for a new outfit.

"Tansy, I can afford to buy you a few new things," she said. "I know I can't take the place of your mother—"

"It's okay, Granny," I said. "Vanessa would have made a terrible mother." My grandmother never talked about her. I missed having a mother, even though people said you couldn't miss what you'd never had. I'd been lucky. I had Granny.

"No, it's not okay," she said. She didn't argue with me about Vanessa, because what could she say? "We're going shopping, and that's final. If you're so worried about the state of my finances, we can hit the outlet mall first."

"It's not that I don't appreciate it," I started to say, searching for a way to get out of spending my granny's hard-earned money. It was frustrating that I had piles of dollars of my own, but I didn't want to use it for something like a dress. That was Queen Tansy cash, and I was going to use it to do some good for my subjects, whether they wanted me to or not.

"Then it's settled," she said. "Drink your tonic. I'll get my purse."

"Granny, it's after eight," I told her. "It can wait until the weekend."

"If you insist," Granny conceded with a wary look my way.

"Thorn, do you and Rose want to come with us?" I asked. I'd offered to be polite, but to my surprise, Thorn said yes, then said good night quickly, as if the fact that she'd voluntarily agreed to go shopping this weekend was shocking and she needed time to recover.

On Saturday, we ate breakfast at home before Granny hustled me out the door with a Thermos full of tonic and an extra one in her bag. Thorn had insisted on driving, so she and Rose swung by to pick us up.

We ended up at the outlet mall in San Clemente. I brought my parasol and my hat.

"I've never been to a dance before," Rose said. She stared at a dress with a white fitted bodice embroidered with red roses and a poufy red skirt.

"How old are you two?" I asked the twins, realizing that they might be younger than I thought.

"A year older than you," Thorn said. She dug into the pocket of her pants and came out with a black card and waved it in front of her sister's face. "You should buy it."

"I couldn't," Rose said, but she didn't stop admiring the dress.

"Well, I'm buying something," Thorn said. She held up a silk jumpsuit in neon green. "This has pockets."

Thorn scooped up the dress her sister was drooling over. "C'mon, Rose," she said. "We're trying these on."

Granny and I continued to search the racks for me.

"This is nice," Granny Mariotti said, holding up a lacy ice-blue number.

"It's cute," I agreed. "But I'm looking for something with more of a wow factor."

"What about this one?" She handed me a long black dress with a deep vee in the bodice.

After I tried it on, I returned it to the rack. "No go?" she asked.

"There was a frightening resemblance to the Bride of Frankenstein," I joked. I took a quick peek on my phone to check the time. "I'm glad you found a place that stayed open late."

"Do you miss it?"

"Miss what?"

"Being able to go outside whenever you want," she said. "Spending all day at the beach. Surfing with Vaughn."

"I wouldn't call what I do surfing. More like falling off a board," I said.

"You didn't answer my question," Granny Mariotti pointed out.

"I know," I said. "Of course I miss it, but it's not like I have a choice."

"What if you did?"

I shrugged. "Granny, drop it, okay? It is what it is."

She touched my arm gently. "We're working on it."

"I appreciate it, but I don't want to get my hopes up, okay?"

She studied my face, and I tried not to squirm. "Okay, I'll drop it. Now let's find you a dress."

There were a lot of good dresses, but nothing just right. It was almost closing time when Granny made a triumphant sound. "This dress is the perfect color," she said. She checked the tag. "And the perfect size." She held it out to me. It was a purple so dark it was almost black.

"It looks…tight," I replied.

She thrust it at me. "Try it on."

I took it into the dressing room. It fit me perfectly and made my green eyes pop. And it was on sale.

I went back out to show Granny, who let out a low whistle.

"I think this is the one," I said.

She nodded. "You look gorgeous."

"Is it weird to be worrying about a dance when I have so much going on?" I asked.

"Tansy, you're seventeen," she said. "A dance is important, too."

"Did my mom go to dances when she was in high school?" I tried for a casual tone, but Granny gave me a sharp look.

"You've never asked me much about your mom before," she commented.

"I've been wondering lately," I said. "What she was like before she was turned. Who my father was. Things most kids know."

"Not everyone," Granny pointed out.

"I know that," I said. "And I realize that not everyone is lucky enough to have someone like you."

"When we get home, I'll dig out the photo albums," she promised. "I'm sorry I can't tell you anything about your father, but I'll tell you what your mom was like growing up."

It wasn't the same as having a mom, but it would have to do.

Chapter Twenty

I wasn't any closer to solving the murder by the time Homecoming rolled around. I'd been hitting the research books almost every night. Another full moon had arrived, but both Connor and Vaughn insisted that their pack was on full alert.

Our football team was terrible, but we went to the Homecoming game before the dance anyway. They had been pretty good before Connor had dropped out of sight. He wasn't the quarterback, but he played some other position where you had to be big and run fast.

I hadn't thought much about whether he'd return to our football team, but then they announced, "Mahoney, number seven," and the crowd screamed out their approval.

"Connor's back on the team?" I asked Vaughn, who sat on one side of me in the bleachers while Skyler sat on the other side.

"They need all the help they can get," he replied.

Since Connor's pack went everywhere with him, I

wasn't surprised when they announced Lucas and Beckett's names, too.

When Connor managed an interception, the crowd roared and started chanting his name. Skyler tried to hide it, but she wore a proud smile as she chanted along with the rest of his fans.

To the crowd's amazement, our high school football team won by three points.

After the game, Skyler and I got ready for the dance at my house.

"What about the tickets?"

"Already taken care of," she replied. My dresser was covered with makeup, with Skyler's collection taking up the greater portion of it.

I wore the purple dress Granny had helped me pick out. I kept staring at myself in the mirror.

Skyler's dress was sunshine yellow. She wore four-inch heeled sandals with it, and her dark hair was flat-ironed and shiny.

"I'm glad I'm not a real vampire," I said, studying the two of us in the mirror, "or I wouldn't be able to see my reflection, and even I have to admit, we look good."

There was a knock on my door. "Connor and Vaughn are here," Granny said. "You girls decent?"

"We'll be right out," Skyler said. She primped in the mirror, and I couldn't resist teasing her.

"Just friends, huh?"

We headed for the living room. "That was before,"

Skyler said.

"What was before?" Vaughn lounged in the doorway, looking handsome in a black suit with a gray shirt. His eyes met mine.

"You look amazing," he said.

"Thanks," Skyler said, giggling.

"I wasn't talking to you," he said teasingly.

"I know," she replied. "But I do look good." She spun around, her skirt twirling.

Vaughn finally tore his eyes away from me. "You look nice, too, Skyler," he said.

"Are you guys ready to go?" Connor asked. Vaughn nudged him, and he added, "Tansy, Skyler, you both look beautiful."

Skyler stuck her nose in the air. "Compliments don't count if they're forced." Connor handed her a corsage, and she allowed him to slide it onto her wrist before she linked arms with me. The guys trailed behind us.

Skyler said, "The answer is before I decided to make him regret leaving."

I looked at her blankly but then remembered my just-friends question. "I think he already does," I told her.

Her face went fierce. "Not enough."

Skyler and Vaughn fought over who would drive, but Vaughn won when he said, "Your convertible's too small for the four of us."

Skyler finally gave in and climbed into the backseat of Vaughn's car before Connor could open the door for her.

Once we were on our way, she said, "Christian asked me to save a dance for him."

I turned around and raised my eyebrow at Skyler.

Connor let out a low growl, but Skyler ignored him. My best friend knew how to hold a grudge, and he'd better be prepared to beg if he wanted to have a chance with her again.

I hesitated. "Christian was acting kind of weird in detention the other day."

"Weird how?"

"He was being a little more aggressive than usual," I commented.

"Everyone always thinks werewolves are aggressive," Connor said. "But it's usually the vampires starting shit."

"Christian's human," I said. But the Thirsty Thieves' music seemed to bring out something toxic in their fans. The band was up to their old tricks.

She shrugged. "It's just a dance. It's not a date."

"Of course it's not a date," Connor said. "You're with me."

"As friends," she reminded him.

"We'll see," he replied.

My best friend had been through a lot. We all had. Maybe the dance would give us a chance to have fun and be normal teenagers for a little while, even though tomorrow, I'd still be queen of the vampires on the hunt for a werewolf killer.

We walked into the gym, which was decorated in our school colors of blue and gold. Haybales and a fake pitchfork were scattered by the photo booth. There were instruments on the stage, but no one was playing them. Instead, someone's phone had been put to use, and Shawn Mendes sang about mercy. We were early enough that there were only a few couples swaying on the dance floor.

"I wonder what band is performing," Vaughn said. There was a poster in front of the stage with the band's name on it, so we went over to check it out.

"I don't frickin' believe it," Skyler hissed.

"What?" I asked.

"The Thirsty Thieves?" she said.

Vaughn and I exchanged looks.

"I saw a bite mark on Christian when we were in detention, and his personality has gone from decent to dickish." A cold shiver was working its way up my spine.

"They booked a band of vampires for Homecoming," Vaughn told me. "And the whole pack is at the dance."

"This is going to be bad." I narrowed my eyes. "I can't believe he'd come anywhere near me," I said. I touched the scar on my face, trying not to remember the pain I'd experienced from Travis's vampire fire.

"He's probably pissed off that you own all his stuff," Vaughn said.

"Not all of it," I said. "They still have their instruments and their tour bus."

"He's used to his dad paying for everything," Vaughn added.

Connor's gaze went from Vaughn to me to Skyler. "I'm missing something," he said slowly. Skyler obviously still hadn't told him about what had happened to her when she followed the band.

She avoided his gaze. "I see Marcus didn't bring a date. I'm asking him to dance." With a little wave, she made a beeline away from the conversation. Connor watched her go with a pained look on his face, and I almost felt sorry for him. Almost.

He watched them talking and laughing for a minute before he grunted something and disappeared.

Christian walked up to us, carrying a clipboard. "Hi, Vaughn, Tansy."

Vaughn tugged me closer. "Hey, Christian," he said. "The gym looks good."

"Thanks," he said. "And the best news is that Thirsty Thieves is performing."

I gave him a polite smile. "I wanted to talk to you about that."

"Later, Tansy," he said. "I have to go see if the band needs anything. They're supposed to perform soon." He bustled off. I stared after him. Christian hadn't been aggressive or hostile. Maybe he'd just been having a bad day? Even as I thought it, I knew it wasn't true.

The band hadn't set up yet, so we sat at a table the farthest from the speakers.

My jaw dropped when I saw Rose and Lucas walk in, arm-in-arm. I nudged Vaughn. "When did that happen?"

Right behind them was Thorn with Beckett and Xavier on either side of her.

"And that," I said. My boyfriend just shrugged.

They spotted us and came over. "Where's Connor?" Lucas asked, but I noticed he pulled a chair out for Rose before he sat. So he did have manners when he wanted to.

Thorn sat in between Beckett and Xavier, smiling widely at something Xavier said.

Xavier picked up her hand and examined it. "That's a pretty bad scar," he told her. "I have some lotion that will help."

"Xavier's our Boy Scout. Always prepared," Beckett

teased, a flirty smile on his face. I just couldn't tell who he was flirting with, Xavier or Thorn.

Someone turned up the volume on the music, and Vaughn said something I couldn't hear to the guys. Then they all stood. He pressed a brief kiss to my forehead. "We'll be right back."

But the guys weren't right back. At least half an hour passed before Thorn said, "This blows. C'mon, let's dance."

"That sounds like a great idea," I said, but then the music stopped. Maybe the battery of the phone they'd been using died. Christian and Skyler came over. She was breathless and glowing from dancing, but I noticed her eyes went to where Connor had been.

"Where'd your dates go?" he asked. Then he started chuckling. "Not too smart of them to leave you girls all alone and unprotected."

Thorn looked like she wanted to tell him to shove his misogyny right up his ass but instead used a form of non-verbal communication and flipped him off. It didn't seem to faze him.

Christian's gaze went from Rose to Thorn to Skyler and then me. "I'd like to taste the rainbow," he said.

"What are you talking about?" I asked, but then I realized we were standing in a line and our dresses were the colors of the rainbow—red, green, yellow, and purple.

Sky caught on, too. "Not even in your dreams, Christian," she snapped.

"Shut up, Bleeder," he said.

"What did you just call her?" I asked.

"I'd move along now if I were you." Connor's cold voice was clear. He and the rest of the guys had finally returned.

Even Christian wasn't reckless enough to take Connor on, and he said a quick, "Oh, I see someone I need to talk to."

I raised a *where have you been* eyebrow at my boyfriend, and he mouthed a *sorry*. He'd been saying that a lot lately. He'd avoided explaining his behavior, which left me uneasy. And, if I were honest, a little insecure.

"Are you guys the reason the band hasn't shown up yet?" I asked Vaughn.

The guys in the pack all grinned at me.

"What did you do?" I wasn't prepared for a fight in the middle of the Homecoming dance.

"Relax," Lucas said. "We didn't hurt the suckers."

"While the vampires were occupied with their fans, we filled their tour bus with water balloons," Connor said.

"Okay, that seems harmless," I said. "If it had been diet soda, they would have been ready to tear you apart."

"They're not particularly fond of holy water, either," Beckett said. Even Xavier snickered at that. I didn't ask where they'd managed to find enough holy water to fill a tour bus.

"Or any water really," Vaughn added.

"The only liquid they like is blood," Connor said. Skyler flinched, and his eyes met hers. "What did I say?"

"Nothing," she said.

"Maybe we should leave," I suggested. It wasn't that I thought Travis would ever try to compel my best friend again, but it had to be hard on her to keep seeing him.

"We're not leaving," Skyler said. "He took enough. He's not going to take this, too."

I wrapped an arm around her. "Okay, we'll stay."

The band took the stage, and Christian shouldered his way to the front. I noticed he was joined by a couple of other guys from our class. What was it about musicians?

"Let's dance," Skyler said, and our entire group went onto the dance floor, even Lucas. Connor wrapped his arms around Skyler, and she put her arms around his neck. He whispered something into her ear, and she turned red but then nodded.

There was some grumbling at first, but since the band played mostly slow songs, the complaints stopped. I spent nearly an hour swaying in Vaughn's arms.

"Thanks for coming with me to the dance," Vaughn said.

"I'm having fun," I replied. "It's nice to have a normal night, even with the Thirsty Thieves showing up."

"The band's not so bad," he said.

I stopped dancing and stared at him.

He started laughing. "Kidding."

I slid my fingers to his ribs and started tickling him. I knew all his weak spots.

"Truce," he finally said, gasping out a laugh.

"What's that on his lip? A hairy caterpillar?" I asked. Travis wore a black cowboy hat, skintight Levi's, and a white satin shirt with way too many buttons popped open. Black cowboy boots completed the ensemble.

He kept shifting back and forth like the probably brand-new boots hurt his feet. I listened for the sounds of compulsion in the music, but I didn't hear any.

I relaxed and decided to enjoy myself. Snuggling up to Vaughn for a few hours wasn't the worst way to spend a night.

"I think Skyler and Connor are going to get back together," Vaughn said.

I gaped at him. "He iced her out. Ghosted her. Broke her heart." It could be said that Vaughn had done two out of the three things on the list to me. I hoped he wouldn't make it a trifecta.

"Yeah, but he has his head out of his ass now."

Skyler bounced up to us, breathless and sweaty. "Isn't this fun?" She wasn't letting Travis and company ruin her night.

"It is," I said.

"Christian's having an afterparty," Skyler said.

Christian's personality had done a complete one-eighty. I could barely stand him now, but I had a feeling it had something to do with his new favorite band. It wouldn't hurt to go to the party and watch them.

I looked at Vaughn. "You up for it?"

"Why not?" he replied.

Then the lights went on and teachers and chaperones started to herd people toward the exits. Vaughn tugged on my hand. "C'mon," he said.

When I glanced back, the band was surrounded by several guys. Christian fist-bumped Travis before the two of them headed backstage. The Thirsty Thieves and their new fans were going to be a problem. I knew it.

Chapter Twenty-One

Christian had a huge place right on the water and mostly absent parents, who traveled a lot for their jobs, if the number of parties he threw was any indication.

"I thought you said this was going to be low-key for a change." I glared at Skyler. "Just a few people." Christian had been acting out of character lately, so it hadn't been completely unbelievable that he'd become less social during his transformation to misogynistic jerk.

She shrugged. "Oops."

Connor chuckled.

"Christian's parties are always loud, drunken debaucheries," I said. "And the last time I went to a party, I ended up getting bitten by a vampire."

"Tansy," Skyler pouted. "I promise you that won't happen again."

I didn't point out that I was already part vamp, so it *couldn't* happen again.

"Okay, but we stick together," I said. "No matter what."

"I promise," she said.

"Tansy, I'm glad you made it," Christian greeted me and ignored Vaughn. He moved into my personal space, and I took a step back. Vaughn put his hand to my waist and drew me close to his side.

Christian was oblivious, but then Vaughn kissed my neck, which got through Christian's dense fog of one too many shots.

"Wait. You two are together?"

I didn't say anything because I thought it was obvious, but Vaughn said, "Yes, we are very much together."

"That's why you turned me down," Christian continued, but it wasn't a question. "Knew there had to be a reason she'd pass on all this." He waved his hand up and down his body.

He'd asked me out right before Vaughn and I had decided we weren't just friends. I opened my mouth but figured I wouldn't wound his ego by telling him I wouldn't have gone out with him either way. He was good-looking with brown eyes that always sparkled with mischief and thick dark hair, but he didn't usually stick with one girl, not even for a night. Besides, I'd been too busy pining over Vaughn.

The rest of the pack were already here, and I noticed that Lucas kept a protective arm around Rose. She looked a little shellshocked at the number of people crammed into the house. Big as the place was, it was still overflowing with bodies.

Xavier and Thorn were talking quietly in a corner, and Beckett's usual sunny smile was missing as he glowered at them from where he sat in the opposite end of the living room, surrounded by girls.

We made our way into the kitchen where the keg was, along with about a hundred of Christian's friends. Okay, maybe not a hundred, but his kitchen was huge, bright, and filled with loud voices. Kelli Martelli sat on a barstool, kissing Samantha Devon, her ex, and a guy who graduated last year, Hunter Somebody, was throwing up in a trash can.

Through the enormous sliding glass door, I could see there were a bunch of people in the pool, but I'd learned not to look too closely, because I was pretty sure I'd see parts of my classmates that I never wanted to see.

I'd changed out my heels for Converse, and my feet were thanking me.

I hadn't spent very much time alone with Vaughn lately, and he looked good. He'd removed his jacket and tie and rolled up the sleeves of his gray button-down shirt. I was too distracted (ogling my boyfriend's forearms) to notice that Skyler had found a bottle of something that looked red and lethal.

"Here's to good times and bad decisions," Sky said. She poured out a shot and then drained it in one gulp and lined up another.

Vaughn scowled at her. "Skyler, maybe you should slow down."

"You're not my dad," Skyler said. "Don't try to boss me around." Obviously, things weren't any better on the dad front. The staying power of each new stepmom was getting shorter and shorter, and Skyler liked Gertie, the current step. Though, if Gertie was pregnant, that might change her dad's M.O.

"I'm not trying to boss you around," he said. "I'm

worried about you. Don't forget about spring break junior year."

Sky's face went from pissed to embarrassed to amused. "Yeah, I forgot about that."

"You puked so much I thought your insides were coming up," Connor said.

"You did, too," she told him. "And both of you did." She pointed first to Vaughn and then to me.

I nodded. "Which is why we think it's a good idea to slow down. No need for vomit comets tonight." I was sticking to water because I had no idea what a drunk vampire queen would do, and I didn't want to find out.

"Let's find the rest of the pack," Vaughn suggested.

Skyler's face lit up with a smile when Connor asked her to dance. We watched them for a moment. Sky was wearing the first real smile I'd seen from her in months.

"I'm glad we came," I admitted. It was worth it to see Skyler smile. I was still not the biggest fan of parties.

"Me, too," Vaughn said. "Especially if you dance with me." He held out a hand. "Please?"

It was a slow song. I almost knocked over a glass in my eagerness to have his arms around me. I took his hand, and we joined the crowd. We swayed in silence for a minute, his hands on my hips, mine locked around his neck.

"I forgot what a good dancer you are," Vaughn murmured in my ear.

He pulled me closer, and I snuggled in. "Nice moves yourself," I murmured back.

When he kissed me, he tasted like the cinnamon candies Granny Mariotti kept in a jar in our kitchen, hot and sweet, but it was probably the shot of cinnamon vodka he'd downed.

Vaughn rarely drank and had limited himself to one shot tonight. The room was packed with people and overripe with the heat of too many bodies in a small place.

"Let's take a break," I shouted over the music. Vaughn nodded.

"It stinks of suckers in here," Lucas said loudly.

That was one thing vampires and werewolves seemed to have in common, an overdeveloped sense of smell.

"What do suckers smell like?" I asked brightly.

He met my eyes. "Like death."

It was true. Vampires smelled of graveyards and decomposing flesh.

"Do I smell like death?" I blurted out.

"What? No," Vaughn said. "You smell like Tansy." He grinned down at me, his dimples flashing. "Like strawberries and vanilla."

"You're not funny," I said. Travis and the rest of the band couldn't shut up about how I smelled like a strawberry milkshake. I was relieved, though.

"I'm going to hit the restroom," he said. "Be right back."

I studied the crowd while I waited. Until I recognized a certain dyed black head bobbing to the music. Travis was here, cuddled up to Christian. I stomped over to them.

"Excuse me for a moment, Christian," I said. "I need to talk to Travis."

He huffed out an okay, and then I said to Travis, "Follow me. That's an order."

Christian gave him a weird look when Travis said, "Yes, your highness." But then Christian must have assumed Travis was being snarky. If he only knew.

I found a spot where we could hear each other, but I could still watch Skyler. One of the things Granny's tonic suppressed was my heightened vampire hearing, so I had to lean in a bit.

"Tansy, I've been wanting to talk to you, too," Travis said.

"So talk."

"I wanted to apologize," he said. I gaped at him. Was this a trick? It was hard to believe that Travis had changed.

"You should apologize to Skyler, not me."

He looked blank, and I put my hands behind my back so I wouldn't smack him.

"Skyler Avrett, my best friend? The girl who you compelled into leaving her family and friends this summer to go on tour with you?"

His face still showed no sign of recognition, so I pointed to Skyler, who was dancing with Connor. Her face was alight as she and Connor competed to see who could do the silliest old-school moves.

"Schuler," he said. "She's hot."

"Skyler," I said through gritted teeth. "And she's off-limits to you and the band."

"I've changed," he said. "I haven't bitten anyone unwilling."

I rolled my eyes at him.

"I haven't bitten anyone unwilling *lately*," he clarified. "And under vampire law, you can't kill me unless I do something you've forbidden."

"Have you?" I asked.

"You don't have to sound so hopeful. Christian's willing," Travis said. "We're not breaking any laws."

He had a point. I didn't necessarily believe he'd

changed, but I didn't have the right to interfere if both parties were willing participants. And it explained Travis's fancy vocabulary. Christian was not only a talented artist, he was smart, too. Was Travis using big words to try to impress him?

"What do you know about the werewolf deaths?" I asked. I'd compelled him to tell me whether he'd killed the werewolf, but I hadn't asked if he knew who did. I didn't like to use my power of compulsion. It would be easy to abuse.

"Why are you asking me?" he replied. "Shouldn't you be asking your boyfriend?"

Travis must be trying to distract me, get me off his scent, so to speak. He chuckled. "You don't know, do you?"

He wanted me to ask. I didn't want to give him the satisfaction, but I couldn't help myself. "Know what?"

His teeth flashed, sharp and deadly. "Do you know how traitors are punished in a shifter pack?"

"Just spit it out, Travis," I said.

"When a pack member is considered a traitor, the pack leader tears out the offending member's heart."

"You're lying." I clenched my teeth with the effort it took to keep my voice even, but my mind was racing. If he was telling me the truth, then why hadn't any of the werewolves mentioned it?

"Am I?" he said. "Ask your boo."

When the song ended, Christian came over to Travis and me. "Are you hungry?" He was obviously talking to Travis, not me.

"Willing donor," he said. "No compulsion. Not against the rules."

"There's nothing you can do about it," Christian said.

I could kill him. The thought must have shown in my eyes because Travis said quickly, "Thank you. For not killing me, I mean."

"The night's not over," I replied. "Christian, are you sure—"

"Stay out of my business, Tansy." He took off, and Travis trailed after him. I'd never seen the expression on his face. Did he *like* Christian? As more than a food source?

Vaughn keeping secrets. Christian a willing food source for Travis. The werewolf deaths. It was all too much.

It was official. I hated parties.

Chapter Twenty-Two

I made my way through the crowd to Vaughn. "You're shaking," he said. He pulled me to his body, and I burrowed in, warm and safe.

"What's happened?" Vaughn asked.

"An extra-large dose of Travis," I said. "Nothing I couldn't handle, though." I didn't want to ask him about what the lead singer had told me. I wanted to hang out with my boyfriend and forget about all the problems piling on me. Just for the night.

We held hands as we wandered outside. Connor and Skyler followed close behind. It was almost as packed in the backyard as it was in the house.

"Pool!" Beckett said. He pulled his T-shirt and jeans off and cannonballed into the water.

Watching him swim made me shiver. It was October, which meant it got cold at night. He went to the shallow end and started splashing around.

"You'll freeze to death," I said.

"It's heated," Beckett replied. Skyler's neighbor Rika gave him an admiring look as he goofed around. She looked like she was thinking about stripping down and joining him.

The boys in the band hadn't listened to my warning. Instead, they joined us in the backyard.

Travis called everyone "darlin'" with that faux twang in his voice. He swaggered from group to group, tipping his hat like they did in old Westerns.

Skyler stood watching Travis as she stood alone by the fire pit. I joined her and bumped her shoulder with mine.

"We can go if you want," I said.

"I'm okay," she said.

"Even though Travis and the band are here?" I asked.

We both stared at the flames until Vaughn joined us.

He wrapped his arms around me and pressed his lips to my neck in a brief kiss. "Sorry it took so long," he said. "I got trapped in the kitchen talking to Marcus about baseball."

Beckett finally hauled himself out of the pool and came over, dripping water all over the tile. I found a towel in one of the storage boxes and handed it to him.

I looked away, and that's when I saw Travis walk up to Skyler and try to hug her. "Oh, hell no," I said.

I started toward them, but Connor beat me to it. "Take your hands off her. Now."

Armando and Ozzie pushed through the crowd. "Is there a problem?"

"There won't be as long as your friend takes his hand off Skyler," Connor said in a growl.

"Is this your new boyfriend?" Travis said. "I see you traded down."

Skyler shook off his hand. "Unlike you, Connor doesn't have to compel girls to get them to go out with him."

"I'm hurt," Travis mocked. "I thought we were in love."

"Travis," I warned. Connor was a hair's breadth from going full-on wolf in front of our whole school.

"I'm not breaking any laws, am I?" he asked.

"Is that how you talk to your queen?" Connor growled.

Beckett shook out his long hair, and a few droplets flew toward Travis.

He jumped straight up, a little higher and longer than normal, to avoid the water.

"Something smells bad," Travis said. "Like wet dog."

"It smells like someone died in here," Beckett said, then pretended to notice Travis for the first time. "Oh, it's just you."

"Shut up, puppy," Travis replied.

I wanted to punch him in his smug face, but Connor did it for me. Without warning, he lunged. He hit Travis square in the nose and then wrapped his big hands around Travis's neck and squeezed.

People were watching. There was nothing like a fight to make everyone pay attention, but a werewolf and a vampire beating the shit out of each other was not what I needed right now.

When they saw Travis and Connor fighting, the rest of the Thirsty Thieves rushed over. Then the werewolf pack joined the fray.

"Connor, let go of him," I said. They were going to go full supe in front of a party jam-packed with humans.

The other vampires' fangs started to come down.

Xavier and Beckett snarled, then a low howl

sounded right before they charged at the other vampires. Fortunately, they still had enough control that they retained their human forms, although Beckett was looking a little shaggy.

I grabbed Skyler and moved her out of the way right before Armando went sailing by. It was werewolves against vampires, and it looked like the werewolves were winning.

"Connor, don't!" Skyler said. "He's not worth it."

His grip tightened as he lifted Travis higher. In a stunning show of strength, he threw Travis across the yard.

"But you are," Connor told Skyler.

There was a *thud* when Travis hit the brick wall that separated Christian's backyard from his neighbor's. Being the kind of vampire who valued his own survival, he stayed where he was.

The drummer growled at Vaughn, but he ignored him. It wasn't a full moon, but the air was fraught with the smell of angry wolf. Would they shift when it wasn't a full moon?

Vaughn's back was to me, but I could tell he was punching someone, probably Boris. When his arm drew back again, it was dripping blood. I couldn't look away from the blood as it spattered onto the concrete.

Xavier and Beckett were still facing off against Armando and Ozzie. It was chaos as the other party-goers tried to dodge the guys who were throwing punches. Ozzie tried to bite Xavier, but he held him off with one hand. Werewolves were crazy strong, but I didn't want Connor and his friends to get hurt.

Thorn and Rose came to stand guard next to me.

Thorn's body was tense, probably from the effort of not joining the fight.

There was the sound of breaking glass, and then minutes later, Christian came running outside. His pants were on, but his shirt was off, and there were telltale bloody smudges on his chest. He'd obviously been in his room with Travis.

Ozzie and Beckett rolled through an open slider door and into the living room. The vampire started throwing knickknacks, probably expensive ones, at Beckett. One shattered, and Christian swore. "My parents are going to freak."

The glass doors gave me a perfect view of the fight going on inside. Beckett tackled Ozzie and lifted him up, using one hand, and left the vampire dangling in the air.

My gaze volleyed from what was happening inside the house to what was happening in the backyard.

"Stop it!" I shouted. I put every ounce of magic I possessed into the command. Everyone froze, even Connor, who seemed to be resisting the magic more than anyone else. "Now, calm down," I said. "Beckett, let go of Ozzie." He dropped him, and Ozzie swore as he hit the highly polished floor of Christian's living room.

Travis groaned, and Connor nudged him with his toe. "When will you learn?"

He groaned again and then shouted for Gary. Gary was the band's familiar slash roadie and probably had the worst job in the world.

Connor jerked his head, and Xavier and Beckett picked Travis up and carried him out. From his screams, I think they threw him into a rose bush.

I tried not to giggle, but honestly, after everything Travis had done, I needed to get my thrills where I could. Since I couldn't actually kill him without breaking my own laws. Which would make me a shitty leader and an even shittier human being.

"Party's over," Christian hollered. "Everyone out!"

Chapter Twenty-Three

It took a while, but gradually, people started to leave. Pretty soon, the only people left were the pack and their dates. Vaughn and I helped with cleanup, but Christian shooed us out. "I'll deal with the rest of it tomorrow," he said.

Rose and Lucas left first, walking to his car hand-in-hand. Xavier, Beckett, and Thorn stood around, obviously waiting for us. Both werewolves were listening intently to something she said, but when Xavier's laugh rang out, Beckett's eyes lingered on him.

"Where's Connor?" Beckett asked.

Vaughn said, "We'll go look for him. You guys can take off."

Thorn gave him a little salute and started walking. "Car's a couple of blocks away," she said.

Xavier put a hand on her shoulder. "We'll protect you."

"More like she'll protect you," I shouted after them. Beckett's laugh was my only reply.

"What a night," I told Vaughn.

"Ready to go?"

"Where are Skyler and Connor?" I looked around but didn't see them. I tried to quell the panic that welled up whenever my best friend was out of my sight.

I sent her a text. **Ready to leave?**

It took a minute, but her reply came. **OMW.**

Vaughn came up to me and draped his arm over my shoulder. "Did you find them?"

"Still no word from Connor," I said. "But Skyler's on her way."

Skyler finally showed. "Did Connor already leave?"

"I thought he was with you," Vaughn said.

"He was, but then said he had to use the bathroom," she said. "I helped Christian take out the recyclables, and we started talking. I guess I lost track of time."

"He's probably asleep inside," Vaughn joked. "He's not much for late nights."

Only a few stubborn stragglers lingered. There were a couple of guys passed out in the living room, but neither of them was Connor.

Skyler went looking outside, and Vaughn and I searched the bedrooms, making sure to knock several times before opening the door, just in case.

"I'm going to check the bathrooms," Vaughn said.

We'd checked every bedroom, except one. As I approached, I caught the scent of blood.

My nerves went on full alert, and I twisted the handle slowly, trying for stealth.

The bedroom was dark, so I flicked on the light. Connor was lying on a white comforter, which was stained red by the blood pumping out of a wound in his chest.

Travis stood over him.

"Get away from him," I said. "Now."

Travis held up his hands, which were dripping with blood. He moved toward me slowly. "I didn't do it. He's still alive."

But Connor wouldn't be if I didn't stop standing there with my mouth open. Blood clots that looked like pitted cherries dripped from the gouges on Connor's chest.

"Vaughn, find Xavier," I shouted. "Now! Connor's hurt."

He swore. "I'll hurry," he yelled back and then I heard him running down the stairs.

I prayed that he'd find Xavier in time.

I didn't know what to do, how to help him, not when there was so much delicious-smelling blood everywhere. I stood frozen as Connor's blood leaked out of him.

I was scared to get anywhere near all that blood. Scared that I'd lose control. I was a vampire queen, but I realized something else—I was also a Mariotti witch. My charm necklace. The chalk. It was worth a try.

I'd never tried to repair skin and bone, but I slowly passed the chalk over Connor's torn flesh, trying not to gag. "Heal."

The minutes went by slowly, but Vaughn and Xavier came rushing in. Finally. He shoved me aside. "What are you doing?" he asked me sharply.

"Trying to help," I said.

"Please don't," Xavier replied. He turned his attention to the prone figure on the bed. "C'mon, Connor, hang in there," he said. Blood was pouring from the wound on Connor's chest, and I couldn't look away.

When Xavier got a good look at Connor, he swore under his breath but rolled up his sleeves and got to work.

Connor's whole body contorted from the pain, and he let out a ragged whimper.

Xavier didn't look at me when he ordered, "Get that sucker out of here."

I yanked Travis by the arm and led him out of the room into the hallway.

"It wasn't me," he said.

"Just in the wrong place at the wrong time again?" I took a deep, shaky breath. "I'm finding it very hard not to stake you right now." I ran my fingers through my hair. "Tell me the truth." I used my most compelling tone.

"I smelled the blood," he said. "Someone ran by me as I went into the room. It was dark."

"You didn't see who it was?"

"They wore a hoodie. Small frame. Taller than you, but not by much." He shook his head. "The werewolf was already cut open." He thought about it for a moment longer. "I think whoever it was had been to The Last Stop recently."

"How do you know that?" I was hoping for an obvious clue, like a cocktail napkin from the bar or something.

"They smelled like it," he said. Vampires did have a highly developed sense of smell, but unless I was prepared to have Travis sniff half of Orange County, I wasn't sure it was a useful clue.

Whoever it was hadn't managed to take Connor's heart or he'd already be dead. Travis might have inadvertently saved Connor's life.

If I didn't get Travis out of here, though, he would be

toast. The pack would not be happy that Travis had been at the site of not one, but two werewolf attacks.

"Travis Grando, you are hereby banned from the California realm," I said.

"What? No," he said. "We have a gig tomorrow night."

"Travis, I know you're using your music to compel angry men," I said. "That was enough to warrant banishment. But you have been seen standing over not one, but two werewolf victims. Do you think the werewolves will let that go?"

Understanding finally dawned in his eyes. "I'm outta here."

"Take the band and leave town," I told him. "Or I promise you, you'll regret it."

"Thank you."

"Don't thank me, Travis," I said. "Because if I catch you compelling anyone again, I'll stake you. Are we clear?"

He gulped then turned and ran down the stairs.

I was still pacing in the hallway when Skyler appeared. "Did you find Connor?" Oh, god. She didn't know. My throat worked, but I couldn't speak.

Lucas was right behind her. Vaughn came out of the bedroom and into the hallway.

"Connor, you have to shift," I heard Xavier say. "Now."

Vaughn took my hand. I could still smell the blood, but the urge to drink it was receding. "He'll be okay," he soothed me. "Xavier is trying to get him to shift to speed up the healing."

Skyler gasped. "I'm lost. Someone fill me in. Now."

"A sucker attacked Connor, that's what happened," Lucas said.

"We don't know it was a vampire," I argued.

They all looked at me with varying degrees of disbelief. "I can't believe you're still saying that after what happened tonight," Vaughn said.

"It was Travis again, wasn't it? Where is he?" Lucas was furious. "I'm going to rip that sucker apart." His body started to shake.

High emotions during a full moon. Bad combo.

I'd made my decision. I was Travis's queen. I squared my shoulders. "I banned him. He's gone."

"You let him go?" Lucas growled, low and deadly. His body started to shake, and his face contorted as his jaw lengthened into a wolf's snout.

"Lucas, control yourself," Beckett said sharply. I wanted to explain that I'd compelled Travis to tell me the truth, that there was no way he'd been lying, but I didn't trust the werewolves not to use it against me somehow.

Skyler sobbed, but when I tried to hug her, she jerked away. Skyler would never forgive me if Connor died.

"This is your fault," Lucas hissed to me.

"My fault?" I was stunned.

"You blame me?"

Skyler nodded. My best friend had turned against me. I bit my lip, hard, to keep the tears from falling.

"You told us Travis wasn't the murderer," she said. "You protected him. And now Connor m-m-might die."

"You really think that?" I asked. "All of you?" Not even my boyfriend met my eyes. "Anyone want to tell me how the pack punishes rogues?"

"Connor's not a rogue," Lucas said.

"So it's true, then?" I asked. "They rip their hearts out?"

"It wasn't a werewolf," Beckett said stubbornly.

"It wasn't a vampire, either," I said. "At least, it wasn't Travis. Unlike you, I'm willing to consider it might be one of my subjects."

"Vaughn, what do you think?"

"I think it's pointless to argue," he finally said. "The pack has to take care of Connor now."

"But I want to help," I said.

Vaughn just shook his head before he went back into the bedroom and carefully shut the door behind him.

He blamed me, too. He wouldn't let me near Connor, not even to try to help. I just hoped that the little bit of healing magic I'd done before Xavier arrived had helped.

Nobody wanted me there, so I took off. I walked home in the middle of the night, in high heels and a pretty dress. I had my drumstick, though. That's all I needed.

That's all I had left.

Chapter Twenty-Four

My grandmother was leaving for a conference, and normally, I'd be ecstatic at the thought of having the house to myself for a few days and maybe inviting my boyfriend over. But since we weren't currently on speaking terms, no invite would be forthcoming.

And he wasn't the only one. "I haven't seen Skyler around much lately," Granny said as she folded her pajamas and stuffed them into her already full case. "Everything okay?"

I winced internally but gave what I hoped was a non-chalant shrug. "Connor's back," I said. "Skyler's busy re-uniting." At least that's what I assumed, but since she wasn't talking to me either, I had no way of knowing for sure.

You couldn't be friends as long as Skyler and I had been without getting into a few fights, but this one was different.

Vaughn did text me that Connor was healing quickly but wasn't up for visitors. Visitors meaning me. I didn't bother replying. Message received. It had been a week since Homecoming, and whenever I saw him or Skyler at school, I headed the other way. I had three weeks to find the real killer, and I'd have to do it on my own.

I didn't want Granny to ask about my maybe ex-boyfriend, so I changed the subject. "We better get to the airport," I said. "Or you'll miss your flight."

"Maybe I should stay home," she suggested.

"Are you kidding?" I replied. "Go. Have fun. Learn some librarian stuff."

She still hesitated, so I shut her suitcase. "Besides, didn't you say the silver fox was going to be there?"

She nodded. "He's a nonfiction writer, and he's going to be a guest speaker."

I managed to convince her, and we made it to John Wayne Airport in plenty of time. "Don't bother parking," she said.

I pulled into the drop-off lane and put the Deathtrap into park. "Have fun, Granny," I said. I gave her a quick hug.

"If you need anything, call Edna and Evelyn," she said.

"I will," I said. "Now get out of the car before you miss your flight."

I returned home to an empty house. I had a few hours before I had to go to work, but I couldn't seem to settle on any activity. I grabbed a book and went to my bedroom to read. My dresser drawer was open. I'd left in a hurry, but I thought I'd closed it. I shrugged off my uneasiness. Usually when Granny traveled, I stayed at Skyler's house or she came here. But this time, I was on my own.

I spotted a gift bag on my bed with *Open now* written on the card. It was in my grandmother's handwriting. The ink on the card looked a little faded, but maybe she'd been holding onto it for a while. Granny must have snuck it in here before she left. It wasn't my birthday, but I tore through the tissue paper anyway.

It was a glass bottle with pretty filigree-decorated sides and stopper. It was half full with a liquid I recognized as the purple-black color of my tonic. It was a slightly different shade, but I assumed that was because Granny had been experimenting.

She had already thoughtfully filled the vial. I put it around my neck. It gave me a sense of security to know that I'd have a small amount of tonic at my fingertips. I wondered if she'd managed to make it taste any better, but it didn't matter.

I checked my official vampire queen email that Rose had set up for me. She'd warned me that many of my subjects had been alive hundreds of years ago and didn't like modern technology, which explained why my email was empty. I did spot a stack of actual letters addressed to Queen Tansy and glanced longingly at my textbooks before diving in. Most of the letters were requests for blood donations, but one letter made me stop.

I would like to buy the Blood of Life ruby. It was unsigned, with just a phone number listed underneath. It hadn't been at the forefront of my research, but I had found the mention that it had been missing for almost a century, and shortly after it disappeared, its owner died under mysterious circumstances.

There was no way I was going to let it go, not until I

found out who sent it to me and its power.

Panicked, I rushed to its hiding spot and was relieved to see it was still nestled in the hollowed-out book.

I had a couple of hours before I had to get ready for work. I was working a cater waiter gig at a fancy home in Corona del Mar. I'd managed to switch shifts with someone so that I didn't have to face Vaughn.

By the time I'd made my way through a stack of communication from my subjects that was whining or threatening in turn, I'd run out of time. I dashed into the shower and threw on my uniform before grabbing my bag with my necessary supplies and left for work.

Since parking was always at a premium, the staff were being shuttled to the event location.

I parked the Deathtrap and sprinted to the white van idling on the far end of the parking lot. The driver tooted her horn at me, and the van door slid open. I plopped down into the only available seat.

"Whew, that was close," I panted out.

"Glad you could make it," Vaughn said. He was sitting in the seat next to me.

"What are you doing here?" I asked.

"Working, same as you," he said. "I thought you were off today."

I didn't say anything else. He'd switched his schedule, too, to avoid me.

"Tansy, we need to talk," he said.

Was he going to break up with me? *We need to talk* was code for *we need to break up*, wasn't it?

"I know we do," I said. "Not at work, though, okay?" I wouldn't be able to make it through my shift.

"I have something to say to you," he said.

"You and your friends didn't say enough last weekend?" I was angry, I realized. It wasn't my fault that Connor had been injured. Their hatred of Travis clouded their ability to see that he wasn't the killer.

"We're here," the driver announced cheerfully. I didn't want to hear what else Vaughn had to say. Instead, I slid out of the van and headed inside.

As soon as I stepped out into the sunset, I started to feel dizzy. I'd thought I'd be okay, since there was only an hour or so left of daylight, but I would have to take my tonic soon.

The wedding was in the backyard, but oh, what a backyard. It had an infinity pool and ocean view. The mystery client made a Kardashian look low maintenance.

The sun beat down, even with the shade provided by the white canopies. I grasped the tiny vial of tonic Granny had put on a necklace for me. It wasn't a lot but would hopefully stop me from vamping out in an emergency.

I also had a Thermos of the stuff stashed in my backpack, along with comfortable flats and an extra white work shirt. I managed to chug some tonic before I saw the head server giving me the evil eye. I stashed the Thermos quickly and then started folding napkins into swans.

I had a headache. My hair was scraped back into a tight bun, which was required of all servers with long hair, by our nameless celebrity client. It made sense because nobody wanted hair in their five-hundred-dollar-a-plate meal.

Vaughn was right behind me. He surveyed the table decor. "This must be where glitter goes to die," he said.

"Shush," I said, playfully swatting him before I remembered we were mad at each other. But he was right—

there was gold glitter on every available surface. The glare from the sun shining on the sparkly stuff hurt my eyes. The menu even included a cocktail called—you guessed it—a Glitter Bomb, which was made with a Russian vodka that had bits of gold and silver in it. It was highly illegal in the U.S., but the client had insisted.

The wedding party and their guests still hadn't arrived, so there were about fifty of us standing around. Vaughn was talking to his dad, but from where I stood, it didn't look like the conversation was going well.

I spotted the high ponytail before I recognized the YouTube celebrity. The bride wore a fitted white dress with so many gold bows on it that you could barely see the white material underneath.

"I'm beginning to understand all the glitter, but is she even old enough to get married?" I was kind of talking to myself, but one of the other servers heard me.

"She's twenty-three," Mariah replied. "But I don't think she's the one getting married."

Two little Chihuahuas pranced in front of her, wearing bride and groom outfits. One dog had on a gold veil and white lace gown, and the other wore a doggie tux with a gold glitter bow-tie.

I kept a smile pasted on my face as I whispered to Mariah, "She dropped all this money on a dog wedding. A dog *wedding*. Famous people have way too much cash to burn."

She shrugged. "It's not hurting anybody."

"Except the poor animals," I replied. The "bride" was trying to eat her dress, and the groom growled when the photographer moved to get him to pose. These nuptials cost enough to put someone through college, and some people didn't even have enough money for rent.

The reception went on forever. Mariah and I were stuck at the least popular serving station, while Vaughn was across from us where his job was to stock the doggie treats.

I watched him as he bent down to restock the water dishes.

Mariah nudged me. "Quit staring at your boyfriend's ass."

"I wasn't," I lied. "Much."

We both snickered.

Her attention shifted to the guests. "I can't believe all the celebrities who came to watch dogs get married," she whisper-screamed.

"I saw someone brought a baby hedgehog," I told her. "It's so cute, but I think they're illegal in California."

I spotted a couple of famous ex boy-banders, a YouTube gamer girl, and a Kardashian cousin. I people-watched for a while, then I realized I needed to find out where my boss wanted the peanut butter animal-friendly cake, but he was talking to the client, so I hovered instead of interrupting.

"My girlfriend is a breeder," Mr. Sheridan said proudly.

"What kind of animals?" The client perked up. Her name was Loretta or Lorraine or something old-fashioned like that, but she went by Lo-Lo.

A gleam of interest lit in her big blue eyes. The rest of the guests were probably equally as famous, but I could tell she wanted to be a trendsetter.

"Cats. Specialty breed. Very exclusive," Mr. Sheridan said. "Very hush-hush." He sounded like a walking infomercial. He held out a white business card, and Lo-

Lo snatched it out of his hand. "Give her a call."

"Maybe I will."

After her dogs got married, they and their doggie friends were given freshly made rice, lamb, and vegetables, no seasoning, and went to sleep in their carriage, which was shaped just like the one in the Cinderella movie.

I'd been standing in the sun too long, so I went inside to cool off, just for a few minutes. After the sun finally set, it was time to serve the human guests their dinners.

A woman sat alone at one of the tables, giving out serious leave-me-alone vibes. She wore a form-fitting red dress and one of those little hats people sometimes wear at events. The server assigned to this area was nowhere in sight, and it was time to clear the dinner plates.

She'd finished the truffle mac and cheese and bourbon-glazed short ribs. There was a tumbler of a dark brown liquid in front of her.

"Can I take your plate?" I asked, and when she looked up, I realized…I was staring at my mother.

I closed my eyes against the sight of her, but when I opened them, she was still there. My mother, the vampire they called the Executioner—the nickname said it all—was at my catering event.

She'd been by Jure Grando's side this summer, but it was still a shock to see her.

I hadn't sensed a vampire anywhere near me.

How long had she been here? The sun had barely set, and she was sitting at a table without an umbrella. I didn't know why she was at this event, but it wasn't to celebrate doggie nuptials.

"What are you doing here?" I asked. "What do you want?"

"I wanted to thank you," she said softly.

"For what?" I braced myself, expecting some comeback about how she thanked me for being a terrible queen or a weak opponent, but that's not what she said.

"For freeing me," she said. "When you killed Jure, you reversed the terrible thing he did to me."

I gaped at her. "Are you trying to tell me that when I killed Jure, it somehow reversed years of vampirism?"

Her smile was warm and soft, the kind of smile I'd always wanted from my mother. Her eyes were bright and her skin was pink, like she'd been out in the sun. It wasn't possible. Was it?

"I know it's a lot to take in," she said. "But it's true. I know it's too soon for you to forgive me, but I hope you might try."

"What do you *really* want, Vanessa?"

"To spend time with you," she said. "To get to know my only child."

"Get to know this," I said, starting to back away. "I have a job to do."

As I served desserts and refilled water glasses, I felt Vanessa's eyes on me.

I gathered up some dirty plates and took them to the kitchen, my stomach suddenly grumbling and my head a bit woozy. Maybe I could scrounge up a snack while I was there. Everything was fine until the dishwasher of the night, Rudy, dropped a glass and it shattered all over the hand-painted tile floor. Andrea tried to help clean up the mess and cut her finger.

I couldn't stop staring at the blood dripping onto the floor. My stomach growled again, and I felt my teeth coming down.

Someone snapped their fingers. "You, there," a female voice said. I looked up. It was our client, the famous child actor turned singer.

"What's wrong with you?" She snapped her fingers again, right in my face this time.

"Get your fingers out of my face before you lose them," I growled. I was going to rip that bow off her head and make her eat it. Or maybe I'd just eat her.

"Do you know who I am?" she asked.

A meal, the vampire part of my brain thought, *she's a tasty meal.* I stepped toward her, but a hand yanked me back.

I turned, snarling, fangs down. Someone was trying to keep me from my food.

"Tansy," a voice said. Who was it? The voice was male, low and soothing. *Vaughn*. It was Vaughn. The knowledge calmed the vampire in me. The bloodlust drained away as quickly as it had come, leaving only shame.

I'd almost eaten a celebrity.

Someone tapped me on the shoulder. "Hey, are you working tonight?" Without thinking, I lunged, fangs descending and claws ready to rip flesh. But Vaughn stopped me again, holding me tight against his body while I thrashed.

"Is she, like, emo or something?" the voice continued.

It was our client again. A little of the tenseness left me. She was alive and unharmed. Vaughn held me and stroked his hands down my back until my breathing slowed and my fangs disappeared. I focused on the sound of his voice, breathing in every time he said my name, until I was calm enough to think again.

He released me. "What can I help you with, Miss Segal?" He led her away while I regained my composure.

I rushed for the closet where they told us to keep our things. I scrambled for my Thermos, but it wasn't in my backpack. I knew I'd had it, though, because I'd drank some of my tonic at the beginning of my shift. I dumped everything out and searched frantically through the pile.

"It's not here," I said. "What am I going to do?"

"Let me drive you home," my mother said, coming up behind me. "You're unwell." I hadn't even noticed her approach. I looked for Vaughn, but he was probably still dealing with our unhappy client.

I remembered the vial and unscrewed the tiny cap and gulped down the liquid.

"It's not working," I said after a few minutes. "What should I do?"

"We need to get out of here," my mother said. "I'll tell someone you're sick and I'm taking you home." Did I trust her? Not entirely, but I didn't have a lot of options right now.

"Take me home, please."

"Will you be able to walk?" she asked.

I inhaled shakily. "Yes."

"Sit here. Give me five minutes and I'll meet you out front," she said. "I'm driving a black Audi."

Some of the nausea passed while I sat there. Before I could head for my mom's car, I had a brief realization that hitching a ride with someone who'd tried to kill everyone I loved wasn't a smart idea. So I stayed put.

What was wrong? Why wasn't my tonic working? I had to get out of there. I'd almost decided my mother was my only hope of leaving without biting someone when

Vaughn returned.

"I'm taking you home," Vaughn said. He hustled me out the back way and into the catering van.

"How will everyone else get back?"

"I'll bring the van back and finish cleanup," he replied.

I nodded. The nausea rolling through me made it impossible to talk.

We drove in silence for a while. Only a week ago, I would have told him right away that I'd spotted my mother. But tonight, something held me back.

Vaughn kept his eyes on the road, but I saw his jaw clench. "Tansy, about Homecoming."

I sighed. "Not right now," I said. "We can break up once I'm feeling better, okay?"

"Break up? You want to break up?"

"You don't trust me," I said softly.

He didn't say anything else, but he reached over and changed the radio station, like he was magically changing the subject.

I'd been kidding myself that the tonic would work as a long-term solution. It was like there was another person inside me, one made up of hunger and greed. Transforming sucked. I'd do anything to ditch my vampire side. I didn't want to crave human blood.

Seeing Vanessa looking so human, though, I realized that I could kill my maker and (hopefully) return to human form, but then some other vampire would only take my place as ruler. And where would that leave the people I loved? Vulnerable. Was there any magic that could solve all my problems? I doubted it. Everything felt hopeless.

When he pulled into my driveway, I was relieved to

see the twins sitting on the front porch. I wouldn't have to figure this out completely alone.

Vaughn carried me into the house. I wanted to protest, but cold chills had overtaken me.

I was shaking. I'd nearly bitten someone.

"Her tonic didn't work," Vaughn said. He showed no signs of leaving, but he couldn't leave our coworkers stranded.

"You'd better get back to the catering gig," I told him. "I'll be fine now that I'm home."

He looked like he wanted to argue, but instead, he said, "I'll come back here as soon as I'm done."

He kissed my forehead and then left.

"The tonic in your Thermos didn't work?" Rose asked.

"It didn't work," I said. "And then I drank the tonic from the vial Granny left on my bed for me, and that didn't do the job, either."

"Tansy, did you put the tonic in the vial?"

"I thought Granny did." The shaking was getting worse. "Before she left for her conference."

The twins exchanged a glance, and Thorn swore under her breath. "Let me see it."

I handed it to Rose, and she unscrewed the topper and sniffed it. "It's grape juice."

"What?"

"Or possibly Kool-Aid," she said. "Something sweet, anyhow." She held the glass vial up to the light. "You have to admit, it's almost the same color."

"How did someone get in here and switch it?" Thorn asked.

I gave her a guilty look. "Remember how you told me

to get rid of the key under the fake rock?"

"Please tell me you did it," she said.

"Not exactly," I said. "Vampires can't enter without an invitation."

"But their familiars can," she said.

"Can you get me some tonic from the fridge?" I asked. The nausea was getting worse.

She nodded. "I'll bring it to you." But she came back empty-handed.

"It's gone," she said. "Tansy, your tonic is all gone."

Someone had deliberately sabotaged me.

The thought pulled me out of my body's desperate cravings for a minute. If I survived this, I was going to find out who hated me so much. First the hellcat, now this.

"Do we have any of Skyler's bloodsicles left?" My stomach was starting to cramp. The thought of blood, any blood, made my mouth water. I tried not to look at the pulse pounding at Rose's throat. I could hear the thrum of Thorn's heartbeat.

While Thorn called Edna, Rose searched our freezer, but she came up empty.

"Edna and Evelyn have some tonic," Thorn said after hanging up. "They'll be over in twenty minutes." I started to sweat, and my eyelids were twitching.

I wasn't sure if I could wait that long. What would happen if I lost control and hurt someone? I was having a hard time focusing on anything but the vein in Thorn's neck.

I ran my fingers through my hair. "Twenty minutes." It sounded like an eternity.

Chapter Twenty-Five

Fortunately, help arrived in less than fifteen minutes, but by then, I was curled up in a ball, my stomach in knots.

Evelyn and Edna burst in. "Hold on, honey, just a minute longer," she crooned.

I started to feel more myself seconds after I'd gulped the drink down.

"Thank you," I told the couple. "You two are lifesavers." I didn't tell them that in the last few minutes, I'd craved blood more than I'd ever wanted anything.

"This is not happening again," Edna said firmly. She started rummaging through the cupboards, searching for ingredients. "Where did I put that lemon verbena?" Her hands were shaking.

I wanted to give her a hug, but my legs were too weak to stand.

"Can we get you anything else, Tansy?" The tonic was starting to work, and that's when I noticed that Evelyn and Edna were dressed up.

"I ruined date night," I said. "I'm so sorry."

"You didn't ruin anything," Edna said. "Pico's will be there tomorrow night."

Pico's was a romantic little restaurant on the water. I was lucky it wasn't far from our bungalow.

"How do you think this could have happened?" Edna asked. "Your grandmother is going to be furious."

"Don't call her!" I said. "Please. I don't want her to miss her conference. Rose and Thorn will stay with me."

Edna looked like she wanted to argue, but Evelyn put her arm around her. "I made a double-batch of tonic."

They whisper-argued for a few minutes, and then Edna said, "We won't call your granny, but you need to tell her what happened the second she gets home."

"I promise."

"And you'll get rid of the spare key under the fake rock," Thorn added.

"Yep," I said.

"This was no accident," Rose said. "Someone in the supernatural community is out to get you."

I hesitated. "There was one other odd thing," I said. "After I came back from dropping Granny off, it seemed like someone had been in my room."

"In your room?" Rose asked. Her shoulders went tense. "Was anything missing?"

"No, I don't think so," I said.

"What about the stone?" Rose was choosing her words carefully, as if she didn't want Edna and Evelyn to know about the ruby.

"Still here," I said.

Her shoulders relaxed.

Granny's friends each kissed me on the forehead before saying good night. I was tired, and my jaw hurt from clenching it. My whole body hurt.

After they left, I lay on the couch and tried to read, but my head was still pounding. Rose and Thorn argued about who would take the first watch, and when Thorn won, Rose went to the spare room to pull out the daybed and get some sleep.

About an hour after Evelyn and Edna departed, Vaughn came back from dropping off the van.

"How are you feeling?" he asked. He rubbed my temples, and I sighed.

"That feels good."

Vaughn studied my face and then stood and held out his hand. "Let's go to your room. You need a distraction."

Thorn made a hooting noise, and I blushed. Vaughn blushed, too. "Uh, I thought we could watch TV or something."

"Or something." Now it was Rose's turn to be a comedian.

I gave them both a mock glare. "We'll be in my room, fully clothed."

But as soon as my bedroom door closed, Vaughn shrugged off his white button-down and the tee he had on underneath, then sat on the bed.

"What are you doing?"

"I read somewhere that skin-to-skin was soothing," he said.

"You want me to take off my shirt, too?" I asked. "But the twins are right outside."

"I mean it, Tansy," he said. "I'd be a total asshole to try to get with you right now. I'm trying to help you relax."

At least I knew that since Vaughn was a werewolf, he'd probably be able to handle it if I lost control and attacked him.

I shivered.

"I'll warm you up," Vaughn said. "Werewolves run hot."

"Yeah, they do," I replied.

He laughed and then kissed me, just a gentle peck, no tongue.

"You're distracting me," I said. I was a weak, weak woman, but he was giving me hope that maybe we weren't over after all.

"I like distracting you," Vaughn murmured, brushing his lips along my neck. I knew he meant for this to be comforting, but I hadn't had the chance to closely examine the changes to his body, so I took the opportunity.

"I like the way you're distracting me," I admitted. I ran a hand across his shoulders and down to his biceps and squeezed. "Is this because you've been lifting weights and eating slabs of protein?"

He choked out a laugh. "Slabs?"

"I don't know how else to describe the amount of meat you've been putting away," I teased. I continued my exploration. "Or are these new muscles because you're a werewolf now?"

He flexed his arm for me. "Are we really talking about my health regimen?"

"Something else you'd rather do?"

"This," he said and rolled so he was lying on top of me. "Is this okay?" He buried his face in my neck and kissed the tiny scar.

"Yes," I breathed. "I missed you," I confessed.

He nipped my lips. "Show me how much."

So I did.

A long time later, Vaughn said, "I have to go home soon."

"Do you have to?"

"As much as I'd love to stay here all night, I have a thing early tomorrow."

"What kind of thing?"

He avoided my gaze.

"You can say it, Vaughn. You have a pack meeting in the morning."

He nodded.

"I'll walk you out."

He ran his fingers through his hair. "Tansy, I'm not choosing them over you."

It sure felt like it, but it had been a shitty night already. I didn't want to add to it by fighting with him.

"I'm not," he insisted, then sighed. "We'll figure it out." He gave me a brief kiss. "Now let's get moving, because I plan to kiss you for at least five more minutes on the front porch."

His words should have soothed me, but after he left, I still couldn't shake the idea that we were on opposite sides.

"Did you two make up?" Thorn asked.

I could feel my face getting red. "It's complicated."

"I bet," she said dryly.

I shifted uneasily. I wasn't used to having chats about

my romantic life with anyone but Skyler.

"What about you and Beckett?" I asked.

"I think he likes someone else."

"Then what about Xavier?"

"I think he likes someone else, too," she replied.

"That sucks."

"Yeah, it does." She brightened. "But at least I can say my first-ever date was with two hot guys."

She and her sister were gorgeous, strong, and interesting. I found it hard to believe that no one had ever asked her out before now.

"Were your parents strict?" I asked her.

Thorn nodded. "You have no idea." She yawned then. "Time to wake up Rose for the second watch."

I watched her go. I got the feeling, again, that Thorn didn't want to talk about her parents. Hard to believe they could be worse than my own unknown father and vampire mother.

If what Vanessa had said was true, then I didn't have a vampire for a mother any longer. Could it really be possible?

Chapter Twenty-Six

I t was Halloween, and normally, Granny made a big deal of it, but she'd been in a rush before she left and had forgotten to buy candy. Which I discovered that morning when I went to pour it into the big plastic pumpkin we used every year.

Rose was in the backyard, watering the plants or talking to them or distilling poison or something. Thorn was on a run, which I'd managed to get out of by claiming I was still achy from my episode yesterday.

Which meant it was up to me to obtain the necessary sweets. The morning was overcast. I threw on a hoodie over my tee; my jeans would cover my legs, and I found a ball cap and covered my head. Sunglasses completed the "don't let the sun touch me" look.

"I'm going out on a candy run," I hollered at Rose. She nodded to let me know she heard me.

I pulled into the grocery store and tried to find a parking spot close to the entrance. It was Saturday morning, the market was already busy, and the Deathtrap wasn't exactly a tiny vehicle, so I had to settle for something in the middle.

I grabbed a cart, deciding that I may as well grab a few other things while I was at it. The candy selection was picked over, but that's what I got for waiting until the last minute.

"I'm a big fan of Reese's Peanut Butter Cups," a woman said.

I glanced up, already prepared to give the speaker my "talking to strangers in a store" smile, but it was my mother. Standing in the middle of Ralph's in broad daylight.

I stared at her. She hadn't been lying. Vampires couldn't walk in broad daylight, yet here she was.

"I'm glad to see you're feeling better," Vanessa said. "I was worried about you. You made it home from the wedding without any difficulty?"

"I did," I said. "Thank you for offering to help me, but my—a coworker took me home."

"Handing out candy tonight?" she asked casually.

"Yep," I said, still stunned by the idea that she had been telling me the truth. My mother was human.

"Want some company?" she asked.

Overwhelmed, I continued to stare without speaking.

"Tansy?" she asked. "Are you all right?"

"It's just a shock," I said, waving vaguely in her direction.

Her eyes twinkled. "You're telling me. When it first happened, I thought it had to be too good to be true. But I've had a few months to get used to being human again."

I smiled at her. I couldn't help it.

"About tonight. Would you like some company?" she

asked. She watched me closely as she waited for my answer.

I really wanted to say yes, but I couldn't. Not yet. "I'm having friends over." Not exactly a lie. Rose and Thorn were becoming my friends. Or at least the closest thing I had to them.

"I understand," she said. "Let me give you my number, just in case you change your mind. Or call me to talk. I'd love to spend some time with you."

I didn't hand her my phone. Instead, I asked her to recite the number, and I put it in my phone myself. It's not that I didn't trust her, but I didn't trust her. Not yet. Maybe not ever. But maybe I could try.

I programmed the number in, and we stood there, grinning at each other. It was kind of awkward, but also kind of nice. Hanging out at the grocery store with my mom. Something a lot of people took for granted.

After a few minutes, she grabbed some candy and then said goodbye. I finished my own shopping and then headed home.

I didn't think I'd call her. I wasn't ready for more, not after seventeen years of silence. Besides, it would be fun to hang out with Rose and Thorn. We could watch a scary movie and admire the costumes.

But it turned out they had other plans. Plans that didn't include me.

"What movie do you want to watch tonight?" I asked.

Rose and Thorn did that twin thing where they didn't say anything out loud but communicated with their eyes.

"I have a date with Lucas," Rose finally said.

"I was going to hang out with Beckett and Xavier,"

Thorn said. "But I can cancel."

"Don't be silly," I said. "I'll be fine on my own for a few hours."

"Are you sure?" Rose asked.

"I am," I replied. "Now tell me what you're doing tonight."

"There's a small party at Con…" Her voice trailed off. They were all going to Connor's house. Skyler and Vaughn would probably be there, too.

"Have fun," I said brightly. "I think I'll read in my room until it's time for the trick-or-treaters." I wanted to cry. Skyler and Vaughn still hadn't forgiven me for what happened to Connor on Homecoming night.

I pretended to be asleep when Rose tapped on my door, but as the night went on, it got harder and harder to smile at the kids in their costumes.

At around nine, the doorbell stopped ringing, and I was alone with my thoughts. I picked up my phone and called Vanessa. When she picked up, I said, "Hi, it's me." I cleared my throat. "Turns out my plans fell through. Would you like to come over?"

"To your grandmother's house?" my mom said. "Are you sure she's ready for that?"

"She's not here," I said. "Nobody is." I winced at the sound of the loneliness I heard in my own voice.

There was a long pause. "Are you sure you trust me enough to invite me in?"

"I do," I said. Besides, I'd keep my drumstick with me, just in case.

"Then I'll be right over," my mother replied.

When the doorbell rang twenty minutes later, I took

a deep breath. Was I really going to let *Vanessa* into my home? What if it was some kind of trick?

The last thing I was expecting was a normal night. But that's what we had.

We made popcorn and threw in the leftover M&Ms, watched a romantic comedy instead of a horror movie, because Mom said, "There's been enough horror in my life," and then we talked about me, mostly.

"What were you like before you became a striga vie?" she asked.

I told her the story of how Skyler and I had met, fighting over a book during story time at the library.

"She sounds like a good friend," my mom said softly.

Some of the pain I was feeling about my faltering friendship with Skyler must have shown on my face, because my mom reached over and squeezed my hand. "Did I say something wrong?"

"Skyler and I aren't talking right now," I admitted. "She's mad at me. But I'm mad at her, too."

My mother was watching me closely. "You were a very good friend to her this summer, Tansy," she said firmly. "I would expect that a true friend would show you the same kind of loyalty."

I didn't want to cry in front of her. She was still a stranger, even though I was starting to think that maybe we could have a relationship. I jumped up. "I'll be right back," I said.

In the bathroom, I locked the door and let a few tears fall. Then I splashed cold water on my face. When I went back to the living room, my mother wasn't there.

Where was she? My mother, the potentially former

vampire, was loose somewhere in my house. And I'd invited her in.

She was in my bedroom. She was examining something on my dresser. "What are you doing in here?" I asked, and she practically jumped as she turned to face me, her eyes wide. I folded my arms across my chest.

"You startled me," she said.

"Why are you in my bedroom?"

"I could tell you were upset," she replied. "I just wanted to comfort you. I'm sorry."

"Maybe we should call it a night," I said.

"If that's what you want," she said.

"It is."

"Maybe we could do it again sometime?" Vanessa asked.

I hesitated and then nodded.

"We can keep it between the two of us," she suggested.

"That we're hanging out?"

She nodded. "And that I'm human."

"Why?" I crossed my arms over my chest.

"I made a lot of mistakes," she admitted softly. "Even before Jure forced me into becoming a vampire. I don't know if my mother will ever be able to forgive me. I don't know if you will be able to forgive me, either."

"I don't know, either," I said honestly.

Tears welled in her eyes. "I understand."

"But I'll try," I said. I wanted to believe her. So much.

Chapter Twenty-Seven

Vaughn called me the next morning while I was still in bed. He called me because I still wasn't answering his texts. I'd slipped a little the night of the doggie wedding, but I wasn't ready to completely forgive him yet.

"What are you doing tonight?" he asked. I wasn't prepared for how angry I felt at hearing the sound of his voice.

I let the silence linger. It was like he'd forgotten that he'd left his girlfriend at home alone to hang out with his werewolf pack. And all my friends.

"Did you have a nice Halloween?" I finally asked before I disconnected the call.

I rolled over and went back to sleep.

Someone was pounding at the front door. Didn't anyone know how to use a doorbell? "Go away," I said, still groggy. The blackout curtains in my room made it hard to tell what time of day it was, but my body told me I'd been asleep for a long time.

I grabbed my drumstick before staggering to the front hall. I gripped it tightly and asked, "Who is it?"

"Tansy, it's me," Vaughn said.

"Then definitely go away," I said. I was sick of the people I cared about betraying me. If that was love, I wanted no part of it.

"Would you let me explain? Please?" he asked.

I had dragon breath and bed head, but I didn't care. I stalked to the door and opened it. "What's there to explain? I can take a hint."

"I'm sorry I hurt you," he said.

"Who said you did?" I crossed my arms over my chest. I wasn't going to admit how much it had hurt that not one of my friends had a problem abandoning me because of one mistake.

"Rose," he admitted.

"I guess I can't count on her, either," I said.

"You can count on me," Vaughn said.

"Very little evidence of that," I said. "At least lately."

"Can we please talk about this?" Vaughn asked. "Why don't we go to your bedroom and talk in private?"

"You don't currently have any bedroom privileges," I said. "We'll talk in the living room."

I made a quick detour to grab a bottle of tonic, but I sniffed it first to make sure it was the real thing. When it passed the sniff test, I drank a whole bottle and then reached for another and took it with me to the living room.

Vaughn was sitting in the middle of the couch. He probably thought I was going to sit next to him, but instead, I chose a chair.

"About Halloween," he said, then stopped.

"You want to talk about the party for Connor?" I asked. "Or about Homecoming? Let's talk about that. You said you didn't want to break up. You said nothing changed. But the first time you had to choose between the pack or me, you chose your pack."

"Travis looked guilty," he said.

"Do you think I don't know that?" I replied. "Do you think that I would let him walk if I thought he'd killed those werewolves and tried to kill Connor?" I had a gut full of mad, and I was spewing it all over Vaughn. "I knew it wasn't Travis, beyond a shadow of a doubt."

"How could you know for sure?"

"I made him tell me the truth," I said. Did he understand what I was trying to say?

By the light dawning on his face, he did. "Why didn't you tell me?"

"You didn't give me the chance," I said. "And I wasn't going to announce it in a room full of angry werewolves." I was determined not to cry in front of him, but my voice sounded clogged anyway.

"I fucked up," Vaughn finally said. "I really, really fucked up."

"You did."

"I wouldn't blame you if you never trusted me again," he said. "But I'd really like it if you would give me another chance. I can do better."

"You keeping bailing on me, over and over again," I said. "I'd never do that to you."

"I know," he said. "I promise you it won't happen again. Please say you'll give me a chance to prove myself to you."

He crossed to where I sat and took my hands in his.

"Say you'll forgive me, Tansy."

"I'll try," I said.

"I'll keep my word," he said. "Even if it kills me."

"What movie is that from?" I asked.

He shook his head. "No movie. Just me."

After a bit of make-up cuddling, Vaughn suggested a moonlight beach run, which was perfect, since I'd been longing for some outdoor activity. The moon was a pale sliver in the night sky, but there were streetlights nearby, so we could see enough to run. And, apparently, for me to ogle my boyfriend.

I was watching his butt flex when he turned around and caught me.

"Doing okay back there?" he asked with a grin.

"I'm loving the view," I said. My boyfriend had gained some muscle mass in a few other places I hadn't noticed until now.

"Race you to the end of the pier," Vaughn said. I ran after him, trying not to huff and puff, but it seemed as though he was faster as well as bigger. I guess a faster sprinting time was a side benefit of being a werewolf.

I pushed through and made it to the end of the pier only five minutes behind him. Vampire speed, I did not have.

I threw myself down on the sand next to him.

He nuzzled my neck and took a deep whiff. "You smell good."

"I'm all sweaty," I said, but I didn't push him away.

He kissed me gently, our tongues meeting. He cupped my head and then took my hair tie out and tangled his hands in my hair.

I leaned back into the sand, not caring about the dampness as Vaughn followed me down, pressing his body into mine. "Tansy," Vaughn growled my name.

We stayed on the beach, kissing, but when Vaughn's hands started to wander, I sat up. "We should go," I said.

"I'm sorry," he said. His brow furrowed. "Did I do something wrong?"

"It's not that," I said, my cheeks heating. "It's just we're kind of in a public place."

Now it was Vaughn's turn to blush. He got to his feet and then helped me up. "Let's stop by Janey's and get something to eat. I'm starving."

We were both covered in sand, so we spent a little time brushing the grit off our clothes and then headed to the diner.

We'd just missed the dinner rush, so we were able to nab a booth right away.

I didn't recognize the server who came over, but Vaughn had barely let him tell us the specials before he was ordering. "Loaded nachos, stat!" I gave him a look, and he added, "Please. I'm so hungry."

After the server left to get our drinks and apps, I studied the menu. Janey's was known for their burgers and fries. They were hot, fresh, and topped with unusual add-ons like truffles and black garlic or brown-sugar bacon.

"What are you going to have?" Vaughn asked. His stomach growled loudly, and I decided quickly. He ordered the largest burger Janey's had on their menu and a side of bacon.

"You are hungry," I observed.

He waggled his eyebrows. "I worked up an appetite."

I nearly spit out my water. "Running," he added, his gray eyes twinkling.

The appetizer arrived before I could comment. Vaughn was practically drooling but still remembered his manners enough to offer me the plate first.

"Go ahead," I said. He dug in, taking a big chip and digging into the cheesy meat-filled goodness. I noticed he tried to find the bits with the biggest chunks of carne asada.

The plate was nearly empty by the time our burgers came.

He bit into his burger, and blood oozed out. It looked like it was nearly raw.

"Do you want to send it back?" I asked. "It seems a little underdone."

"So good," he mumbled.

My boyfriend was craving raw meat and had bulked up rapidly. I was learning a lot about being a werewolf's girlfriend.

When his food was finally gone, he said, "I need to find our server." Then he added, "I'm still hungry."

I gaped at him. "You're kidding."

He smiled at me and ducked his head. "Only a little."

"Do you…want dessert?" I'd never seen him eat so much.

"I'm gonna get a couple more burgers to go," he said.

"Are you training for a competitive eating contest?" I asked. "I mean, from what I can tell, a werewolf would be a shoo-in."

He laughed. "No," he said. "But I have been running with the pack lately, and those guys burn a lot of calories."

"Have you shifted since the first time?" I asked, then

added, "Or is that question too personal?"

"It's not too personal," he said, laughing. "At least not coming from my girlfriend."

"I don't know the rules," I said, rolling my eyes.

"I don't know all of them, either," he replied once he stopped laughing. "You are my girlfriend, right?"

"Right."

"You can ask me anything. No more keeping things from you."

I felt so guilty when he said that, but my mother had asked me not to tell anyone about her until she'd had the chance to apologize to everyone.

"Vaughn," I said softly.

"It'll be fine," he said. "I'm fine."

We paid our bill and left the restaurant, but I couldn't help worrying. We'd already ended up on opposite sides once. I could only imagine Vaughn's response if I told him I'd been talking to my mother.

When we got to my house, he gave me a brief good night kiss and then left. I hadn't been completely honest with Vaughn, but I told myself I needed to protect myself this time. No one else was going to do it for me.

Chapter Twenty-Eight

School was slightly less awkward now that I only had to avoid my best friend, instead of my best friend *and* my boyfriend.

When my class before lunch ended, Vaughn came to walk with me to the cafeteria.

"Did you hear that Christian got suspended for fighting again?" Vaughn said. "They kicked him out for good this time."

"No, but I think he's been listening to too much Thirsty Thieves music," I said. "It's making him too aggressive."

We walked into the cafeteria, hand-in-hand, talking about how Christian had changed. Vaughn's pack was sitting at a table. I was relieved to find Connor was back at school. He was washed out and sickly-looking but alive. Next to him was Skyler. When our eyes met, she looked away.

My stomach sank, and I dropped Vaughn's hand, but he picked it up again. "I promised," he said in a low voice.

"They'll get over it."

"And if they don't?"

"Then I guess I'll have to find a new pack," he said.

I hoped it wouldn't come to that, but judging from the glares being sent my way, I wasn't ruling it out, either.

Vaughn and I took a seat at a table as far away from our former friends as possible. "Do you want to hang out tonight?"

I bit my lip. "I can't," I said. "I already have plans." I didn't want him to ask what those plans were, so I added quickly, "I'm free tomorrow night, though."

"It's a date," he said with a grin.

Tonight, I was going out to dinner with my mother.

She picked me up a block down from my house, as I'd asked her to. Granny wasn't home yet, but Rose and Thorn were still staying with me. I couldn't risk Vanessa being seen.

"I thought I'd introduce you to my boyfriend," she said, looking down.

"You have a boyfriend?"

"He's really great," she said. "And he's looking forward to meeting you."

"Sounds good," I said, but I was taken aback. I had so many questions. "How long have you been dating?"

"Not that long," she said. "But I think he's the one."

We ended up at Janey's. "You like this place, right?" she asked.

"How did you know that?"

"You must have mentioned it," she said. "You said something about their waffles?"

"I do love their waffles," I said.

We'd arrived during the dinner rush, but we managed to get a booth after a very short wait.

I looked at the number of people waiting for tables. "Maybe we should have taken a smaller table. There's just the two of us."

"Actually." She clapped her hands. "I have the best surprise. My boyfriend will be joining us. In fact, that's him now."

I craned my neck, but I didn't spot anyone who looked like they'd be dating my mother. I did see someone I wasn't expecting, though. *Vaughn.* Standing next to his dad, who was talking to the hostess. She grabbed two menus and headed our way.

Part of me wanted to duck, but they'd seen me. Even worse, it looked like they were coming to our booth.

"Sorry we're late," Mr. Sheridan said. He slid into the booth and kissed my mom's cheek, a lovesick smile on his face.

Mr. Sheridan did a double take when he saw me. "Tansy?"

Vaughn's dad…was dating my *mother*?

Vaughn sat next to me. I couldn't look at him. My stomach rolled, and I started to sweat. I'd made a big mistake. I'd been angry at Vaughn for hiding the truth, but I'd done the same thing.

"What the fuck?" Vaughn muttered. He recognized my mother, of course. It was hard to forget the person who'd tried to kill you.

My hands clenched into fists, but Vaughn took my hand and laced our fingers together. "I promised," he whispered, and the tension inside me subsided. "Dad got one thing right about her," he continued. "She *is* beautiful, at least on the outside. You look like her."

It was true. There was no denying she was my mother. We had the same red hair, pale skin, and green eyes.

"Panda, this is my son Vaughn," Mr. Sheridan said.

Panda?

"Vaughn, this is my girlfriend," Mr. Sheridan said. "Tansy, it's nice to see you. I didn't know Vanessa was your mother."

"I didn't know Vanessa was your girlfriend," I said lightly, but I was trembling. This couldn't be a coincidence. But what did it mean? "Why do you call her Panda?"

They exchanged a gooey look and grinned at each other. "Because she was wearing a black-and-white top the night we met."

"Cute," I said, but I couldn't help feeling that my mother was up to something.

"It's quite a coincidence that I randomly met your mother and we started dating," Mr. Sheridan said.

Vaughn's grim expression told me he didn't believe it was a coincidence, either.

"It's so lovely to meet you, Vaughn," Vanessa said. "How do you know my daughter?"

Vaughn made a big show of glancing at our entwined hands. "She's my girlfriend."

"Oh?" Vanessa gave me a sideways glance.

"Tansy, I haven't seen you lately," Mr. Sheridan said.

I didn't look at Vaughn when I said, "I've been busy." Busy almost breaking up with his son.

There was a frown settling between my mother's eyes.

"So how'd you two meet?" I asked.

"A happy accident," Mr. Sheridan said. "You tell it, honey."

"No, you tell it," my mother cooed.

Vaughn's hands were wrapped so tightly around his water glass that I was worried he was going to shatter it. It looked like he was seconds from wolfing out. I rubbed his knee comfortingly, and his body relaxed into mine.

"We were at the same country-and-western bar, and I couldn't take my eyes off her," Mr. Sheridan continued.

"What's the name of the bar?" I asked. My throat felt tight. It couldn't be a coincidence. I would bet my whole paycheck that they'd met at The Last Stop.

Which Mr. Sheridan confirmed with his next words. "It's kind of a dive."

I had a bad feeling it was a vampire dive. Vaughn and I exchanged a glance.

"And then I ran into her again." Mr. Sheridan picked up Vanessa's hand and kissed it.

"I volunteer," my mother continued the story, "selling tickets for an animal shelter fundraiser." She sounded so believable, but could I really trust her? Vampires lied to your face and made you believe every falsehood, no matter how blatant. Besides, she hadn't been a great mom even before she'd turned into a vampire. I was suspicious, but if she wasn't human, how was she able to walk around in broad daylight?

"Which shelter?" I asked.

"A golden retriever rescue," she said.

"And you just happened to bump into each other?" Now

it was Vaughn's turn.

"Adam made such a generous contribution," Vanessa cooed.

"I've always wanted a pet." Mr. Sheridan's eyes lit up.

"Yes, you've told me," Vanessa said. There was an almost undetectable edge in her voice.

"Are you still volunteering?" Vaughn asked.

"I've turned to other pursuits," she replied.

"What kind of pursuits?" I asked.

"This and that," my mother replied. She was trying to change the subject, but Vaughn's dad didn't get the hint.

"Darling, don't minimize what you do," Mr. Sheridan said.

"What do you do for a living?" Vaughn asked Vanessa.

"It's not just a living," she replied. "It's my passion. I'm a cat breeder."

"A cat breeder?" I tried and failed to keep the shock from my voice. It was the last thing I thought she'd say.

"What breed?" Vaughn asked.

"A new breed of designer cats," she replied. "Very exclusive."

I waited, but she didn't elaborate. She gave Vaughn a challenging smile. "I was thinking of giving your father a kitten."

"Isn't Mr. Sheridan allergic?" I asked, but he gave her a sappy smile.

"These are hypoallergenic cats," she replied. Vanessa had an answer for everything, but I still didn't know if I could trust her. Sure, we'd been spending some time together, but did I really know her at all?

"I'll help you pick one out," Vaughn volunteered.

"The cats are very special," his dad said. Vaughn and I exchanged a "what the hell" look across the table.

"What kind of cats exactly?" I asked. "Like a Sphynx?"

"Something new." Mr. Sheridan's smile was so proud it made my heart hurt. "Very hush-hush."

She smiled at him. "I'm not ready to unveil the concept yet." When she caught me staring at her, she smiled at me, too. "I wanted it to be a surprise."

She looked human and, even more importantly, she smelled like a human. I couldn't detect even a hint of vampire.

"So this bar where you two met…" I started.

"She was the cutest cowgirl I'd ever seen. I asked her to line-dance, and the rest is history," Mr. Sheridan said. My mind boggled at the thought of my mother in a denim skirt, a cowboy hat on her immaculately styled hair, and shitkickers on her feet.

"Was it The Last Stop by any chance?" Vaughn asked.

"You've been there?" His dad sounded delighted.

"With my grandmother," I said. I glanced at my mother, wondering if the mention of her mother, the woman she'd tried to kill, would upset her.

"I'm hoping to see your grandmother soon," Vanessa said. Was it my imagination or was there a hint of menace behind that statement?

My grandmother could take care of herself, especially if she was up against a human and not a vampire who had an unfair advantage.

Hope and suspicion fought in my mind. Had I let my loneliness and desire for a parent of my own overrule my better judgment? Or was it just a coincidence that my mother was dating Vaughn's dad?

Field trip? Vaughn mouthed, and I nodded. My mother was watching us, and I gave her a sweet smile.

An awkward silence fell. "Everyone ready to order?" our server asked. She looked like she might be new. She plunked down a basket of rolls in the middle of the table.

Mr. Sheridan offered the basket to my mother, who waved it away, and then to me.

"I'll have the garlic chicken," Vanessa said. "With extra garlic, if possible. And a diet soda."

That ticked the "not a vampire" column.

Vaughn and I both ordered spaghetti with extra garlic, and Mr. Sheridan ordered a medium-rare steak.

Vaughn thought about it for about two seconds. "I'll have that, too."

"You want a steak instead of spaghetti?" the server asked.

"No, I want steak *and* spaghetti," he replied. "Please."

After we'd placed our orders, my mother asked, "Tell me how the two of *you* met."

I rolled my eyes. "Vaughn and I have been friends since we were little."

"But you're dating now?" she persisted. "When did that happen?"

"This summer," Vaughn said. "It was a very interesting summer. You might even say life-changing." For a second, I thought he was going to say something shocking, like how she'd tried to kill him, but instead, he bit his lip and scowled.

I took a bite of the spaghetti. It had tons of garlic in it. "It's delicious." Maybe my mother's plan was to poison us all. I hoped it wasn't poisoned. Where was Rose when

I needed her? She was the expert.

My mother took a big bite. "I love garlic."

Mr. Sheridan gave her an indulgent smile. "Anything for you, my love."

"Dad, it doesn't bother you that she ditched her kid?" Vaughn asked.

"Vaughn, I've taught you there are always two sides to a story," his dad replied. He gave my mom a kiss that started out innocently but then turned into full-on making out.

Vaughn covered his eyes with one hand and my eyes with the other. "You can't just do that without warning," he said.

"Mom, I beg of you, please stop or I'll be scarred for life," I said.

"Okay, it's safe to look now," Mr. Sheridan said with a good-natured chuckle.

"I hope our relationship isn't upsetting to you," Vanessa said.

"Since I'm Tansy's boyfriend," Vaughn said, "it does make you dating my dad a little awkward."

To add awkward on top of awkward, we finished the meal in silence.

"Thanks for dinner, Mr. Sheridan," I said. He nodded, but there was a troubled look on his face.

"I'm going to take Tansy home now," Vaughn said, and we left our parents making out in a booth at Janey's Diner.

But he didn't take me home. Instead, we ended up parking at the beach to talk.

"So, when did you start hanging out with your mother?" Vaughn's voice was carefully neutral.

"I'm so sorry I didn't tell you sooner. But remember

at that wedding when I almost vamped out?" I asked. "She was there just walking around, and it wasn't even sunset. She told me that when I killed Jure, it reversed her vampirism."

"And you think it's true?"

"I want it to be true," I said. "But it can't be a coincidence she's dating your dad."

"What do you think she's up to?" he asked me.

"I have no idea. Did you notice that she didn't smell like a vamp?" I asked Vaughn.

"It's not impossible that she's human," he said. "Jure is dead."

"And your dad seems to be mark-free, unless his bitemark is in a less obvious spot." Most vampires went with a traditional neck bite, although some liked the wrist or a thigh.

"I can see the appeal," he said. "She's a beautiful redhead, you're a beautiful redhead," he replied.

I hated the idea that I was anything like the woman who'd almost killed both my boyfriend and my grandmother.

"Jesus, I'm screwing this up," he said. "I'm trying to say that, objectively, I understand why my dad would be attracted to her."

"What does my mother see in *him*?" I wondered aloud.

"Hey, that's my dad you're talking about," Vaughn said.

"I can see the appeal," I added, parroting his words. "Your dad is awesome and handsome and kind, just like his son."

"Your mother must have a hidden motive," Vaughn said. "Some agenda."

"Maybe. But what if she doesn't?" I asked.

"You mean what if the woman who was called the Executioner just happened to meet my dad and they fell in love? I don't think so."

"The only link is me," I said. "Is it wrong to hope that it's true that she's human? That she's in love?"

"She isn't capable of love," he said, then hurried to clarify. "Not because she's a vampire, but because she hurt you," he said.

I leaned in and kissed him. "I know what you meant." We'd promised to trust each other.

"Even if she's not a vampire any longer, which I doubt, she's still the kind of person who would abandon her child," he said.

"Thank you for not freaking out when you first saw us," I said. "I didn't mention it to you because Vanessa asked me not to say anything. And you weren't really talking to me then, anyway."

"Why did you decide to spend time with her?" There was no judgment in his tone.

"Part of it was that I wanted it to be true," I admitted. "Because if it was, then there was still hope for me. That there's still a possibility that I can return to normal. It would be such a relief to be a Mariotti witch again, instead of a striga vie."

Instead of replying, Vaughn's lips met mine. Before I knew it, we were in the backseat and Vaughn's shirt was off. He brushed his fingers down my arm, the calluses setting off little shivers everywhere he touched.

"You've been practicing," I said.

He stopped the motion and lifted his head. "What?"

"Your hands," I said. "New calluses. You've been playing

the drums again."

"Yeah," he said. "Is it weird that I picked it up again after playing for The Drainers?"

"No," I said. "I think it's nice."

He started stroking my arm again. "Sorry about my hands," he said.

"I like it," I admitted.

"Tansy, you know I lo—"

I covered his lips with my hand. "Not yet," I whispered. I wasn't ready for him to say it, not when we'd just found out our parents were dating.

He kissed my hand still covering his mouth and nodded.

I dropped my hand onto his shoulder and leaned in and kissed him again.

We broke apart, both of us breathing heavily. "What are we going to do?" Vaughn asked.

"About our parents?"

"About everything."

"I'm going to have to tell Granny," I replied. I needed to figure out if my mother was telling the truth about how she'd become human. I tried not to think about how much I wanted it to be true.

Chapter Twenty-Nine

When we got home, Granny was in the family room with a few of the Old Crones Book Club. Judging from the open bottle of wine and the fancy snacks, we'd interrupted the tail end of a book club meeting. Or a coven meeting. I got those two things confused sometimes.

I went over to Granny and gave her a hug. "How was your conference?" I asked. "I missed you."

She chattered a bit about what she'd learned and casually mentioned a night out with the silver fox. I tried to remain calm, but the pressure was getting to me. Finally, I blurted it out.

"We need to talk to you," I said. I had to break the news quickly, like ripping off a Band-Aid. "Adam Sheridan is dating Vanessa Mariotti."

Granny's hands flew out and she almost tipped over her glass of wine, but she caught it at the last second. "Your mother is going out with Vaughn's dad? Are you sure?"

"I'm sure," I said. The whole story came tumbling out.

"How long?" she asked.

"Vaughn's dad started dating someone this summer," I said. "But neither Vaughn nor I knew it was her." I paused. "We both met her for the first time tonight. She looks… human."

Granny was silent for a long time. "Did you ask her how she managed that?"

"You don't trust her," I said.

Her face softened. "I know she hurt you."

I ignored that. Granny wasn't talking about when Vanessa had hurt me this summer.

"She doesn't look or smell like a vampire," I said.

"Maybe Vanessa was who took your tonic and that's why she looks human," Edna suggested.

"I wouldn't put it past her to take the tonic," Granny said. "But the tonic doesn't work on a full vampire."

"Interesting," Evelyn said.

I wasn't convinced that my mother was sincere, but I'd made my own mistakes. "Granny, do you think it's possible she's just reverted? I did kill Jure. He could have been her maker."

"I've learned that many things are possible," she replied.

"She looks human now," I protested. "Smells human, too. I couldn't detect a trace of vampire."

"She's up to something," Vaughn said.

"What if she's not?" I replied. "What if killing Jure freed her? What if she's human now? There could be another reason she's with Vaughn's dad," I insisted. "Something non-nefarious. He is good-looking."

Evelyn gave a snort. "Vanessa is up to no good," she

said. "It's not a coincidence she's dating your boyfriend's father."

"I thought that was a possibility, too," I admitted.

"Maybe she is human," Granny Mariotti said. "But I've never heard of someone like the Executioner returning to human. After all, traditional belief is that once you kill a human by draining them dry, the process is not reversible."

"She nearly killed you," Vaughn said. "She nearly killed me. I can't believe we're even arguing that woman's humanity."

"But she didn't," Granny pointed out.

"But what if?" I asked hoarsely. "What if she's really human?"

I secretly hoped in my heart that my mother was coming back to us.

On Saturday I was working at the main office of Sheridan Catering. It was mostly filing paperwork, but it kept me inside, away from the sunshine and customers I may or may not have tried to bite.

I was filing without really paying much attention to anything except the file they went into when I glanced down and noticed a familiar name. Vanessa Mariotti had used the company credit card to charge a hefty sum, but there was no description. I wrote down the name and address on a sticky and shoved it in my back pocket.

My mother walked in the front office while I was staring at the paperwork and stood in full sunlight.

"Tansy, what are you doing here?" she asked.

I slipped the papers beneath a batch of invoices and turned to face her. "I work here. What are you doing here?"

My mother was beautiful, with creamy skin, green eyes, and hair a shade darker red than my own, but I'd never seen her look so human before. Hopeful. Alive. Not the Executioner, but a woman in love.

Maybe we were wrong about her?

"Is Adam available? I thought I'd take him to lunch," she said. The fond smile that crossed her face was almost perfect.

"I think he's still on the phone with one of our suppliers," I said. He hadn't been to the catering office much lately. Now it was my turn to frown. A lot of people relied on the jobs he provided, and I didn't want his infatuation with my mother to mess with that.

"I'll wait," Vanessa replied. She sat on the small loveseat in the reception area. I turned around and went back to my job.

When I next looked up, my mother was hunched over, vomiting something into a waste basket.

"I'll get Mr. Sheridan," I said.

"No, don't leave me," she groaned. "Can you help me?"

"What's wrong with you?"

She started to pant, and her face went pale. "Could you get me some water?"

I got a bottle out of the small fridge where we kept beverages for guests and handed it to her. She gulped it down and then motioned for more. She drank that one quickly as well.

"I must be coming down with something," she said. "I'll

go home to rest. I don't want to infect Adam."

She hurried off, and I stared after her.

My mom was still young. What if she was pregnant, like Gertie? The thought didn't thrill me. I'd always wanted a sibling, but the thought of my boyfriend and I both introducing a kid as a sibling made me want to throw up, too.

I'd gotten used to the human-looking version of my mother, but after she'd thrown up, she'd looked cold. Pale. Dead? Like the Executioner.

Was my mother truly human or was she just faking it? I had to find out.

Chapter Thirty

That weekend was dinner with Mr. Sheridan and Vanessa, but this time we were eating at a restaurant owned by one of Mr. Sheridan's friends. The closer we got to the next full moon and the longer I went without finding the werewolf murderer, the harder it was to act like everything was fine. And since my boyfriend was a werewolf, there was a chance he could be the next victim.

Vaughn and I hit traffic on our way to Laguna Beach.

"Remember when we had that tide pool assignment?" I asked. From sunup to sundown, we'd scrambled over the rocks, searching for gooseneck clams, sea stars, sea urchins that looked like underwater flowers. The seagulls begged for scraps in their loud, demanding calls.

He thought about it. "Near the end of seventh grade. You got sunburned."

I nodded. "I'd forgotten my sunscreen. And you hiked to the store to get me some aloe vera lotion while we waited for Skyler's dad to come pick us up."

"That was no big deal," he said gruffly.

"It was to me," I replied. "That's when I knew I liked you."

"I was so…I don't even know how to describe it. Awkward? Oblivious? I liked you then, too," he said.

"You're joking," I said.

He kept his eyes on the road. "Nope. I had it bad for you. Almost as bad as I have it for you now."

What would it have been like to have dated Vaughn back then? Simpler, for sure.

I sighed.

"Everything okay?" Vaughn asked.

"I miss the sun," I said.

"I know," he replied. "But we still have the stars."

My boyfriend was romantic, something I hadn't known when we were just friends. I put my hand on his knee, and he put his hand over mine, for just a second, before returning it to the steering wheel.

Our parents were already at the restaurant when we arrived.

Vaughn and I sat next to each other, and he slung his arm across my chair. He trailed his fingers across my arm, and goose bumps prickled all over my skin.

"Are you feeling better, Vanessa?" I asked.

"Yes, much better," she said smoothly. "It must have been a touch of the flu. And I thought you were going to call me 'Mother,'" she said.

"I'm not quite ready for that," I admitted.

She frowned but didn't respond.

We ordered tiny appetizers, and Vanessa ordered a glass of red wine, her go-to drink. After realizing there was no way the appetizers would be enough to quench Vaughn's appetite, we waved the server back and tripled our order.

"We have something to tell you," Vanessa said. *Please don't let it be that they're getting married.* It was awkward enough that they were dating.

Mr. Sheridan cleared his throat. "We wanted to tell you Vanessa is moving in with me." He reached for Vanessa's hand, but she was watching me.

"We'll be one big happy family," Vanessa said. "Once Tansy moves in, too."

"One big dysfunctional family," Vaughn said. "Since your daughter and I are dating."

"I am not leaving Granny's, Vanessa," I said. I kept my voice even and firm. "You've never even had custody of me. Besides, I'm a senior in high school. I'll be in college next year."

"More reason to spend time together now," she said. She sounded sincere.

"I don't mind spending time with you," I admitted. "But I'm not moving into my boyfriend's house with my long-lost mother. That would be too weird."

"We'll see," she said. I excused myself to go to the bathroom, and when I got back, Chef Paretti was at the table, chatting with Vaughn and his dad.

I didn't know why, but I stood just out of everyone's sight line and watched. Vanessa took something out of her purse and poured it into her glass.

I took a step forward, and when she looked up, she noticed me and gave me a bright smile. I slid back into my seat. Vaughn put his arm on the back of my chair but didn't interrupt his conversation with his dad and Chef

Paretti. They were talking about the best recipe for sweet breads, which meant they wouldn't be done for a while, and I decided to use the opportunity to have a little side chat with Vanessa.

"You understand that it's hard for me to trust you, right?" I asked her.

She studied my face. "I do. But I want a relationship with you. And I have stories I can share."

"What kind of stories?"

"Am I right that you'd like to know about your father?" she asked. She smiled. "Now's not the time, but I won't let you down."

I shook my head. "Not good enough."

"For every hour you spend with me, I'll tell you one thing about him. Starting with his name," Vanessa said. "And where to find him."

"You will?" She'd already told me something. My father was *alive*.

I don't know why my curiosity about my father made her so happy, but she was practically glowing. "I'll tell you everything."

I nodded my agreement just as Vaughn and his dad finished up with the chef.

"You don't know who your father is?" Mr. Sheridan asked.

My mother said, "It's just too painful to talk about." She could be telling the truth. Why didn't I know?

I bit back a comment and then wished I hadn't when Mr. Sheridan wrapped a consoling arm around her.

My mother let out a sob, and Mr. Sheridan whispered something in her ear that seemed to cheer her up. Vaughn laced his fingers with mine, causing shivers to climb up my arms.

Vanessa smiled and pointed at our joined hands. "I love to see you two getting along. You'll make great siblings." She gave Mr. Sheridan a shy smile. "Someday."

Siblings? Omigod, ew.

"Tansy's my girlfriend," Vaughn reminded her.

"Of course," she replied airily.

"We're together, Vanessa," I said.

"Puppy love," Vanessa said. "So adorable."

I narrowed my eyes at her. "What do you know about love?"

"I'm sorry," she said. "I didn't mean to offend you. It's just…high school romances rarely last. You even said that you'd be off at college next year. Unless the two of you plan on going to the same university?"

"Tansy and I are staying together," he said. "Even if we go to different colleges. Even if you two get married."

"How will you date with us all living in the same house?" Vanessa's voice was sugary sweet, but her eyes flashed.

"We won't be living together," I said. "I'm staying at Granny's."

"We'll see," she replied. It sounded like a threat. There was no way I'd let my mother break up Vaughn and me.

Vanessa had a strange expression on her face. I'd never seen her look like that before, although my experiences with her were limited. Her lips were turned up, and her eyes sparkled. She looked *happy*.

"Next weekend, we are going to see the band that was playing the night we met," Vanessa replied.

"What's their name?" Vaughn asked casually.

"You wouldn't know them," Vanessa replied. "Unless you're into country music?"

I gripped Vaughn's knee under the table, but he didn't even flinch. The Drainers. It couldn't be a coincidence.

Vaughn was probably thinking the same thing, but he remained calm. "Not really my thing."

Mr. Sheridan had been silent almost the entire time, but he perked up. "Vaughn is quite musically inclined," he said proudly. "He plays several instruments."

"The band is Thirsty Thieves," Vanessa replied.

Vaughn and I exchanged a glance. She was wrong. We had heard of them.

"We'll have to catch a show sometime," I said. I still didn't trust my mother, so I'd do what it took to protect Vaughn and his dad. Even if it meant going line-dancing with our parents.

"That's a great idea," Mr. Sheridan said, but my mother frowned until he turned to her. "I'm so pleased that we're all getting along so well."

I fought the urge to roll my eyes. That was wishful thinking if I'd ever heard it. Mr. Sheridan was usually much better at gauging people. Vaughn was suspicious, and Vanessa was pissed off, although she was trying not to show it.

I took my Thermos out of my purse and took a swig. My mother's eyes narrowed. "You're taking Granny's tonic."

It didn't seem weird that she called her own mother Granny. Everyone called my grandmother "Granny" or "Granny Mariotti."

"How do you know about Granny's tonic?" I asked. "You're not a witch. How did you find out?"

"You're the queen of the California vampires," she replied. "I'm not the only one watching you."

I shuddered, suddenly rethinking the whole mother-daughter bonding thing.

Vanessa smirked. "She *didn't* tell you."

Was she lying to me? "I don't believe you."

Her eyes gleamed. "Ask your grandmother."

My mother went off to reapply her predator-red lipstick, and Mr. Sheridan went with her.

"She's using him to get to you," Vaughn said.

I didn't want to believe it. I wanted a normal mom. But Vanessa seemed human, even if she wasn't a particularly nice one.

"I know," I said. "I'm sorry." Tears welled. I couldn't stand that my own mother had played me.

He wrapped an arm around me, and I buried my face in his chest, both for comfort and because I didn't want my mom to see me cry. I needed for her to believe I was still falling for her act long enough to figure out why she was doing it.

"We can't choose our parents," Vaughn said. "But we're not responsible for their mistakes, either."

"Do you think she's human again?" I asked. "Even if she does have ulterior motives?" I winced at the hope in my voice. I hated that even a tiny bit was there. But it wasn't even about Vanessa, not really. If killing Jure had made her human again, it meant there was hope for me. Even if it meant Travis had to be staked.

"I don't know," Vaughn said. "But human or not, she's a terrible person. Though I can't kill her if she's human."

I studied his face. "But you could if she's a vamp?"

He nodded but didn't meet my eyes.

"People make mistakes," I said. I was certainly proof of that.

"She only cares about power. She's been trying to get close to you, then she'll go for a power grab."

"I don't know how dating your dad would accomplish that," I told him.

"She's shown you who she is, Tansy," he said. "Believe it."

Our parents finally came back, holding hands.

"Thanks for dinner," I said. "Vaughn and I have to get going."

They didn't protest, but I felt my mother's eyes on me as we left.

Vaughn took my hand, and instead of heading toward the valet, he asked, "Want to take a walk?"

"Sure," I said. The restaurant had an ocean view, so we walked down to Main Beach.

The crowds had thinned out, and we found a quiet spot to watch the waves crashing to the shore.

I snuggled into Vaughn, grateful for a moment of quiet, but my pulse accelerated when he laid his soft lips on my neck.

Then my pulse leaped for a different reason. Another hellcat appeared in the distance. It wasn't the same one that had stalked me to the diner, but it raised its head and sniffed the air with the same air of a predator.

"Vaughn," I said. He didn't stop kissing my neck. "Vaughn," I said again in a whisper. "There's a hellcat tracking us."

His lips stilled, but he didn't move. "Where?" he said against my neck.

"To your left," I said.

The feline had picked up our scent and was stalking closer. Vaughn tilted his head a fraction and studied the animal.

"Damn," he muttered. "That thing's huge. Bigger than a tiger."

"They're fast, too," I said.

"We'll get up slowly," he said. "Head back to the restaurant. We should be able to make it to the street."

I scooped up a handful of sand and closed my fist.

Vaughn helped me up. I glanced at the animal out of the corner of my eye, but it hadn't moved yet.

He put his hand on my lower back, and we started moving. "What's happening?" I asked, trying to sound casual.

"The hellcat is getting closer," he said, then, "Jesus, it's fast. Run!"

Before I could do anything, the animal was on me. It jumped on my chest and knocked me to the ground. For a moment I was frozen, unable to move, unable to breathe.

Then I threw the sand in its face, and it yelped. While it tried to shake the sand out, I ran. "Vaughn!"

"I'm here!" he shouted.

I stumbled a couple of times, but then Vaughn was there to help me. The big cat was on our heels, but we were almost at the restaurant when I felt my ankle give underneath me. *Snap!* I screamed from the pain. I wasn't going to be able to stop myself from going down, but before I hit the ground, Vaughn scooped me up and then continued running.

"Almost there," he said.

"You're not even breathing hard." Guess a muscled-up werewolf boyfriend did come in handy sometimes.

I peered over his shoulder and saw the hellcat gaining on us.

"Stay!" I shouted, then tried it in Latin, German, and French. It didn't work. There had to be a way to stop it, too. I only needed to find out how.

Its muzzle was an inch away, so I took my long fingernail and flicked it. The animal yelped, and I flicked it again. I flashed my fangs and said, "No! Leave. I command you."

The hellcat retreated, but I wasn't sure if was because I'd commanded it or because we'd reached Main Street, where there were more people.

Vaughn continued to carry me.

"Let's follow it," I said.

"What? We were just running from it!"

"And now we aren't. We need to know who's behind this—"

"You're *hurt*," he argued. "We should get you home."

"It's just a tiny sprain," I said. "I'm fine." Pain was radiating up my ankle, throbbing like the beat of a drum, but I had to find out who was sending hellcats after me. I whispered a little healing spell and hoped it would be enough.

"There it is," I screamed right into Vaughn's ear. Down the street, a white minivan pulled over, the side door slid open, and the hellcat bounded inside it.

"Hurry," I said. "They'll get away!"

"Tansy—" he started to protest, but I cut him off.

"This is just going to keep happening again and again until we either stop it or I'm dead. I can't do this alone, Vaughn, please."

He glanced down at me and nodded.

Fortunately, the hellcat van was stuck at a red light on PCH.

By the time Vaughn eased me into the passenger seat and jogged around to the driver's side, the van was just turning right.

I kept an eye on it. "They're taking the toll road. Hang back a little, so it's not obvious we're following them."

Vaughn tailed them like a pro. Eventually, we ended up on the same road as The Last Stop.

We passed the Christmas tree farm where we bought our tree every year. Granny called it our winter solstice evergreen. The streetlights were spaced farther and farther apart until they were completely gone.

"Which way?" Vaughn asked.

"Turn left," I ordered.

We followed the minivan to Wildcat Canyon Road. It was only a few miles from the city, but it was like a different world here. The one-lane road was lined in ancient oak trees.

We passed horses grazing in their pastures and a yard full of chickens and turkeys before the van finally slowed down. Then it turned into a driveway with an unmarked mailbox at the front, but we couldn't see the building from the main road.

"What should we do?" I asked.

Vaughn drove by slowly. "I think there's a turnout up ahead."

We parked and hiked back to where the van had gone, then hid behind the overgrown bushes that lined the driveway. The house was an older-looking ranch with chipped and peeling paint.

Yeah. This wasn't creepy at all.

A few moments later, a shadowy figure got out of the van. They didn't move when someone with a hoodie hanging over their face came out of the house, letting the front door bang closed.

I jumped and managed to stifle a scream, but the hooded figure stopped and seemed to stare right at our hiding spot. My pulse accelerated, but the mystery person finally got into the van, and they tore out of there like the devil was chasing them.

"Who do you think that was?"

"It could be your mom," Vaughn replied. "She could have seen us go to the beach, so she knew where to find you."

"Maybe. But I don't think so." The hooded figure was stockier and taller than my mother. They were gone now, but I wondered what the other person was waiting for. Why didn't they go in the house? I glanced away for a minute, and when I looked back, the human was gone and an enormous four-legged wolf stood in its place. A werewolf.

"That's definitely not my mother," I said, then shot Vaughn a look. "The werewolves are the ones trying to kill me."

Vaughn sucked in a breath. "You don't know that for sure."

"You're right, I don't," I said. "But they could be involved somehow."

"So could your mom."

Okay. He had a point. The only way to settle this was to stop guessing and find some hard evidence. "Let's go check out the house," I suggested.

The front door was locked, so we went around to the fenced backyard. When Vaughn rattled the gate, a chorus of snarls and hisses started. He stepped back quickly. "That's a dead end. Literally."

"What now?" I asked.

"Maybe there's an open window somewhere."

"Good idea." It wasn't like the neighbors would see us. There wasn't another house for a couple of miles, just trees and brush.

We went around to the front, and I checked under the mat for a key, but no such luck. At least there weren't any security cameras that I could see. But I did see lines of salt along every window and doorway.

"What's the salt for?" Vaughn asked.

"Keeps the demons out," I said. "It's the fastest and easiest way to protect a house."

"Demons," he said. "We have to worry about demons now, too?"

"Not if we get inside," I said, still checking for any possible entrance. I was almost ready to give up when I spotted an open window near the front door. It was too small for Vaughn to get through, even before he'd beefed up, so he boosted me up and over.

I landed with a *thump*, but fortunately, my butt took the brunt of the fall, keeping my sore ankle from any further injury. I hurried to stand and unlocked the door, and Vaughn stepped inside. The other windows were covered with aluminum foil or old blankets, so it was hard to see. He turned on his phone's flashlight.

The first room was bare, except for a beat-up leather

sofa with the stuffing coming out and a folding table.

A room at the back of the house led to a crude addition that had been built by an amateur carpenter. The floor was filthy, sticky, and smelling strongly of blood and urine. I tried not to gag as we kept moving forward, into a large space with gray concrete floors and walls that used to be white but now were a dingy beige.

"God, it stinks in here," Vaughn whispered. "What do they feed them?"

We doubled back down the hall and checked what was probably a bedroom. The last door was locked.

I frowned. "There has to be a key around here somewhere."

We went searching for something to unlock the door. I knew Vaughn was capable of using his enhanced strength to break down the door, but instead, I slid my credit card into the gap between the frame and the door and prayed it would work. The doorknob turned, but the door still didn't open.

But when we finally got in the room, it was anticlimactic. There was nothing inside except a long table with a row of plants under grow lights.

I used my phone's camera and snapped a couple of quick pics, but I was baffled. I wasn't an expert, but the plants had tiny purple flowers and almost looked like something you'd find at any home and garden center. Almost. There was something unusual about them, but I didn't have time to figure it out right now. I'd have to study the photos later.

We tiptoed into another room where a dozen adorable kittens played. These cuddly kittens turned into hellcats?

Then low growls filled the air.

It was coming from two enormous black hellcats, who were the size of small horses. They had something cornered—a black kitten with a white star on its nose. There was a vicious-looking bite mark on its flank, and blood dripped from its nose. The hellcat's eyes glowed an emerald green when it looked at me.

The other animals circled the kitten. Their lips were curled into snarls. One of them lunged at the smaller animal, teeth snapping, but I grabbed the bigger one by the tail and yanked.

I used all my strength, but the cat barely budged. It turned and looked at me, its expression telling me it was trying to decide if I'd make a better dinner than the kitten. Glowing green eyes, fangs slathered with drool. There was something not quite right about the sounds they made.

I scooped up the smaller animal and tucked it into my hoodie. It shivered and then burrowed into my warmth. I thought it would smell bad, considering the condition of the room we were in, but it smelled like nutmeg and, strangely, roasted marshmallows.

"Tansy, we need to get out of here, now!" Vaughn shouted. The two hellcats weren't alone. More cats advanced, cutting off our exit.

"Let's make a run for it," I said. The cats' ears pricked, almost like they understood me.

But I wasn't going to wait around to see if I was right. I ran as fast as I could with my injured leg. Vaughn was so close behind me that I could feel his hot breath on the back of my neck. Which was a good thing, because my ankle reminded me it was weak, and I almost fell. He lifted me without breaking his stride, but then he suddenly stopped short.

There was a large hellcat blocking the exit—the same animal from the diner. Blackberry. I recognized it from its torn left ear. Our only chance was to get through Blackberry, or I had no doubt we'd be torn apart by the pack of animals chasing us.

Blackberry didn't stay in front of the door long. Instead, it came running straight for me, but instead of attacking, it jumped over Vaughn, landing between us and the other animals, and hissed at any cat who tried to advance.

The kitten in my arms started to whimper as we reached the front door. I realized why the salt was everywhere. To prevent the hellcats from leaving. "Vaughn, the salt," I said. "Get rid of it."

He kicked at the lines of salt until a gap formed. The kitten stopped crying, and we exited the house.

We didn't wait to see if the hellcats followed us. Vaughn picked up speed as I clung to him.

"What the hell just happened?" he asked.

He didn't stop until we reached the car. Once we were safe, he set me down gently in the passenger seat. I still had the kitten held tight against me.

The hellcats' growls sounded closer. Blackberry must not have been able to hold them all off. "Get in!" I said. Vaughn threw himself into driver's seat and slammed his door closed.

"Is she coming with us?" he asked as he started the car.

"We can't leave her here," I said.

"Will Granny let you have a hellcat as a pet?"

"I guess we'll find out," I said. A witch with a black cat?

Stereotypical or what?

"I guess we will," Vaughn said with a grin. The animals in the backyard were now slamming their bodies against the fence as we drove by, snapping and snarling at us. I didn't breathe again until we were safely back on the road. We both let out a long sigh.

"What should we call her?" Vaughn asked.

"Hecate," I said. I stroked the kitten's fur, and she gave a little rumble of contentment.

"Like the goddess?"

"Yeah," I said. "The name just sounds right for her."

"You know, if Granny won't let you keep her, I'll take Hecate," Vaughn offered.

"You will?" I smiled at him.

"I'd do anything for you, Tansy."

My whole body flooded with the knowledge that he was the one for me. That we were meant for each other, no matter what.

I leaned over and kissed his cheek softly.

I held Hecate in my lap while Vaughn drove us through the twisty canyon road. When we reached our neighborhood, he parked the car, and we both exhaled noisily.

"That was a successful recon," I said. "We found out where they're keeping the hellcats. We can research who owns the house. We can get some answers, finally. But I have a new question."

Vaughn raised a brow. "And that is?"

"What kind of plants need to be behind a locked door?"

Chapter Thirty-One

Granny Mariotti's car was in the driveway. We let Hecate out into the backyard, and Vaughn stayed with her while I went inside to break the news to Granny.

"We're home," I hollered.

It was late, but I knew Granny always stayed up reading, and as I expected, she was in the family room, curled up with a book. She put a bookmark in the pages and closed her book. "Did you and Vaughn have a good night?" she asked.

"It was unusual," I admitted. "We found something."

She didn't say anything, just cocked her head in inquiry.

I stood by the open slider door. "Hecate, here, kitty, kitty," I called. The kitten came to the door and meowed but wouldn't cross the doorway.

"What kind of animal has glowing green eyes and smells like toasting marshmallows? And there was salt by every doorway to contain it?" I asked.

"I've never heard of any animal smelling like

marshmallows, but the rest sounds like a hellcat," Granny replied. "I've never actually seen one, though."

I smeared away the line of salt to see what would happen. Salt kept demons away, but maybe a hellcat was a sort of demon? It did have the word "hell" in its name. Once the salt was cleared, Hecate bolted through the slider door and skidded to a stop in front of Granny.

She gasped. The kitten let out a pitiful whimper and nudged her hand. Granny cooed, "Aren't you the sweetest thing?"

"That's Hecate," I said.

She bent down and scratched her. "She does smell like marshmallows." She sniffed again. "And blood. And brimstone. Where did you get a hellcat?"

I sucked in a breath. "We followed a grown one after it attacked us. We're fine, though—I swear."

Granny eyed me with concern, but she didn't stop petting the kitten. "We need to bandage that cut on her face. And don't think I didn't notice you're limping and trying to hide it. Get a wrap for yourself, too."

It was no use denying I was injured, even though I'd just claimed I was fine. Granny noticed everything. I got the first-aid kit out of the bathroom and set it next to Hecate. "The other cats were picking on her."

While Granny took care of the little kitten's face, Vaughn came in from outside and helped me wrap my sore ankle.

"There were other hellcats?" Granny asked.

I nodded. "The one that attacked me on the beach got picked up by a minivan, and the driver was a werewolf. We followed them to this place out in the canyon," I explained.

"Once they left, we checked out the house. It was full these kittens and adult hellcats."

"They were hungry, and the whole place reeked," Vaughn added.

"Can we keep her, Granny?" I asked. "Please?"

Granny sighed, then asked, "Does she have a name?" That meant yes.

"I've been calling her Hecate," I said.

Granny's eyes twinkled. "That's a perfect name for our new pet. Hecate. Goddess of the boundary between the natural and hidden worlds."

I hugged my granny. "Thank you."

"I'm not sure she'll stay with us," Granny warned. "Hellcats move through boundaries with ease. Unless something prevents them."

"The salt wasn't to keep demons out," I said. "It was to keep the hellcats in."

"I expect so," she said. "But the bigger question is, what are werewolves doing with a litter of hellcats?"

"It's not anyone from my pack," Vaughn said abruptly. "I would have recognized them by their scent. But something about that werewolf smelled familiar."

"We have to do something about it," I said.

Vaughn nodded. "I agree. We need to get those creatures out of there."

"You have something in mind?"

"I'm not sure," he replied. "It's not like we can call animal control."

"I know. And we don't exactly have the room here."

"Maybe the Old Crones Book Club can give us some ideas," Granny suggested.

"It's worth a shot," I agreed.

Vaughn's phone pinged with a text. As he read it, he started to frown. "I've got to go," he said. "Dad forgot to leave the catering order for a big client event tomorrow, and he's not answering his phone."

"That's not like him," I commented.

"No, it's not. I'll take care of it." He kissed the top of my head and took off.

After Vaughn left, Granny went to bed, and I curled up with a book, but Hecate wouldn't stop meowing, the sound high and frantic. When I tried to open the back door to see what had her so agitated, she stood in front of it and growled at me.

"What's gotten into you?" I flicked the motion sensor lights on and peered out the kitchen window, but I didn't see anything out of the ordinary.

"Why's she making all that racket?" Granny asked. Her untied robe flapped behind her, and I snorted at her *Ask Me About My Coven* T-shirt and cut-off sweats.

"I don't know," I admitted.

She peered out into the darkness. "Time to shore up our defense charms."

"Do you think it's a vampire?"

"You tell me."

I inhaled and tried to focus. "Cold like a vampire, but something smells different." I took another breath. Something about the scent repelled me. It made me queasy, like I was going to throw up. Disoriented, like the time I'd been on the Tea Cups at Disneyland and had spun so hard I could barely walk.

"Very good," Granny said.

Hecate finally stopped howling and came over and nudged my hand. I scratched her under the chin.

"Whatever it was, it's gone now." Granny rubbed Hecate on the head and then got a glass of water before she went back to bed. I stared into the night and wondered what had been upsetting Hecate.

I went to Granny's library to get a different book to read.

Granny's bookshelves were better than any search engine, at least for the kind of information I needed, so I started there.

There was conflicting mythology about the hellcats. Some sources believed they were guardians of women and girls, and others believed that hellcats were harbingers of death.

So, which one was Hecate?

Chapter Thirty-Two

I spent the next day with my mother, keeping up the act that everything was fine until I knew for sure why everything wasn't fine. And maybe she'd tell me more about my father while we were "bonding." She was pleasant enough, but she really liked to shop. And I didn't.

"You have to let me buy you something," she insisted.

"I don't really need anything," I said.

But we weren't leaving without buying me something. "Why don't we head to Old Navy?" I suggested.

"Don't you want something designer?" she asked.

"Not really," I said.

"I'm buying you this," she said. She held out a cute but designer green silk dress.

"Don't you think it's a little too expensive?" I asked.

"Don't you like it?" She sounded disappointed. Maybe she'd missed doing mom-type things like buying her daughter clothes. I gave in.

"I do like it." I shrugged. "Whatever. It's your money."

She dug through her wallet and slid out a credit card, then handed it to the guy behind the register. A black AmEx. Unlimited spending. Where'd my mom get that kind of money? Did cat breeding really make her rich? Some of those purebred cats were expensive, but there were hundreds of cats in shelters just waiting for a home.

"Oh, wait, I just saw a necklace I might want," Vanessa said. I stayed put while she wandered a few feet down to look at a jewelry display. She'd left her wallet open on the counter, and I caught a glimpse of the address on her driver's license.

I slid out my phone from my back pocket and snapped a picture, then caught sight of Vanessa. I pretended I was reading a text while she chatted away with the salesperson. Something about that address bothered me. I typed it into the map app.

"What—" I slapped a hand over my mouth. Vaughn had been right not to trust her.

My mother lived at the same house where we'd found the hellcats.

That night, Vaughn called Thorn, Rose, and Skyler over to my house for a meeting.

Skyler and I still weren't friends. Not exactly. But she wasn't glaring daggers at me, either. We were trying.

"Can any of you think of a reason why someone would want to kill Tansy?" Vaughn got straight to the point.

"It's likely," Thorn said. "Almost inevitable, really. A

vampire king or queen is bound to make a move eventually, to try to take your kingdom from you."

"Exactly how many kings and queens are there?" What I wanted to say was how many vampires with oversize egos was I going to have to deal with? I had enough on my plate with my mother.

"In the U.S.?" Rose said. "There are nine regions, which are divided geographically. California and Texas are the only realms that are also single states. The Western region is Alaska, Hawaii, Washington, and Oregon, although there are actually no vampires in Oregon."

"Maybe hipsters don't taste good," I suggested.

Thorn snorted. "Alaska's full of them, though."

The twins took turns giving me the low-down about each vampire realm. This summer had been too intense for a vampire political structure lesson, and now we were busy dealing with murders and hellcats and werewolf boyfriends. By comparison, this stuff didn't seem that urgent.

"But sometimes," Thorn said, "there are high populations of multiple paranormal creatures within a certain region, so there might be conflicting groups."

"Like there could be a vampire queen and, say, a werewolf king?"

Rose shook her head. "Werewolves don't have kings. They have pack leaders."

"Then that makes Connor the leader of the pack?" I giggled.

They both gave me a blank look, and Vaughn kissed the top of my head. "They don't get your music humor," he said. Honestly, very few people did, but I thought Granny might have recognized the song, at least.

"There are several pack members in your realm," Rose continued, "but they are considered to be some of the most peaceful werewolves in the country."

"We did see a werewolf with the hellcat. And there are a few werewolves who wouldn't mind seeing me staked."

Skyler and Vaughn exchanged a glance. "Connor would never," Skyler said.

"Are you sure?" I asked. "He's done some pretty hurtful things in the past. Some of them to you."

"This doesn't seem like his style, though," Vaughn said. "He's very direct. And besides, he was attacked, too. He almost died. It just doesn't add up."

"Okay, who does that leave?" I asked.

"What about Vanessa?" Vaughn replied. "We know she's somehow involved. And she almost killed your grandmother."

"Except she's not a vampire anymore, so she couldn't rule even if she wanted to," I said, annoyed that I couldn't fit all the pieces together into anything that made sense. Yes, my mother was involved, but who was leading all of this? Who wanted to take my place? "What about Travis?"

"You banned him from your realm," Vaughn reminded me.

"That doesn't mean he listened," I replied. "And there is a werewolf in his band now."

"I don't think it's Travis, as much as I would love to blame him for everything," Skyler said. "Travis is interested in blood, groupies, and music. In that order. But being in charge of his father's realm? Not so much. He never even mentioned it when I was…"

She didn't finish her sentence. She didn't have to.

"The Thirsty Thieves are long gone," I said. "But it's the drummer I'm really worried about. Boris. He just seemed off."

Vaughn went still. "That's because he's a rogue werewolf."

"How do you know?" I asked.

"Connor mentioned it after the first time we saw him at The Last Stop. I didn't make the connection then."

We all stared at him, waiting.

"But *what*?" I said. "You can't leave us hanging."

"A loner without a pack can be more dangerous than a whole pack," he finally said.

"Why?" Skyler asked.

Vaughn drew in a deep breath and let it out slowly. "Because they go by their own rules, and the only loyalty they have is to themselves."

What was in it for Boris? Would a rogue werewolf be willing to kill other werewolves? And if so, why?

Chapter Thirty-Three

We only had five days until the next full moon, but every time I thought we were closer to an answer, a zillion more questions came up.

Tonight, I was at Vaughn's house, but instead of hanging out with my boyfriend, I was in his living room—with Vanessa. Vaughn and his dad were both working at the catering company. My mother had asked me over, and I couldn't exactly say, *No, thank you, I'd rather not spend the evening with an evil mastermind right now. Try me again on Thursday.*

Vanessa was calmly flipping through a fashion magazine, as if she wasn't part of some sinister plot, while I tried to remind myself why spending time with her might actually help me.

Oh right. I was cozying up to a vile possibly not so ex-vampire because I needed to find out what she was up to and to squeeze some information out of her about my biological father. The usual.

"How are you coping with managing all of Jure's properties?" she asked. "I'd be happy to help you organize your new possessions."

"They're not mine," I said. "They belong to the realm. My job is to decide what's best for my subjects. I've been donating a lot."

Her head snapped up. "Like what?"

"The ranch where he took my friend," I said.

She relaxed. "I've already been there."

"What's that supposed to mean?" I asked.

She hesitated like she'd just realized what she'd said, but she covered smoothly. "Just that it was a wise decision to get rid of that place. It was tacky. Jure had no design sense."

Why had she been at the ranch where they were abusing girls?

"Are you ever going to tell me anything about my father?" I asked. "Besides the fact he had horrible taste in women."

She smirked at me, but not before I caught a flicker of something that resembled hurt in her eyes.

I sighed. "Sorry." Insulting her wasn't improving the situation, and it made me feel like a jerk. She'd promised she'd tell me about my father, and she'd gone back on her word. I shouldn't be surprised, but I was. It was a good reminder not to get too close to her.

"I have something for you." She dug through her wallet and handed me a photo. It was a strip of shots taken from a photobooth. I stared at it. My mother, young, human, and judging by the way she was looking at the guy next to her, in love. In the first, they were both staring at the camera, the second, she was in his lap, eyes on each other, and in the third, they were kissing like they didn't even know they were being recorded.

"Is that him?" He was thin but muscular, and there was something wild in his dark eyes, something hurt and trapped.

I didn't think she was going to answer me. She just stared down at her younger self. "I haven't looked at this for a long time."

"Is that him?" I repeated.

"Yes." He was tall and handsome with dark eyes and hair, but I didn't see even a little bit of him in me.

"Can I have a copy of it?" I cringed at the pleading note in my voice.

She nodded.

"Thank you," I replied.

She slipped the photo back into her wallet without looking at it.

I didn't tell her, but I'd noticed the writing on the back. Vanessa and Mason, Balboa. My father's first name was Mason. Interesting. Mason was the first name of the PAC leader. If my father was Mason Alicante, he'd know where I was and hadn't even bothered to introduce himself.

"Mason Alicante is my father?" I asked.

"You already knew?" she asked.

My stomach dropped, and I couldn't form words. It was true?

"I suppose you know about Rose and Thorn, too."

That snapped me out of it. "What about them?"

"They're your sisters," she said. "Half sisters, to be exact. Mason already had twin toddlers when we met."

What?

The same man that Thorn resented so much because he favored Rose, the same man who had sent hellcats after his own daughter? That asshole was also *my* father?

Did they know, too? Was *everyone* keeping secrets from me?

"You're lying," I said, but my heart was pounding.

"I'm not," she said. "Ask them if you don't believe me."

"I will."

I sent an SOS text to Skyler. My hands were shaking so badly I could barely type. **Extraction needed. I'm at Vaughn's. With my mom.**

On it, drama llama. Ten minutes later, the doorbell rang.

"I've got to go," I told my mother, but she barely looked up from her phone.

"Have fun with your little friend," she answered absently.

I got into Skyler's car. "You are a lifesaver."

"Where's Vaughn?" Skyler asked. "Maybe we can all hang at your house."

"He's working. Let's go out to Janey's for dinner instead." Rose and Thorn might be at my house, and I wasn't ready to confront them yet about what my mother had told me. Sisters? Vanessa had to be lying. "That way I can bring some pie home to Hecate."

"Is it good for hellcats to eat pie?" She pulled out and started heading in the direction of PCH. I texted Vaughn and asked him to meet us at Janey's when he finished his shift.

"They're not like regular cats," I said. "So far, Hecate can and has eaten almost anything."

Skyler found a great parking spot near the front door.

"You didn't even have to use your magic!" she crowed triumphantly.

"I'm not doing that anymore," I said firmly. The last time I'd used my magic to get a parking spot, Travis had bitten me.

Vaughn beat us to the restaurant and was sitting at a booth in the back when we arrived. "Dad let us close early," he explained. He made a face. "He wanted to go see Panda." The mention of Mr. Sheridan's pet name for my mother's barely made me shudder. I was just glad to see my boyfriend.

"Rough day with your mom?" he asked.

"You have no idea," I said.

Sky shot me a look. "I thought you were getting along."

"She showed me a picture of my dad," I said.

"You've been spending a lot of time with her," Vaughn said cautiously. Skyler looked equally as concerned, and I realized I needed to fill them in.

"She said she'd tell me about my father," I said. "But I have to spend time with her for that to happen."

"You know she's about as stable as a toddler on a sugar binge, right?" Vaughn said.

A woman who looked a lot like Vanessa walked into the diner. "Speak of the devil, and in she walks," I said in a low voice.

She was alone as she took a seat at the counter. When she put her bag on the chair to her left, I noticed her hands were shaking and her skin looked gray. She seemed like she was in desperate need of a meal. Or maybe some blood.

Janey, the owner, said something to her, but Vanessa

waved her off.

"Duck," I said. I scrunched down in the booth and hoped she didn't see me.

"What's going on?" Vaughn said, craning his head.

Boris walked in and said something to her. How did she know him? She lifted her bag, and he sat in the seat where it'd been.

"Don't look," I hissed, tugging Vaughn down. "My mother and Boris are here. Together." I hated the fact that I was disappointed in my mother, that I'd started to believe, even a tiny bit, that she had been telling the truth. Now her story was unraveling. Fast.

She'd been lying to me the whole time. Maybe she'd even lied about who my father was. And that Rose and Thorn were my half sisters, not just vampire hunters I'd met this summer. I wanted to stand up and scream *liar* at the top of my lungs, but instead, I watched her.

They sat at the counter with their backs to us. They both ordered something to drink. It looked like iced tea for the werewolf and black coffee for my mother, but neither of them touched their orders.

Boris said something to her, and she reached into her bag and came out with what looked like a wad of cash. She slid it quickly across the counter to him. He didn't count it, just pocketed it, then put something small down on the counter and left without another word. My mother scooped it up, put down a couple of bills, I assumed enough to cover both their drinks, but didn't leave. Instead, she poured something into her coffee and sipped it slowly.

When she got up to leave, her face was in profile. Her skin was flushed pink, her eyes sparkled, and her hungry look was gone. She exited without having seen us, and I slowly straightened.

What had Boris given her? Some kind of drug, but *what exactly*? And why was a werewolf selling it to her?

"Are you ready to order?" Dave's voice cut into my thoughts.

"Just some water," I said, and he turned to Vaughn, who I knew would be ordering plenty enough to spare me a bite of his. I had bigger problems than deciding on dinner.

I thought back to when Skyler had run off with The Drainers. Vaughn's dad had just started dating an unknown woman back then. Was my mother the mystery woman from the summer? Had she been planning this the whole time?

After Dave left to put in our orders, I turned to Vaughn. "Can you find out from your dad how long they've been dating?"

"I think so," Vaughn said. "Is it important?"

"I'm not sure," I admitted. "But I can't help thinking this is all part of a bigger scheme."

Realization flashed in his eyes. "You think your mom has been planning something since this summer?"

"Possibly," I said. "I don't know what she's up to, but I think your father is in grave danger." After all, my mother never stuck around, not even for her own daughter, unless there was something in it for her.

Chapter Thirty-Four

Vaughn was spending more time at my house now, probably to get away from Vanessa. He arrived just in time for dinner. Vaughn playfully suggested we order a pizza, but Granny Mariotti was not having it. "Mine is better," she said firmly.

"Really?" Vaughn's eyes twinkled as he teased her. When he wrapped an arm around me, I leaned into his embrace. The deeper into this mess we got, the more I appreciated these moments with him.

"Better than Gino's?" he whispered to me once Granny was getting dough out of the fridge.

"Much better," I confirmed.

"Time to chop the vegetables," Granny said.

We broke apart and then washed our hands before we helped with dinner prep. We chopped a mountain of veggies.

"How many people is your granny feeding?" Vaughn asked.

I shrugged. "Who knows? Probably around twenty?"

"Twenty?"

"Book club, Skyler, and us," I said. Then I added, "Probably Rose and Thorn, too."

"I was hoping we'd have a chance to spend some time alone," Vaughn said. "There's something I wanted to talk to you about."

"We could take a walk after dinner," I suggested.

Vaughn was chopping tomatoes when it happened. A muffled exclamation and then his finger dripped bright blood onto the white quartz counter.

I stared at the drop of blood, unable to look away as the scent of copper and sunshine and the ocean at dusk filled my nostrils.

I forced myself to look away, and my gaze collided with Vaughn's. There was something different about him tonight.

He held out his hand.

"Here," he said, offering his blood to me.

I shook my head, but he put his finger to my mouth and traced the blood around my lower lip.

"Open up," he said, and this time I did. Vaughn's blood smelled delicious and tasted even better.

I drew his finger into my mouth and sucked gently. Vaughn's eyes fluttered closed, and his head fell back.

Worry conflicted with the pleasure I was feeling. Had I compelled him?

"I know what you're thinking," he said. "I wanted to, Tansy. You didn't force me."

I made a doubtful noise, but he continued. "This was freely given."

Blood freely given tasted good, no hint of fear or pain.

I tested the drop on my tongue and relaxed. He was telling me the truth. My lips moved from his finger to his mouth. His blood tasted different, though. The werewolf tasted wild and sweet.

Our kiss deepened. Vaughn's arms tightened, pulled me closer, but then we were interrupted when his phone buzzed with a text. I tried to step away to give him some privacy, but he held on to me.

He grabbed his phone one-handed, keeping his arm around me as he glanced at it.

I stiffened when I saw the name on the screen. *Connor.* I moved to free myself, and this time, he let me.

"I don't know why he's texting," he said.

"It's none of my business," I said.

His face clouded, but then it cleared. "It's your business," he said. "You're my girlfriend."

I tamped down the insecurity I was feeling and said, "I know that. It's just awkward that your best friend hates me."

"He doesn't hate you." He reached in and pulled me close. I relaxed into his arms.

I studied his face. "He's not my biggest fan, then. Does that make it hard for you?"

He inhaled sharply and then admitted, "A little." When he saw my face, he added, "Not because Connor's pack leader. Because he's my friend."

I was still angry at the whole pack, but Connor was Vaughn's best friend and had helped him through a confusing, stressful time.

Granny bustled in. "Tansy, it's a beautiful night. Let's eat outside."

We took a citronella candle and the utensils, which

were stored in a handy container with a handle for summer dinners and headed outside. For as long as I could remember, Granny had owned the two long wooden tables with owls carved on the legs.

Vaughn and Granny went back inside to grab plates, but I stayed where I was and breathed in the night air.

When I was little, I'd hung out under the table and talked to the carved owls. I used to tell everyone they talked to me, but I soon learned to keep that information quiet.

On impulse, I ducked under the table and said hello. When I popped my head back up, Vaughn stood there, a half smile on his face. "I remember when you used to talk to them," he said.

I looked at my feet, embarrassed to have been caught committing such a childish act.

"I think it's cute."

Rose came in without her twin.

"Back from another PAC confab?" I asked casually. Inside I was tied up in knots wondering if everything my mother had said about the twins was true. "How'd it go?"

She smiled, but it wasn't a real smile. "As expected."

"So my mother told me my father's name," I said. "It's Mason."

Rose flinched.

And my stomach churned.

"You flinched when you heard his name," I said. "Why?"

Rose didn't say anything.

I crossed my arms over my chest, suddenly cold. "You may as well tell me what you know. I'll find out somehow."

She hesitated but then nodded. "Mason Alicante is the

most powerful and most hated man in the hidden world. The king of kings if you will."

"I want to know everything there is about him."

Rose shook her head. "I'm sorry, Your Majesty—"

"I prefer that you call me Tansy," I said. "We're friends, right? Just start with what he is. Is he a vampire?"

She frowned but did as I asked. "There are many other creatures in the PAC," she said.

"Then what is he?"

She shrugged. "It is a well-kept secret."

"Maybe he's a witch," I suggested. "Or a werewolf."

"The werewolf representative is Cormac Mahoney from Ireland," Rose said. "Connor's uncle." She'd changed the subject and probably hoped I didn't notice.

"So back to my dad," I said. "Does he know about me?"

"Yes," she said flatly.

I sucked in a breath, trying not to let the knowledge stab me in the heart. "Then he just doesn't care."

"You're putting words in my mouth," she said.

"Sorry." It had been a long week. I was stressed out, and my mother's return brought all those feelings of abandonment back. Why hadn't she wanted me? Why didn't *he* want me?

Evelyn and Edna arrived, with Skyler trailing behind them. "Are we interrupting something?" Skyler asked.

"No," Rose said at the same time I said, "Yes."

"I forgot the tablecloths," Rose said and rushed inside before I could ask her anything else.

The book club ladies brought flowers in potted plants and three bottles of wine, which Granny did not let me sample. But dinner was amazing.

While everyone was organizing dessert, I again tried to corner the twins.

"Why were you two gone so long?" I asked Rose and Thorn, but I was not expecting their reply.

"We wanted to talk to you about that," Rose said. "It's private, though." She glanced around the house, which was filled with friends and family.

"I don't have anything to hide," I said, crossing my arms.

"We're your sisters," Thorn said flatly.

"What did you just say?" My mother *had* been telling the truth. I felt like throwing up.

"Our father is Mason Alicante, the leader of the PAC, and he sent us here," Rose said.

I gaped at her. I heard the words the twins were saying, but they weren't making sense.

"You're my sisters and your dad—no, our dad sent you here to spy on me?" I asked.

"I know it must come as a shock," Rose said.

"A shock? I thought we were friends," I said. "But you were spying on me for Mason Alicante." A stray tear dripped down my cheek, and I wiped it away.

"He's not your enemy," Thorn said. "He's your father." From the few things she'd told me, he wasn't a very good one, not to the twins and certainly not to me.

This wasn't happening. I glanced at Vaughn. My boyfriend looked as shocked as I felt, wide-eyed and openly staring at Rose and Thorn.

My sisters were introducing themselves like they were strangers. Which Rose and Thorn were. I'd never even known I had a sibling, and now I had two.

I needed to get away from all the people staring at me.

I rushed into the house and took my frustration out on the dirty dishes. Rose and Thorn followed me in, though, and all three of us stood at the sink and got to work.

Thorn washed while Rose and I dried, and while I toweled off a plate, I tried to think of a way to ask them. I kept giving them sidelong glances when I thought they weren't looking, but finally, Thorn lost patience. "Ask your questions, Tansy."

Where to start? I went with the first thing that popped into my head. "How long have you known?"

Thorn said, "We found a picture of your mother when she was pregnant with you. We asked our dad who she was. He told us they'd been together when we were little. He told us a few other things."

"Like how in love they'd been?"

"Like how she wanted to slit the throat of the man who'd knocked her up."

"Mother of the year award goes to Vanessa Mariotti," I said.

"Why is it so important to you, anyway?" Thorn asked. She handed me a glass, and I started drying it to give myself time to think. Why did I want to know so badly?

"Vanessa is a terrible parent," I said. "Would it be so awful to want to know if our dad isn't? If both of my parents are awful, what does that make me?"

"We aren't our parents, Tansy," Thorn said. "At least, we don't have to be."

"Why hasn't he reached out to me?" I asked. "Especially now that I'm part of the PAC?"

"Your boyfriend is a werewolf, part of the most powerful pack in the world, your grandmother is a witch, and you're a striga vie," Thorn said.

"Why does that matter to someone who's the head of a paranormal organization?" I asked.

"He only sees a consolidation of power," Rose said.

"My own father thinks I'm a threat?"

"Yes," Thorn said.

"Do you?" I asked them both, but my newfound sisters didn't answer me. Great. The only thing worse than this would be if—

"Last question," I said. "Does my granny know?"

Suddenly, both twins had never been so interested in the art of dishwashing before.

I set the glass I'd been holding down onto the counter so hard it cracked, then stomped into the family room to confront my grandmother.

Chapter Thirty-Five

Granny was good at keeping secrets. I'd thought my mother was dead (meaning dead-dead, not vampire undead) until last summer, so it wouldn't shock me that my grandmother had hidden my siblings' existence, too.

She was in the library, studying some ancient text intently, taking a break from playing hostess. When she saw my face, she closed the book without even putting a bookmark in it. Shocking for Granny. "What's wrong?"

"Why didn't you tell me I have siblings?"

Her face went white, then flushed red. "Because you don't."

"According to Rose and Thorn, I do," I said. "And it's *them*." I'd always wanted a sibling. Someone to hang out with, someone who would know me at the cellular level. But even though we'd been spending some time together, my sisters were practically strangers.

Granny was shaking her head, either in disbelief or denial. "That's not possible."

Seeing her distraught, my anger left me. I sat down next to her. "They said they knew about me the whole time. They're a year older than me."

Her lips trembled. "I don't understand how it's possible," she explained. "It wasn't that long after she left you with me that Vanessa became a vampire. She never talked about your father and definitely never told me he had other children."

"How do you know when she became a vampire?"

"I saw her," Granny said. "About a year later. And she was definitely a vampire then. She even tried to kill me."

"So she tried to kill you not once, but twice?" I asked. "God, I hate her."

"No, you don't," she replied.

"I wish I did," I said softly. "It would be easier that way."

"I know." She wrapped an arm around me, and we sat silently for a long time. Finally, Granny stirred. "What are they like? Your siblings?"

As if on cue, Rose and Thorn burst into the room. "Tansy, we're not done talking to you."

"Granny, meet my siblings," I said, waving my hand at the twins.

Her mouth dropped open. "How? When? *What*?" Granny asked. We gave her a few minutes to get over the surprise, but I shifted in my seat, unable to get comfortable.

"Can you tell us anything about your father?" she asked the twins.

"Mason is a sorcerer," Thorn said. "Head of the pack."

"A sorcerer?" Granny didn't sound pleased by that.

"Our father is a complicated man," Rose said. That was tantamount to me calling him a total asshole. Great.

I studied them more closely. I didn't see any resemblance, but maybe we had similar noses? Rose and Thorn must take after their mother.

I could tell that something about the description of my bio dad had caught Granny's attention. "What's his last name?"

The twins exchanged a glance. "Alicante," Thorn said.

Granny gasped. "Your father is the *serpent* sorcerer? The one they call Serpent King?"

My parents were the Executioner and the Serpent King. It sounded like a match made in a horror movie.

"Yes," Rose confirmed. "Our mother died when we were a year old."

"I don't stand a chance with parents like mine," I said.

Thorn gave an exasperated sniff. "Just because our dad is a terrible person doesn't make us terrible people."

"You belong to the light, your parents belong to the darkness," Granny Mariotti said.

"I'm still in trouble." I ticked the reasons off on my fingers. "My mother is a vampire, an evil one, who abandoned me, hid the fact that I have twin sisters, tried to kill my boyfriend, and is now dating my boyfriend's dad for some yet unknown but probably nefarious purpose. Oh, and someone is sending hellcats to try to kill me."

The secrets were all too much for me. It was almost impossible to not feel sorry for myself, at least until Granny said, "I know it's hard, but suck it up, sweetheart. This is the hand you were dealt."

What could I say? I knew she was right, but I just wanted a little time to wallow in it.

Granny Mariotti was not going to let me wallow. "Now,

are you going to sit there like a lump or are you going to get off your tush and handle business?"

My grandmother, the motivational speaker, ladies and gentlemen.

"I'm scared," I admitted.

"I'll tell you a secret," Granny said.

"I'm not sure I can take another one."

"Everyone is scared, Tansy," she said. "It's what you do with the fear that makes the difference."

"I just want my life back," I said quietly. "The life I had before Travis decided to take a bite out of me without my permission."

I missed the smell of coconut oil, the way Skyler spent ten minutes searching for the perfect spot and then putting her towel down in the exact same spot she always did, the sight of Vaughn at the end of a good beach day, shrugging out of his wetsuit. I missed it all.

"If you want your life back?" Granny replied. "Then *take it*."

Chapter Thirty-Six

Another full moon and I hadn't found the killer yet. I tried to blame it on my mother, since my life went completely sideways when she showed up, leaving me with no time to investigate. But I couldn't really blame her. Whoever was on this murder spree was just too damn good at covering their tracks. We had plenty of suspects but no hard proof.

Still, I wouldn't quit. We all agreed that the best way to find this person—or creature—was to catch them in the act. But without any clues about where they'd strike next, there was a lot of ground to cover.

So we split up. Because nothing bad ever happens in horror movies when everyone splits up.

Vaughn went with his pack to check out the Christmas tree farm, which was usually deserted this time of year, while Rose, Thorn, Skyler, and I headed to the Black Star Canyon trail. A trail that went through dark, creepy woods with a zillion places to hide. But with Skyler on lookout just ahead of me, and my twin half sisters on either side of me, I felt pretty confident that the four of us could handle anything that came our way. Or at least that's what I kept telling myself.

I'm a badass vampire queen. I'm not afraid.

It would have been pitch black, but the light from the full moon filtering through the bare tree branches lit our way. The twins kept looking at each other, and once, I thought I caught Thorn nudging Rose like she was prompting her to say something, but neither one spilled.

We were still figuring out how to be sisters. I had a lot I wanted to say to them, too, but it never seemed like the right time. We were out here hunting down a murderer. I couldn't just casually strike up a conversation about our dysfunctional family. We all needed to stay focused.

But after hours of searching, we still hadn't found anything. The car was parked a few yards away. I headed straight for it but then noticed Rose and Thorn hanging back, and it sounded like they were whispering to each other.

"Is something wrong?" I asked.

Neither of them answered, so I kept moving toward the car with Skyler, but my sisters stayed behind, arguing in hushed tones. Obviously about me.

"Oh," I said when we reached the car. "I forgot Thorn has the keys."

Skyler sighed, but with a smile. "I'll go get them from her. You can stay here."

"Thanks, Sky." Her feet had to be as sore as mine, but she'd have to be dead to not have felt the tension between me and the twins tonight. She was doing what a good friend did. She was looking out for me.

I glanced over at the bench near the end of the trail. I could wait for them there. Except someone was already occupying it, and I wasn't about to go sit next to a strange man in the dark.

As I glanced at him, though, something about his slumped-over posture didn't seem right. I called out, "Are you okay?"

He didn't answer, and there was a trail of something dark and liquid running down his chest. I sniffed the air. Blood. Lots and lots of blood.

"Rose, Thorn, Skyler!" I shouted. "Come quick!" There was too much blood. I wasn't sure I would be able to control myself.

There was no doubt in my mind there'd been another murder—right under our noses. And the closer I got to the man's body, the more the awful truth looked me in the eyes.

Like the others, his heart had been ripped out of his chest.

I sent Vaughn a text, letting him know we found another victim, and asked him to pick me up for a little sleuthing. Enough was enough—it was time I figured out who was doing this for good.

I remembered my mother had charged a big-ticket item on the company credit card.

"We need to stop by my house," I told him. I prayed that I hadn't washed the jeans I'd been wearing when I discovered the expense.

"I'll only be a minute," I told Vaughn. I ran to my room and dug through my clothes hamper. It had been hot out, so I hadn't worn that particular pair of jeans lately. Or done my laundry. I snatched up the sticky note and headed back to Vaughn's car.

While he drove, I used my phone and searched the name and address and found out she'd bought something from a retired professor who specialized in rare flora and fauna. My gut told me he would be able to help us identify the mysterious plant. Maybe Vanessa had even bought the plant from him.

Vaughn and I had to drive to the back roads of Silverado Canyon to look for clues.

A sign with peeling paint indicated we were close to the address I'd found on the internet, our destination. We turned onto a narrow, paved road and at the end, found a greenhouse made of what looked like old windows. Plants had nearly taken over and pushed up and through the panes of glass in some spots. It looked abandoned, but then I noticed the tiny house next to it.

It was on wheels and adorable. It looked like someone had blown up a Christmas gingerbread house.

We sat in the car for a minute, observing the place.

"Isn't it kind of weird we're spying on her?" Vaughn asked.

"It feels like Vanessa is running a scam," I admitted. "I just don't know what her end game is."

"She seems to like spending time with you," Vaughn commented.

"I think that's just a front," I said. The thought that

my mother was just using me hurt more than I let on. My voice quavered, and he grabbed my hand and squeezed it.

"Her loss, Tansy," Vaughn said.

We got out of the car, and when I slammed the door, I heard the now-familiar sound of a hellcat roar.

"Hush now, Fluffy," a man's voice said, and then an elderly man hurried out of the tiny house and closed the door swiftly behind him. I didn't miss the thud as a hellcat's body hit the door as it shut.

"Hello," I said. "We're here to do a follow-up about a purchase Sheridan Catering made."

"You must be Vanessa's children," he said.

"I am, he's not," I said. "Vaughn's my boyfriend."

"Tansy, right? You look so much like your mother," the older man said.

"And Vanessa is dating my dad," Vaughn added. "It's complicated."

"I'm Felix," he said. "Professor Felix."

His hands were covered in dirt, so we didn't bother shaking hands. Felix was human, which meant he probably didn't know he owned a hellcat instead of a regular old tabby.

"I set aside some black lilies," Felix said. "Black velvet lilies and a few bat orchids."

"Could we see some roses as well?" I asked.

"I'm afraid not," he said. "Vanessa was clear. No roses. I wouldn't want her to take away my precious Fluffy."

I snort-laughed at the idea of a hellcat called Fluffy.

"Big cats need love, too," Vaughn whispered.

"That's not a cat," I whispered back. "That's a hellcat."

I already knew the answer, but I asked anyway. "Did

you get Fluffy from my mother?"

He beamed. "Why, yes. Bargain, too."

"What kind of bargain?" Vaughn asked.

The hellcat heard us talking and began to hiss and growl and throw itself against the door more determinedly.

"This way," Felix said.

We followed him into the greenhouse. The path was slick with moss and dead leaves.

My breath caught when we stepped into the moist dark interior of the greenhouse. In one corner, where the light still reached, tiny seedings sat atop a wooden table, neatly in rows, but in other parts of the large greenhouse, some of the plants stood taller than Vaughn.

The earthy green smell mingled with the perfume of a multitude of different flowers.

"Bit of a mess right now," Felix said. "The plants are at my lab at the university, but there's a good sample of specialty plants in my personal collection."

"You teach at a university?" I asked politely.

"Retired, but I keep my hand in," he replied. "But Vanessa is so special that I wanted to provide her with flowers from my own personal collection. My favorites are just in here."

We stepped into another room where the plants grew even more closely together.

It wasn't just a career, it was an obsession. Flowers I'd never heard of, many of them in dark purple or black, grew in riotous chaos. I admired black star lilies, calla lilies, and tiger lilies. Queen of the Night tulips.

Then I sneezed. I couldn't help it.

"My mother mentioned that she'd traded a cat for

something special," I said, as casually as I was able. I was lying, but he didn't know that. I needed information.

"Your mother has also requested something from the *Solanaceae* family," Felix said.

"What's that?" I asked.

He cleared his throat. "It's perhaps more commonly known as flowering nightshade."

"Isn't nightshade poisonous?" Vaughn asked.

"Some plants, yes," Felix replied. "But potatoes and tomatoes are also in the nightshade family."

"Of course," I said. "Can we look at your recommendations? Obviously, not potatoes."

"Or anything poisonous," Vaughn added. His brows scrunched together. He was probably wondering the same thing as I was.

"She mentioned another really cool plant," I said. "Cursing violet or something like that?"

"The plant is commonly known as the crying violet," he corrected me.

"Can we see one?" Vaughn asked.

He tsked. "Unfortunately, the plant is virtually extinct."

"Virtually?"

"I did have two seeds," he said. "But they were purchased."

"What did the buyer want to do with them?"

"It doesn't matter," he said. "Those seeds were so old, it would be impossible to get them to germinate."

Impossible, unless you knew a few spells.

• • •

The Old Crones Book Club were all waiting for us when we got back home. Their faces were grim, and Edna was crying. Her wife Evelyn had her arms wrapped around Edna.

"Who was it?" I asked.

I hadn't expected to know the victim, but I did. It was Ms. Ferrell's uncle Tobias Ferrell. Edna had known Tobias for years because he'd come to her dermatology practice for excessive facial hair issues.

Granny unlocked the door, and we all went inside.

We were barely settled in the living room, though, when someone pounded on the door. "Granny Mariotti, I know you're inside. I want to talk to you," a woman's voice came through loud and clear.

The voice sounded familiar somehow. I wasn't taking any chances, though. "I'll get it."

I threw open the door. "How can I help you?"

"Tansy?"

"Ms. Ferrell?" I asked. "What are you doing here?" Her eyes were bloodshot and swollen from crying.

"Is your grandmother home?" she asked.

"You might as well come inside," I said. I had a feeling Ms. Ferrell wasn't here to talk about my English Lit grade.

Granny and the crones were in the kitchen. She was heating up something on the stove but turned when she heard me come in.

"Ms. Ferrell, this is my grandmother," I said.

"You're here about Tobias," Edna said.

"Yes," Ms. Ferrell replied.

"I'm sorry for your loss," Edna said. "I knew him well."

Ms. Ferrell took a long, shaky breath. "So you know?"

"That he was a werewolf?" Edna replied. "Yes."

"Did you kill him?" Ms. Ferrell's accusation sent the witches in the room into a stunned, angry silence. Ms. Ferrell was in dangerous territory.

"Witches, at least the kind of witches we are, do not take lives," my grandmother said, her voice cold and absolute.

"I believe you," Ms. Ferrell said carefully. "But I'm not certain others in the werewolf community will."

Skyler and Connor arrived as I was walking Ms. Ferrell out. "What's going on?" Connor asked, looking from Ms. Ferrell to me curiously.

"There's been another murder," I said. I was a witch. I knew paranormal creatures existed, but it wasn't like I could tell just by looking at them that they were werewolves, at least when they were in their human form. So how did the murderer know?

He took Ms. Ferrell's hand. "I swear to you I will find out who did this."

I stared at him. "Why are you really here, Connor?"

He sighed. "Let's go inside and I'll explain."

We went back inside and sat in the family room. It was a little crowded, so Skyler perched on Connor's knee.

"You know there's been a slew of werewolf killings," he said. "We think the killer has a reason."

"Who's we?" I asked.

"My uncle Cormac, who I went to live with in Ireland, sent me back here to figure it out. But he heard I was attacked and he's here." Connor's dad was dead, and nobody talked about how he'd died. "It's an understatement to say he's not happy."

He glanced at my grandmother and the Old Crones.

"This can't leave this room. You have to swear."

"I swear," they all said.

"Are you sure you can trust Tansy?" Skyler asked.

I sucked in my breath. Low blow. "Get out of my house."

"Tansy—"

"No," I said. "I can't believe you said that. I was there for you when Connor was off drinking whisky and flirting with Irish lassies or whatever he was doing. We put our lives in danger when you were in thrall to a vampire."

Skyler shot me a dirty look. "Way to spill the tea," she said.

"You didn't tell him yet?" I asked.

"She didn't," Connor confirmed. He wrapped Skyler in his arms and pulled her tight against his chest. "I'm so sorry, Skyler. Sorry I wasn't here for you."

"So now that we know why you really came back," I said, "why don't you tell us what you know about the murders?"

"Some of the werewolf folks think that black magic is involved," Ms. Ferrell said.

Granny gave her a long look. "And you thought you'd just stroll into my house and ask me about it?"

"We're pretty sure that they're using the werewolf hearts for a spell," I admitted. "To turn vampires human again." I wasn't ready to share my suspicions that my own mother was the killer. What if I was wrong? I could tell by Connor's face that the pack would tear the killer apart when they found them.

"How does a werewolf heart turn a vamp human?" he asked.

None of the Old Crones spoke, but I could tell by the way they were avoiding my eyes that they knew something.

"It takes dark magic," Granny finally said, "to use a werewolf's heart."

"I figured," I said dryly. "But what exactly does the spell do?"

"Some say it can reverse effects of certain transformations," Edna said.

"Or?" I asked. Because I knew a dodge when I heard one.

"Or it can reverse the effects of vampirism," Granny finally said.

I sucked in a breath. "Who would kill to return to human form?"

"The real question is who wouldn't?" Evelyn said.

Granny shook her head. "That's the thing. It doesn't do that. Only the death of a maker can truly return a vampire to human form. But if the vampire has drained someone completely, even the death of a maker isn't enough to cure them."

"A werewolf heart does that?" I asked.

"The effects are only temporary, though," she said. "And the cost is great. Most vampires don't even know it's a possibility."

"And the ones who do?"

"Even those vampires hesitate," she said.

"See?" Connor said. "This is why we wanted to talk to you."

"To me?" Granny's brows drew together. Her lips were in a straight line when she looked at Connor and said, "You need to leave."

"I didn't mean to offend you," Connor said.

"You didn't think waltzing in here and accusing me of

practicing the dark arts would offend me?"

Connor looked comical as my small but determined grandmother started pushing him out of the living room. He probably outweighed her by a hundred pounds.

"I don't think you're practicing black magic," he said. "I thought you might know of a spell that would explain why they're taking a werewolf's heart?"

Granny stopped shoving him, and her face went blank. "If they are taking the werewolf's heart, it won't do them any good without a crying violet."

Edna and Evelyn jumped to their feet. "It's not possible," Edna gasped. "That plant is lost to time."

"Unless someone had an in with a rare flower guy…" I said, some of the pieces clicking into place in my mind. I didn't like this at all.

I got out my phone. "I took a picture of Vanessa's driver's license when we went shopping."

"She has a driver's license?" Vaughn asked. "That's pretty law-abiding for a vampire." The quip made everyone chuckle, and some of the tension left the room.

"Anyway," I said. "It turns out that the address on her license is the same place we found the hellcats. And Vanessa has access to all sorts of exotic plants." I turned to Vaughn. "We need to go back to the hellcat house."

Everyone agreed that Vaughn and I would go. Since we had the most experience, we would be the ones to check it out, but Skyler stubbornly insisted on going with us.

After her dig about not trusting me, I felt awkward and uncomfortable around her.

"I'm driving," I said. Skyler got into the Deathtrap's backseat without arguing.

The murders and the hellcats were connected somehow, but I couldn't figure out how. They were guarding something. We needed to take another look at those plants, locked away and guarded by two of the biggest hellcats I'd ever seen.

We said our goodbyes and made a stop at Janey's for half a dozen pies before we visited the hellcat secret lair. From what I knew, hellcats liked pie, so loading up on baked goods couldn't hurt.

"What do you think they're hiding in there?" I asked. "It can't just be some random plants."

"A conscience," Vaughn said.

"The secret to why Tom Cruise doesn't age," Skyler said. She shuddered. "He looks exactly the same at seventy as he did at twenty."

"He's not seventy," I said.

"So what you're saying is that we have to break into that creepy house on a deserted canyon road," Skyler said.

"That's exactly what I'm saying." It was a risk, but I didn't see how I had any other choice.

The house was dark, and I didn't see the white van anywhere, but we still moved quietly and cautiously.

The front door was unlocked this time. I paused to listen. "Do you think anyone's here?"

Vaughn shook his head. Eager to learn my mother's secret, I was the first one to step inside. As I moved deeper into the house, I realized that I didn't hear the adorable mewing of the kittens. We were almost to the hallway that led to the locked door.

Something clawed at me. Pain went down my arm. One of the kittens must have been in a playful mood. But when

I looked down, my arm had a deep gouge on it, and my blood was dripping onto the floor.

Two full-grown hellcats blocked the exit. The adorable kittens had been replaced by huge cats the size of tigers.

Vaughn spotted the animals the same time I did. He threw one of the pies and then yanked open a bedroom door and shoved Skyler and me inside. I slammed the door and locked it.

One of the hellcats let out a roar that shook the doorframe. Judging by the way the feline was slamming itself against the door, it wouldn't hold the animals for long.

I had to get us out of here, but I couldn't bear the thought of hurting animals, even if they were murderous beasts trained to kill.

I slid two more pies out, and the animals pounced on them. "I don't think anyone's been feeding them," I said. What kind of dickhead abused animals?

We were down to the last two pies. I texted Connor. **Can you come to the secret hellcat house? And bring as much beef as you can find. Or pie. Or both.**

A few seconds later, his text came back. **Do you need my help or do you just have the munchies?**

HELP, I texted back. **Skyler and Vaughn and I need you here**. While I texted with one hand, Vaughn ripped a sleeve off his hoodie and used it to bind my wound. The gouge stung, but we had bigger problems. Like getting out of here without getting eaten.

On it. But do I even want to know what happened?

That was a definite no.

. . .

I knew that Connor had finally arrived when the beasts started to roar. "Here, kitty, kitty," I heard him say.

"It's safe to come out now," Connor said. He'd brought Beckett and Lucas with him. "Xavier is studying," he said. "I'm only supposed to interrupt him if someone is dying."

"Minor injuries," I said. "I'll ask Granny for a poultice when I get home. Besides, we have bigger problems. We can't leave until we find out what's behind that locked door."

"We don't have much time," Connor said. "We brought about thirty pounds of raw hamburger, but that won't last long."

"They like pie, too," Skyler said.

Connor brushed a lock of her hair back and then murmured, "I was worried about you." I looked away. I was warming up to the idea of him with my best friend, and his tender expression almost convinced me.

I cleared my throat. "Let's go."

We hurried to the room with the locked door. Connor stuck out his hand to turn the knob, but it occurred to me that it might be booby-trapped.

"Wait!" I shouted. Nothing had happened the last time, but I didn't want to take the chance that someone had figured out we'd been there. We had taken Hecate, which might have clued someone in on the fact that someone had been snooping around, but it was also possible they'd thought she'd wandered off on her own.

They watched me as I closed my eyes and tried to sense

if there was any magic. I didn't detect anything but still recited a quick anti-curse spell.

"Is your mom growing weed?" Beckett asked.

I rolled my eyes. "That's not cannabis," I said. "It has purple flowers."

"Then what is it?" Skyler asked.

"I'm not a botanist," I said. "But I think it might be a crying violet." Despite my disappointment at not finding concrete evidence about who was murdering werewolves, I took a photo with my phone anyway.

It was important enough that my mother hid it behind a locked door. I'd figured out who the murderer was, but it didn't make me feel any better.

Chapter Thirty-Seven

Vaughn and Connor took off to let his uncle know the latest discovery while Skyler and I drove home in silence.

Solving the murder wasn't nearly as satisfying as I thought it would be. I'd been so gullible. The murderer had been right in front of me, and I'd been too distracted—too hopeful, too lonely—to notice.

"I'm going to drop you off at home, Sky," I told her. "There's something I need to do."

"Tansy?" she asked me, her voice sounding on the verge of panic. "What are you going to do?"

What *was* I going to do? It was hard to remember what my goals had been before this summer. Now I just wanted to survive. And I wanted the people I loved to survive.

I vaguely remembered wanting to finish *Infinite Jest*, get some sun, and get Vaughn to notice me. I still wanted Vaughn to notice me. He was a werewolf, and I was a vampire queen, but we loved each other. I would lose everything if I didn't stop my mother.

Skyler got out of the Deathtrap and slammed the door. "Be careful."

"Like you care," I muttered under my breath, but she heard me and flinched. Her back went straight and she marched into her house without another word.

I cruised by Vaughn's house, but no one was home. I drove by the house in the canyon. There were no cars there, so I continued to drive around.

I considered the werewolf I'd found at The Last Stop. Most of the attacks had occurred near or at the bar. That was where I might find the killer.

Within a few minutes, I pulled into the empty lot and parked, then ran up to the bar.

It was empty, too, from what I could see through the windows, but I could hear the faint sound of someone moving around inside. I sent Vaughn a quick text to let him know where I was and why.

The door was unlocked, so I went in.

My mother stood there. Her grin chilled me. I'd seen glimpses of the Executioner before, but my mother had managed to fool me into thinking she was human.

All traces of humanity had vanished, and I knew that she needed to kill again because the effects of the werewolf hearts she'd already eaten had faded. My mother was gone, and the Executioner was back.

People had died because I'd been so distracted by the hope that I would finally have a real mom, finally find out who my dad was, that I'd trusted a murderer. The werewolves were right. This *was* all the fault of a vampire. Or at least a vampire-witch hybrid. Me.

"Not very fair odds, Vanessa," I said. "Or should I call you by who you really are? The Executioner."

"I like these odds," she said. "Four to one."

Hecate bounded into the room and let out a low, challenging growl. The other hellcats cowered. Hecate had been the runt of the litter, but now she was a massive hellcat and stood head and shoulders above the others.

"Two to four," I said. "I like my chances."

When I was little, I'd longed for the day my mother would return and we'd be a family again. Now I wanted to travel back in time and slap that kid until she wised up and remembered to be careful what she wished for.

"Give up, Tansy," she said. "I've outwitted you. Honestly, it wasn't even my best effort."

"I don't think so." Instead of a scowl, I gave my mother a smile. I think it confused her. "You were looking for something, weren't you? That's why you were cozying up to me. You think I have the Blood of Life."

I'd surprised her. The cloud of hatred Mom sent my way couldn't be missed, but I felt good for standing up to her for a change. I was a queen. It was time I started acting like one.

"I was right. You do have it, don't you?" She studied my face, and then a grin crossed her face. "You don't even realize what you have."

"Why don't you tell me?" I replied. "I already know about the crying violets and the werewolf hearts."

"Tsk, tsk," she mocked. "Dabbling in the black arts. I didn't know you had it in you."

I held onto my temper with difficulty and prompted her, "The Blood of Life?"

"There are some vampires who would give me everything they own for it," Vanessa said.

"Because it makes them invincible?" I guessed. The thought made me shudder. Vampires were already hard to get rid of.

"Because it makes them human." She smirked. "Not just the appearance of a human, truly human with all their vulnerabilities and emotions. I don't really see the appeal."

"Then why kill all those werewolves just to appear human?"

"A means to an end," she replied. "There was no other way to arrange our reunion."

"I should have killed you when I had the chance," I hissed.

"But you didn't," she said. Her smile grew wider until I could see all her teeth. She didn't have fangs. "Why didn't you?" she asked. "Don't tell me you didn't let a little thing like biology stop you. I wouldn't have."

I didn't point out that she hadn't killed Granny because I didn't want to give her any ideas.

She made a sharp motion with her hand, and one of the hellcats ran for me.

Then another cat growled, in challenge, and the hellcat's ears perked up as Hecate bounded into view.

I needed another job just to keep her in kitty treats, but she earned every bite when she came to my defense.

She jumped, landing on the other cat and knocking it away from me. Hecate had her teeth on the other cat's neck before I could tell her to stop, but she didn't break the flesh. Instead, her eyes, blood red and scary, looked at me like she was searching for answers.

They exchanged a series of growls, and then the rest of the pack retreated, leaving only Hecate and the other feline. Hecate held him, her teeth near a vein in the other cat's neck, until it whimpered. Hecate released her grip, and the other cat rolled over and showed its belly, then slunk out of the room.

Hecate's jaws snapped and got one of the hellcats on the flank, but they kept coming after her. She was going to have to fight her own battle because I had to pay attention to my mother or she'd kill me without thinking twice.

"Why are you pretending to be human?" I asked her.

Something dark and devious passed over her face. "I'm not pretending."

"Give it up, Vanessa," I said. "We already found the plants. We know what you're doing. Why you killed those werewolves. The pack will rip you apart when they hear about this."

"They won't get the chance," she said. "You haven't told them yet, have you?"

"Of course I told them," I lied, but my mother saw the flinch I'd tried to conceal.

"You are a terrible liar," she said. She snapped her fingers, and Boris came through the double doors that led to the kitchen. "And I don't need to kill you. He'll do it for me."

I thought she'd leave, but she stood there as Boris came toward me. I realized she wanted to watch me die. That wasn't going to happen.

I hit him in the stomach before he had a chance to shift. I wasn't sure I'd stand a chance against a rogue werewolf, and I didn't want to find out.

He bent over, wheezing, but threw off his gloves. His

hands were long claws, sharp and deadly. I hit him again, and he swiped at me and missed. I turned my head to smirk at my mother, and by the time I'd turned around again, he'd gone full wolf.

His first blow sent me flying across the room until I landed against a wall. My head was ringing, and I staggered as I stood. His claws slashed out, narrowly missing my face.

I kicked at his feet, but it was like kicking a tree. I tried to clear my mind and focus on using my power, but I felt like I'd been hit in the head with a brick.

"Stop it!" I ordered, using my power.

My mom laughed. "The wolf can't hear you when blood lust is on him."

"Why did you need him anyway?" I asked. "You had the plants and the hellcats." And the werewolf hearts, but I didn't want to think about how my own mother had been running around brutally murdering people.

"He was dating a witch who would make the potion," she said. "For the right price, of course."

Vanessa had needed a witch to cast the spell, since she was no longer a Mariotti witch. No witch in her right mind would mess with such an evil spell, but Vanessa had managed to find someone.

An unnatural witch? Here? Granny was going to lose it when I told her. If I ever got the chance.

I hadn't been paying attention, and Boris's jaws snapped dangerously close to my neck.

Vanessa was going to get her wish. He was going to kill me.

His eyes were black, his jaw snapping as I dodged him. His arms wrapped around my waist and lifted me in the air and then slammed me to the floor. My head hit the hard wooden planks, and red exploded behind my eyes. I tried to focus, to see where Boris was, what he was doing, but all I could see was a curtain of red.

My fangs came out, and I bared my teeth. "Boris, be reasonable."

I dodged and feinted, but knew I was losing valuable time.

"Don't hit me ever again," I said.

But he resisted my compulsion. This blow was to the face, harder this time. I doubled over.

He backhanded me. Rage suffused my whole body, and I had to force myself to take a deep breath. It was either that or bite him.

Frantically, I tried to remember what werewolves were vulnerable to during a full moon. I remembered the silver moon Granny had given me. I'd taken it off, but maybe it was still in my pocket.

My fingers found it as Boris's teeth caught at the leg of my jeans.

I reached out and pressed the silver moon into his flesh. He howled, and his fur-covered flesh began to sizzle. I used all my strength, pried open his jaw, and forced him to swallow the charm.

My mother put up a hand like she was going to give me a high five. "Look at you." She smirked. "A natural born killer. You've made your mother so proud. I thought he'd kill you and I'd have to find another werewolf, but now I'll kill you first and take his heart later."

In response, I doubled up my fist and popped her in the nose.

Her head snapped back, and her hellcats growled at me. One of them took a running jump at me, but Hecate slammed into the other feline mid-jump, snapping and tearing at its flesh.

The other two attacked, but I took out my drumstick and smacked one of them on the head.

That caught its attention, and I started to run. It chased after me, and I jumped on the bar, sending beer bottles and glass tumblers to the floor as I slid across it and into the back room. The big cat followed, but it overshot and went past me. I stepped back into the main room and locked the door.

There was a *thud* as if a two-hundred-pound enraged animal had thrown itself against the door. I hoped Vaughn could get here before the cat broke down the door. It was a temporary fix. The other two hellcats ran out, and Hecate followed them, howling her fury as she went.

Somewhere in the room, a cell phone began to chirp with text notifications, one after another. I vaguely wondered where my phone was, but it didn't matter at this moment. I needed to concentrate on staying alive.

The texts stopped, and then seconds later, a phone began to ring and ring. Someone was trying to call me.

I returned my attention to the bigger problem, Vanessa Mariotti, the woman who was willing to dabble in the dark arts.

"Where's your boyfriend?" she sneered. "Out with his buddies instead of you?"

I ignored her. What kind of mother preyed on her own daughter's insecurities like that? A terrible one.

"You don't know what you're talking about," I said

calmly, but my heart raced.

"He'll choose his friends over you every time," she snarled.

She called them his friends, not his pack. So she didn't know Vaughn was a werewolf. Good. I had no doubt if she had known, she would have tried to kill him. Just to hurt me.

I gagged when she punched me in the stomach, but then I summoned power from somewhere deep inside me. My mother hit me over the head with something heavy. A bottle of booze maybe? My skull felt like it was cracking wide open.

Vanessa knocked me down and had her hands wrapped around my neck.

I couldn't breathe. I couldn't speak to try to use my magic. I used my legs to push up and got her off me. I jumped to my feet, wheezing. I was going to have to hurt her, and I didn't even feel bad about it.

She wrapped her hands around my neck again and squeezed so tightly that I thought I was going to black out. "You'll never find the ruby if you kill me."

She stared down at me for a long moment and then dropped me to the floor.

My mother thought she'd won, but I wasn't ready to admit defeat. I used a move Thorn had taught me and kicked her feet out from under her. As she went down, her head hit the edge of the solid wooden bar. She lay there motionless. I got to my feet and stood over her, waiting for a counter-attack that didn't come.

She hadn't exploded into ash and goo, so she was still alive, or whatever the vampire equivalent of that was.

My drumstick was sticky with my sweat, and I gripped

it tighter as I stared at my mother. Could I actually stake Vanessa? Staking a vampire in self-defense was reasonable. She'd never stop trying to mess with me, but I couldn't drive my drumstick through my mother's heart when she was unconscious. I could, however, give her to the Paranormal Activities Committee and let them decide her punishment.

I turned away to look for something to tie her up. There was a sharp pain in the back of my skull, and then I went down.

I wavered in and out of consciousness as the adrenaline rush faded. I didn't know how long I lay there before I heard Vaughn's voice.

"Tansy, what happened?" he asked.

"My mother happened," I rasped out. My throat hurt. My neck felt like it was starting to bruise.

He helped me up and carried me to a chair. "Shh, I've got you," he crooned and sat down, with me cradled in his lap. I wrapped my arms around his neck and put my head on his chest.

"My mother was behind it all," I said.

Vaughn growled. "I'm going to kill her."

I put a hand on his shoulder. "I'm okay." My bruises would fade.

"You look like you could use a trip to urgent care," Vaughn replied.

"No hospital," I said. There was no way I would be able to explain my injuries.

"At least let Xavier check you out," he said.

I nodded. Even that hurt.

He fished his phone out of his pocket, careful not to jostle me, and made a quick call. "I need you at The Last

Stop. As soon as possible. Tansy's hurt." After he hung up, he put me down and went behind the bar and came back with a plastic bag full of ice. "Put this on your face. Your eye's already starting to swell."

"Okay," I said.

"Xavier, Beckett, and Lucas are on their way," he said. "They'll be here in less than five minutes." He scooted a chair next to mine. "How are you doing? It looks like you got hit pretty hard."

I didn't want to think about what could have happened if my mother got her hands on the Blood of Life. Now that I knew what it could do, at least according to Vanessa, who had demonstrated once more that I couldn't trust anything she said.

Who had sent me the ruby, though? And why?

"I'm okay," I said. Hecate returned, her muzzle black with blood. The ferocious look on my cat's face vanished and was replaced by my cuddly kitten.

I scratched her under the chin and then handed her one of the kitty treats I kept in my pocket. "Good kitty, Hecate."

The pack of hellcats had vanished as quickly as they'd come.

I couldn't just leave Boris's body on the floor I had to wait until the pack arrived to go after my mother. And for my head to stop spinning.

It was just after dark when I heard the door open, and the Thirsty Thieves walked in. They'd showed up for their gig. Even though I'd banned Travis. No one was surprised.

"Not again," Travis bellowed when he saw Boris's body. He'd died mid-shift. I couldn't look at Boris's corpse.

It didn't make me feel any better that I'd had to kill the werewolf or he would have killed me.

"You're gonna need a new drummer," I said. I was trying not to throw up, but the guys in the band would pounce if they sensed any weakness.

"You killed our drummer again?" Travis asked.

"He attacked me," I replied. "He didn't leave me any other option."

"I had nothing to do with that," Travis said.

I narrowed my eyes at him. "He was working with my mother. Killing werewolves to appear human. I don't suppose you know anything about that?"

"Why would we want to be human?" Armando said. He swept his hand down his body. "And give up all this?"

Lucas, Beckett and Xavier entered the bar, and when they saw the Thirsty Thieves, they immediately shifted to werewolf. Werewolves really disliked vampires, or at least they disliked *these* vampires.

"There's no time for that," Vaughn said. "We need your help."

It took a minute for his voice to get through to them.

I stood there shaking.

Vaughn draped his coat over me. "I'll call your grand-mother."

A few hours later, I was home and resting in my room with an ice pack and a tall glass of tonic.

"Tansy, how are you feeling?" Edna asked.

"It looks worse than it is," I said.

"Your face looks terrible," Skyler said. "Like nightmarishly bad." She'd shown up, even though she was still mad at me. I was still kind of mad at her, too. But we'd both get over it because that's what friends did.

"Thanks a lot," I said.

"Just being honest," she said with a small smile. "Your eye is almost swollen shut."

Vanessa had given me a black eye. I sat on the couch, Hecate curled up beside me, and I drank another tonic, this one spicy and laced with honey and herbs.

"To help you heal," Evelyn said.

Granny and her friends coddled me with tonics and snacks, but I wasn't home long before I got a call from Connor.

"My uncle wants to talk to you," he said.

"When?"

"Now," he replied. "Vaughn knows where."

"I have to go see Connor's uncle," I told my grandmother. Edna left the room while we were arguing.

"You're not going alone," Granny said. "And that's final."

"I'm going with her," Vaughn said. I'd been so busy bickering with my grandmother that I hadn't heard him come in.

"Maybe I should come, too," Granny said.

"I'll be fine," I told her. Whatever was waiting for me, I didn't want Granny to get hurt.

Vaughn drove. We didn't talk, but his hand held mine in a comforting grip. I wondered if we were walking into an ambush.

Instead, it felt like we were at an interview of some

kind. Only if you didn't have the right answers, it wasn't the job you'd lose, it was your life.

The GPS told us that we'd arrived, but I still couldn't see the house. Then the road curved around and suddenly, there it was. The driveway was near a barn, where more cars lined up in neat rows.

I sucked in a breath. "There are so many people here." Apparently, there were more werewolves within traveling distance than I'd thought.

I surveyed the green lawn, the horse pastures, and the woods behind the house. "There's plenty of space for the werewolves to roam."

A group of people were on the front lawn, sitting at picnic tables and deck chairs.

An older man sat on a carved teak chair, surrounded by his loyal pack members. "I'm Tansy Mariotti. Queen of the California vampires."

There was a low grumble of complaint from somewhere. I looked over at the group of Connor's friends, but didn't see Connor. Lucas gave me shifty eyes and Vaughn shoved him. It must have been Lucas complaining.

They snarled at each other, but then Lucas bent his head. An older woman said something to them both and they shut up.

The man stood and extended his hand. "Cormac Mahoney. Please take a seat."

"What should I call you?" I asked. "Boss or alpha or king or what?"

"We don't use titles. Call me Cormac."

Title or not, there was no doubt this man was in charge. His dark eyes examined me from head to toe, assessing me, probably searching for weaknesses. He had a closely trimmed beard and looked to be about thirty or so.

"You don't look like a vampire queen," he said. He kept staring, and I realized his eyes were brown, like his nephew's, but while Connor's were an eerie amber, Cormac's were almost black.

I stared back at him. He was extremely tall, at least six foot six, with pale skin and a streak of white in his black hair. "Sorry I forgot my tiara."

Cormac got right to it. "A Mariotti witch is to blame for the deaths of my people."

I squared my chin. "Vanessa Mariotti is not a Mariotti witch." My mother was technically a Mariotti, but from now on, I'd remember what she really was—a deadly vampire who would do anything to get what she wanted. No matter who it would hurt.

"But she is a Mariotti," he said. "Reason enough to put you and your family to death."

Someone, probably Lucas, snarled in agreement, but I didn't look away from Cormac. Vaughn started to move in front of me, to protect me, but I put my hand on his arm, and he fell back to my side.

"I found out who was responsible and why," I said.

"And the plants?" he asked.

"The ones we found were destroyed," I said. I didn't want to meet his cold dark eyes, for fear of what I'd see there, but I did anyway.

I shifted on my feet when the silence extended. Cormac appeared lost in thought, but the other werewolves started to crowd around Vaughn and me. Lucas got too close to me, and Vaughn snarled out a warning.

"What about the hellcats?" Cormac asked.

"They've been taken to the Paranormal Activities Committee headquarters," I said. His dark eyes studied me, like he was searching for any untruth, and I added, "Except for one."

Cormac frowned. "Where is the missing hellcat?"

"She's not missing," I said. "Hecate's mine."

The werewolves crowded closer. I searched for Beckett and Xavier, looking for any allies, but I didn't see them. A skinny teen reached out a hand to touch my hair, and Vaughn shoved him hard enough that he fell into a group of his friends. The teen swore, and I thought a fight would break out, but Cormac growled. The other werewolves stopped but didn't stop pressing close.

"How is Connor?" I asked. Homecoming seemed like ages ago.

Cormac's solemn look lightened. It was almost a smile. "He is nearly recovered."

He waved his hand. "Give our guests some room." The other werewolves stepped back, finally giving Vaughn and me enough space to breathe.

A wise queen owned up to her mistakes, and it was time that I admitted mine. "I was wrong," I said. "I underestimated my mother, but I did my best to correct my mistake."

"Your mistake cost good werewolves their lives," Cormac said.

Vaughn's low growl could be heard. Cormac's gaze went to Vaughn's, and they exchanged a long glance. "But you saved my nephew's life, and for that, I am grateful."

"How did you know?" I hadn't told anyone I'd used a healing spell to save Connor after he was attacked. "I mean,

Xavier is the one who saved his life."

The pack leader didn't answer my question. "But your spell is what kept him alive until Xavier arrived," Cormac replied. "And because of that, you have our pack's loyalty. You may go."

Vaughn's sigh of relief was barely audible. We started to leave, but then Cormac added, "If you want my advice, Queen Tansy, you will take care of Vanessa Mariotti once and for all."

It was good advice, and I planned on taking it.

Once we were back in the car, I finally relaxed my tense shoulders. "Well, that went well."

Vaughn laughed, but there was no mirth in it. "If Vanessa's smart, she's already left town," he said. "Because Cormac Mahoney won't be so forgiving next time."

Chapter Thirty-Eight

My mother had escaped, but the good news was that nobody else had died. She probably would have killed me, except she knew I had the Blood of Life but didn't know where I'd hidden it. We'd destroyed the last crying violet so no one would be able to cast that terrible spell ever again.

When we got to Vaughn's house, there was no sign of Mr. Sheridan. I wasn't sure how we were going to break the news to him that his girlfriend was a killer.

Vaughn shouted into the silence. We walked through the house, but it was empty.

"She has my dad," Vaughn said, waving his phone at me. His dad had sent him a text. "They're eloping. Damn it, they've gone to Vegas to get married."

A piece of paper was pinned to the fridge with a magnet. It was a wedding announcement for Vanessa Mariotti and Adam Sheridan. Underneath, written in pen were the words, *Trade you. Bring the ruby.*

He stomped to his room, and I followed him.

He started shoving clothes into a duffel bag. "What are you doing?"

"Call the pack," he said. "We're going after them."

I wouldn't bet on our chances of making it back home unscathed, but I couldn't let my mother marry Vaughn's dad, especially not now that I knew how many werewolves she'd killed to seem human.

My best friend was barely talking to me, though, and I couldn't really blame her. She loved Connor, and my inability to see my mother for who she really was had almost gotten him killed.

"I'm coming, too," I said.

Vaughn and I agreed we'd pack a bag and meet at my house.

He texted me that he was at the bungalow, and I stepped outside, carrying my duffel, snacks for the road, and my trusty drumstick. The Blood of Life ruby was in the duffel, still concealed in the hollowed-out book. I could feel the cloud of menace that hung over it. I didn't want the gem anywhere near me, but I didn't have a choice.

I wasn't expecting to see all our friends waiting for me.

Skyler and Connor were on the porch, talking to Vaughn. She had an overnight bag at her feet.

"You're coming with us?" I asked. I didn't want to smile at her, but I couldn't help it. No matter how mad she was at me, there was no way my best friend would let me go to Vegas without her.

"I have to make sure your mother doesn't try to kill my boyfriend again," she said coldly, but there was a hint of a smile in her eyes.

For the first time, I noticed the large passenger van parked in my driveway. It was purple and black with some sort of mural painted on it.

"What is that monstrosity?" I asked. "It looks like Prince puked up on the Magical Mystery Machine."

"It's mine," Beckett said from the driver's seat. "Now get your cute butt in the van. We need to get on the road. We're going to Vegas, baby!"

I was going back on the road, this time with a pack of werewolves. What's the worst that could happen?

Acknowledgments

Thanks to Shana Norris, Mary Pearson, and Melissa Wyatt for having their (virtual) stakes at the ready to slay all those writing vampires. My agent Stephen Barbara isn't afraid of vampires, werewolves, witches, or difficult contract negotiations. And thanks to Curtis, Heather, Meredith, Riki, Jessica, Lydia, Stacy, and Liz, who make the publishing magic happen. And to my husband and kids, who are simply magic.

I'm with the Banned is a laugh-out-loud paranormal romance with vampires, werewolves, and witches. However, the story includes elements that might not be suitable for some readers. Blood, fatal wounds, death, and a strained mother-daughter relationship are included in the novel. Readers who may be sensitive to these elements, please take note.

*Don't miss the global sensation
everyone is talking about!*

c ra_ve

by Tracy Wolff

My whole world changed when I stepped inside the academy.
Nothing is right about this place or the other students in it. Here
I am, a mere mortal among gods…or monsters. I still can't decide
which of these warring factions I belong to, if I belong at all. I
only know the one thing that unites them is their hatred of me.

Then there's Jaxon Vega. A vampire with deadly secrets who
hasn't felt anything for a hundred years. But there's something
about him that calls to me, something broken in him that
somehow fits with what's broken in me.

Which could spell death for us all.

Because Jaxon walled himself off for a reason. And now
someone wants to wake a sleeping monster, and I'm wondering
if I was brought here intentionally—as the bait.

This epic angels-and-demons YA series combines all the tropes readers are looking for: pulse-pounding romance, epic worldbuilding, and plenty of twists and turns.

EMBER
OF
NIGHT

MOLLY E. LEE

I've never been a stranger to the darkness. But when darkness comes knocking and looks *that* good, who wouldn't invite him in?

Draven is mysterious, evasive, and hot as sin. The only thing more infuriating than how much he won't say is how obnoxious he is every time he *does* open his mouth. But when a group of strangers attacks me and he fights back, causing them to vanish into a cloud of black dust, I know Draven is more than he seems.

He finally shows me there's a veil separating the world I know from a world of demons living all around us. Turns out, good and evil are just words. Some of the demons don't fall into either category. And I'm realizing just how easily I fit in among the ancient warlocks, the divine soldiers, and the twisted supernaturals...

There's so much more to me. To my past. And to what I am truly capable of than I ever thought possible. So when all signs point to me having the ability to unleash Hell on earth? I'll have to decide if I want to do the world a solid and save it, or give it one hell of a makeover.

An exciting new voice in paranormal romance,
Vanessa Barneveld's Under the Milky Way
is a supernatural thrill ride.

Nothing ever happens in Dawson, Colorado.

Until high school senior Cassidy Roekiem's mom checks into a "wellness center," but nothing is wrong with her.

Then people start seeing lights in the sky and missing chunks of time, but the town insists nothing is going on.

And now Hayden, the new boy at school who keeps to himself and is more than a little mysterious, starts to notice *her* like it's nothing out of the ordinary.

Suddenly, "nothing" is starting to feel a whole lot like *something*. And everything leads back to Hayden. The boy she's starting to fall for. The boy with too many dark secrets for his kind heart. The boy she's pretty sure isn't human…

Let's be friends!

@EntangledTeen

@EntangledTeen

@EntangledTeen

bit.ly/TeenNewsletter

entangled teen
an imprint of Entangled Publishing LLC